THE EARL
CLAIMS HIS WIFE

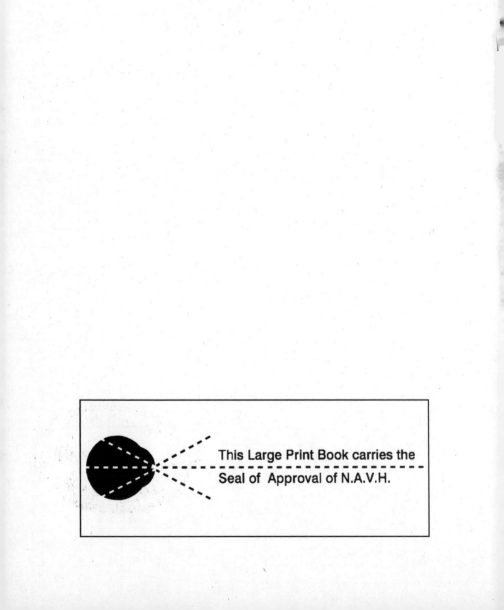

This Large Print Book carries the
Seal of Approval of N.A.V.H.

THE EARL
CLAIMS HIS WIFE

CATHY MAXWELL

THORNDIKE PRESS

A part of Gale, Cengage Learning

GALE
CENGAGE Learning™

Detroit • New York • San Francisco • New Haven, Conn • Waterville, Maine • London

LIBRARY OF CONGRESS CATALOGING-IN-PUBLICATION DATA

Maxwell, Cathy.
    The Earl claims his wife / by Cathy Maxwell.
        p. cm. — (Thorndike press large print basic)
    ISBN-13: 978-1-4104-2513-3 (hardcover : alk. paper)
    ISBN-10: 1-4104-2513-4 (hardcover : alk. paper)
    1. Napoleonic Wars, 1800–1815—Veterans—Fiction.
    2. England—Fiction. 3. Large type books. I. Title.
PS3563.A8996E17 2010
813'.6—dc22   2009050003

Published in 2010 by arrangement with Avon Books, an imprint of HarperCollins Publishers.

Printed in the United States of America
1 2 3 4 5 6 7 14 13 12 11 10

This one is for you, Andrew.

*It's about a wonderful man
who is sometimes mutton-headed
but believes in love,
doing the right thing,
and living life to the fullest.*

**Couldn't think of a better book
to dedicate to you . . .**

CHAPTER ONE

January 1810

Gillian Ranson, Lady Wright, knew how to embroider a straight stitch or darn a sock, make soap that was as good as Pears, and run Huntleigh, the country estate of her cousin the Duke of Holburn, with efficient profitability. She was the model of propriety, a gentlewoman in every way, and knew her Bible forwards as well as backwards.

She was also ready to take a lover.

Andres Ramigio, barón de Vasconia, was the most handsome man she'd ever laid eyes on. He was also gallant, thoughtful, witty, adventurous, and a host of other stellar qualities that made her heart beat faster than it ever had in her life.

At last, she understood why married women risked all for a lover.

At last, she felt alive again.

In truth, Wright had ignored her for years. His military career and his mistress were far more important than a wife. Since he'd returned to London he'd started writing her, one curt note after another ordering her home — hardly the stuff of lovers.

Gillian had decided it was *her* turn to *ignore* him. She'd had quite enough humiliation from her husband to last a lifetime. In spite of recently marrying, her cousin was happy to let her stay at Huntleigh and manage things and now there was Andres. Wonderful, amazingly handsome Andres.

Her cold, indifferent English husband was no competition to a Spaniard.

This morning, she had accompanied Andres and many of Huntleigh's houseguests, left over from the annual Christmas gathering of friends and relatives, down to the stable yards. Andres had announced over breakfast he planned to put the spirited Andalusian mare that had been delivered to the estate the day before through her paces. The love of seeing good horseflesh up close was all that was necessary to cause almost every man at the table to push back his chair to join him.

Gillian was the only woman to tramp down the path from the house to the stables with them. She hoped for a moment of private conversation with Andres. Huntleigh's walls had ears when it came to any affairs of the heart and she didn't want gossip to sully what they felt for each other.

It was a good day to be out. After days of rain, the sun had decided to grace them a rare taste of glory, chasing away gloomy spirits in spite of the nipping cold.

Gillian didn't mind the weather. She was bundled up in her blue wool pelisse and velvet muff with its matching hat. She stood at the base of the path leading up to the house, a few steps away from the gathering of men forming a large circle around Andres and the horse.

The mare was magnificent — everything Andres had promised she would be. Holburn would be overjoyed when he returned from his trip north to Scotland with his new wife Fiona to find such an addition to his stables.

Of course, Gillian's attention was on Andres's tall, lean figure. He held the leather lead rope with a light hand, speaking Spanish to the mare in soft, soothing tones.

The horse was skittish and uncertain in her new surroundings. She was one of a small herd of prime bloodstock that had been hidden from Napoleon's cavalry. The French had already decimated almost all the other Spanish herds with their demand for war horses. Andres's friend, a priest, had smuggled the horse out of Spain and sent her to Andres and Holburn for safekeeping against the day the French were thrown off Spanish soil.

The sleek, refined horse with her black legs and silvery gray coat seemed designed to enhance Andres's handsome elegance. Every time Gillian looked at him, she felt a bit dizzy. His jaw was lean, his thick hair a mass of blue-black curls, but his eyes were his most stunning feature. They were a silvery gray that could look straight through to a woman's soul — and there wasn't a woman under Huntleigh's roof immune to their power.

However, what had finally turned Gillian's head was his kindness. Andres Ramigio treated everyone with respect from the scullery maid to Uncle Walter, the oldest relative in the house, who had a terrible time hearing any conversation. Gillian noticed how Andres would patiently repeat himself for the older man and didn't duck and hide when he saw him coming as everyone else did, including herself.

By the eve of the Epiphany, something magical had happened — Andres had made her believe again in the finer qualities of men. He was chivalrous and yet bold, playful and yet wise. A man worthy of her trust.

What woman could *not* fall in love with him?

"It would not be prudent, you know," her Aunt Agatha's tart voice said, intruding on Gillian's adoring thoughts with a strong dose of common sense.

Gillian turned, surprised to see her favorite aunt. Aunt Agatha rarely ventured outside. Afraid her aunt could read her thoughts, Gillian pretended to misunderstand. "What would not be prudent? Coming out in this weather?"

Aunt Agatha was a petite woman dressed in regal purple wool who appeared frailer than she truly was. Her strength was in the alert intelligence of her eyes. She wore a fox fur hat on top of the turbans she favored, this one being purple that matched her coat and scarf. It was Aunt Agatha who had sponsored Gillian's first season in London when she'd met Wright.

"You know what I'm talking about," her aunt said. "And it *isn't* the weather."

Gillian wanted to pretend she didn't understand. She also wanted to change the subject. She glanced up the path, expecting to see servants with a sedan chair, and seeing none went on the attack. "Did you walk down here?" she demanded.

"I did," her aunt said, offended at anyone

11

questioning her actions, as Gillian had known she would be. "I have two legs."

"Legs that beg you to have care. Do you wish to fall again? It's a steep walk." The irritation in Gillian's voice was real.

"That it is," her aunt agreed. "But coming here would bring me to the one place where I might catch you alone and have a stern word or two." Her gaze drifted over to Andres and the horse. "Pretty filly. I take it our Spanish friend is a master of horses, too."

"Apparently," Gillian said. She pretended nonchalance.

Her aunt slid a glance in her direction. "Don't try to humbug me, girl. I helped your mother change your nappies. I can read every thought that passes across your face. And when I say it would be very unwise to carry forth with what you have in mind, I'm not talking about the mare, but the stallion."

Meaning Andres. Gillian felt the usual flash of alarm whenever she was caught doing or even thinking something she shouldn't, but she also felt a flare of temper. Ever since she'd left Wright last summer, she'd had the run of Huntleigh to herself. She'd served as her cousin's household manager and few had told her what to do or what to think. After years of living with her husband's parents, the haughty marquess and marchioness of Atherstone, while Wright had been off to war, the freedom had been heaven.

She would not allow a host of people to poke their noses in her business. She didn't answer to any of them. She was six and twenty, old enough to know her own mind.

"Oh, granted he is handsome," Aunt Agatha continued when Gillian didn't reply immediately. "All those Latin men are. Even a woman my age becomes a little giddy looking at them. However they are no substitute for a good English husband."

"Like mine? A man I haven't seen in years?" Gillian asked, forcing herself to remain calm as Andres chose that moment to smile over at her. She gave him a small wave.

Disapproval radiated from her aunt. "First, you should know that those Spaniards are like the Italians, daffy headed over anything with yellow hair. Don't fool yourself into believing he sees anything else but your hair, your hair, your hair. Second, *you* are a married woman."

"I know what I am," Gillian replied, not looking at her aunt but watching Andres set the mare into a trot on the lunge line. The idea that a man as accomplished as Andres would chase a woman because she had blond hair was ridiculous. There was more between them than mere lust. They had discussed their feelings last night while pretending to play a serious game of chess. "I have no feelings for Wright and I doubt if he thinks of me at all."

"He thinks of you every week when he writes that letter demanding you return to London."

"Demands are not requests, Aunt."

"Since when must a man request his wife to come to live under his roof?"

"Since he practically ran from our wedding bed back to his mistress. Since he went off to war without a backward glance in my direction, leaving me to reside with those two horrid people he calls parents. Since he rarely wrote or gave any consideration to me for four *long* years."

"He was at war, Gillian. On the front."

Gillian brought her brows together, pretending to consider the matter. "I wonder if he wrote his mistress or forgot to pay *her* bills each month."

Aunt Agatha's brows rose to her hairline. "Did Wright forget to pay your bills?"

"No," Gillian conceded.

"Was he *ungenerous*?"

"With his affections or his money?" Gillian shot back.

"Money," her aunt snapped.

"I received my allowance but not much else. Not even a home of my own — which his mistress did indeed have." Gillian turned to watch Andres, not wanting this conversation with her aunt and yet unable to stop herself from adding, "There is more to a marriage than money . . . such as affection and companionship."

"And you believe you will find that with some penniless Spanish nobleman?"

"I believe I want a divorce," Gillian said, the words flowing out of her mouth with a will of their own. *Divorce,* the unthinkable word, had been on her mind ever since she'd finally had enough of living under Wright's father's roof where not even the servants held respect for her. Divorce. Freedom. A chance to choose again and this time pick a life of love.

It sounded right. Absolutely, perfectly right.

But not to her aunt, who appeared struck dumb by such an admission — but not for long.

"Di— ?" Aunt Agatha came near to collapse, clutching a hand to her heart. Gillian placed a hand to stabilize her, glancing over her shoulder to see if any of the men noticed the dramatics.

They didn't. Their eyes were on the Andalusian.

Aunt Agatha gasped for air and tried again, "Divor— ?" She couldn't go on without a swoon, and so she gave up attempting to say the word "divorce" to demand, "Would you ruin us all? The scandal would be horrific."

"It would impact no one but myself," Gillian snapped.

Her aunt made a disbelieving sound. "It would shame us all and send me to an early death."

"Aunt Agatha, please. You must understand how unhappy I am."

But her aunt wasn't listening. Instead, she was reasoning the matter out in her head, speaking aloud as she did so. "Wait, you can't petition Parliament for a divorce. Only a husband may present such a petition — and Wright would never attempt such a thing."

She seemed so relieved to know Gillian's plans were thwarted that Gillian felt a little mean as she said, "Actually, there is a growing movement amongst important, intelligent women to see such a circumstance changed. Women should have some voice in a marriage. It shouldn't all be the husband's wishes and we deserve the right to petition

Parliament for a divorce."

Aunt Agatha's brows snapped together. "You have been associating with those bluestockings again, haven't you? You complain about not having freedom but it hasn't stopped you from forming friendships with those radical, educated females. Why didn't I write Wright and warn him? This is my fault as well as yours —"

"It's *not* your fault," Gillian insisted before her aunt could work herself into another frenzy, "or your affair. I will protect the family from scandal as well as I can. But, Aunt, I will not continue living a solitary life. Or a lukewarm one. I've fallen in love with Andres Ramigio. I want to be free to be with him. Of course, Wright may very well not divorce me. He isn't interested in my doings. I could live openly in the heart of London with the barón and I doubt it would matter to him." She hated the resentment in her voice. It took away from the bravado.

Her aunt was even more aghast by that suggestion. "You've known that Spaniard less than a month and yet you would throw your life away?"

"Time has no bearing. What I feel for him is so vivid and strong. It is as if we were fated to meet."

"Fated for disaster," her aunt corrected.

"And what of Wright? I remember when you thought you were fated to meet him. Don't attempt to dye this wool. I was there. You told me you fell in love with him at first sight. He walked into Lady Sybman's ballroom and you all but ran to me begging for an introduction. Your feet didn't touch ground until three months later when you married. And correct me if I'm wrong, but I remember that he wasn't all that attentive back then."

That was true. Back then, she had thought there was no man more dashing, more gallant, more wonderful than he — but he *had* been distant and distracted, something she'd been too lovesick to register before their marriage. "He didn't turn out to be what I had expected." *Which was a man who loved her.*

"Husbands rarely are." Aunt Agatha moved closer to her. "Gillian, Wright is a man slated for high positions in government. It was because of your father's writings and connections that the marquess of Atherton," she referred to Wright's overbearing parent, "would even consider you for his youngest son. The scandal of divorce would ruin many of Wright's prospects. Or is that what this is about? Are you just so angry at his treatment of you that you wish to pay him back in kind? Do you wish to destroy him?"

"I have no desire to hurt him in any way," Gillian answered, offended at the suggestion. "I'm merely saying that we have a sham of a marriage and should go our own ways. Truly, Aunt, Wright sat me down the day after our wedding and told me of his mistress. They'd played together as children on his father's country estate. He grew up with her and professed he loved her. He's always loved her."

"Every man says that about his first mistress —"

"He meant it." Gillian glanced over at the crowd of men. Andres was cantering the mare, something far more interesting to the gentlemen than two women with their heads together.

She tried to make her aunt understand. "Wright was very sincere. He loves Jess."

"Jess?"

"That is the name of his mistress. He'd married me because I was his father's choice. Wright said he'd known he would have to marry someday and if it could not be Jess, then he hadn't cared whom he married. So, it was me. Lucky . . . lucky . . . me." Gillian turned away, tears stinging her eyes.

19

"My dear niece," Aunt Agatha said in commiseration, her expression softening. "What pain you must have suffered. I've been blind to your unhappiness."

"I don't want your sympathy, Aunt. I want your understanding. I held on to the marriage. I really did believe Wright and I were supposed to be together. The 'magic' you teased me about. I dutifully wrote Wright every week after he returned to his post, trying to sound happy when I was completely miserable. He wrote occasionally to ask how I was doing but little else. I was an afterthought in his life. Well, I no longer want to be an afterthought. He broke my heart, but I'm stronger now and know my own mind. Six months ago, he returned from the war and instead of coming to see me, he went to his mistress. *That's* when I found the courage to leave that cold, cold house his parents live in and come here. I'm happier than I have ever been. I want love in my life. I want a family. If I can't divorce my husband, then I shall happily live in sin with my lover and our children."

"Your father will have a fit."

"My father and stepmother are so busy with all their children, they won't care. When I wrote and told them I had changed my residence, they didn't even raise a question. Well, my stepmother wished to know when I could visit again because I'm so good with the children. You know she's had another baby."

"*Another* one?" Aunt Agatha rolled her eyes. "The woman is past the age of reason for such nonsense. Why, it is almost *indecent*."

Gillian couldn't help a bitter smile, struck by the irony. "Yes, I've been four years married and no children because I have a husband who doesn't want me. Meanwhile, my father is three and fifty and he just sired his eighth."

Aunt Agatha dismissed her concern with a wave of her gloved hand. "He married a younger woman."

"Who is very fertile," Gillian added.

The quip startled a laugh out of her aunt. She reached over and patted Gillian's arm. "At least I did one good thing. If I hadn't swept you out of there, you would still be tending your stepmother's babies. I had so wanted happiness for you, Gillian. I'd feared they'd keep you a spinster for their own selfish reasons."

"Please, Aunt, believe me when I say I am grateful you gave me a Season. And my marriage could have turned out differently. But you see, Wright was never committed to me. And he was honest about it . . . although after the fact. In a way, I have to say I respect him for loving someone. After knowing his parents and the way they think, I realize Wright probably didn't imagine I would mind his loving another woman. Both the marquess and the marchioness have lovers. Sometimes several at a time. It's absolutely dizzying the way they carry on —"

Gillian broke off, embarrassed to be carrying tales. "My father would say they are quite hedonistic," she concluded.

Aunt Agatha stared thoughtfully up at the bare tree branches over their heads. "Do you believe Wright is?" She lowered her gaze to Gillian.

The question caught Gillian by surprise. "Hedonistic? No. In fact, I believe he is amazingly loyal. I think that loyalty made me the most envious of Jess. To have a man care that deeply for you. Don't mistake me, Aunt, there is much to admire about Wright. He has a purpose in his life, much more so than his parents. And his brothers didn't give a care or concern for anyone other than themselves."

"They both died, didn't they?"

Gillian nodded. "Yes, last year. Almost within four months of each other. It's very sad except both of them died of causes that could have been avoided if they had been more moral and upstanding. Their deaths are the reason the marquess had Wright ordered home. He didn't want to run the risk of the third and last son being shot by the French."

"Was Wright happy about that?"

Slipping her free hand inside the warmth of her velvet muff, Gillian confessed, "Sadly, I don't know. I have no idea of how the man I made the mistake of marrying thinks or what he feels."

"My dear, dear girl. I am so sorry," Aunt Agatha said. "But perhaps Wright has had a change of heart and wants you in his life, something you should wish. Now that he is his father's heir, you will be a marchioness."

Gillian sighed heavily. Aunt Agatha could be very single-minded. "Wright doesn't care about me."

"He has been writing you, every week."

"To order me home." Gillian turned to watch Andres bring the horse to a puffing halt. "And he certainly holds no passion for me."

"Are you discovering you are a passionate woman?" her aunt surmised.

"Yes," Gillian said softly. "I am." Andres caught them watching him and smiled. She smiled back until her aunt's new theory intruded upon the moment.

"Or are you attempting to strike back at Wright?" Aunt Agatha wondered. "That's what this divorce talk really is, isn't it? You want to humiliate him. If you do, that must mean you still care for him —"

Shocked by her aunt's conclusion, Gillian interrupted her to insist, "I love another —"

"Or do you just *think* you do. That silver-eyed Spaniard is handsome. I'll give you that. But you are better than he, Gillian. If you aren't wise, you could be making the same mistake all over again —"

"What mistake?" Andres's accented voice asked.

Both women turned in surprise, neither having expected or anticipated his approach.

Andres was still in shirt sleeves, but a stable lad hurried up to him with his jacket and gray wool greatcoat.

Gillian knew he had to be aware they'd been talking about him. Andres always picked up on the nuances, especially since both she and Aunt Agatha had guilty expressions on their faces. However, he gifted her aunt with his easy, confident smile and bowed over her hand. "Hello, Lady Kensett. Have you had the opportunity to see the lovely new girl in my life?"

"If you are discussing the mare, I barely noticed. I don't like *foreign* horseflesh," Aunt Agatha answered, the undercurrent of unpleasantness to her tone leaving no one to doubt she referenced him behind the word "foreign."

Gillian wanted to take her by the hand and march her to the house as if she was a willful child but Andres took it all in stride. Unlike Wright, who had been born into privilege and wealth, no one had handed Andres anything. He may have been Spanish nobility but circumstances and the war had robbed him of all that he owned. Yes, he'd lived by his wits but life had taught him compassion — and perhaps that was what Gillian admired the most about him. He was unfailingly respectful in his dealing with everyone, including the servants and noticed the slightest details such as when Gillian changed her hair style or appeared to have had a difficult night's sleep.

"I have a great appreciation for your fine horses," Andres said smoothly. "However, for breeding it is good to introduce a new bloodline from time to time. It makes for stronger, more intelligent offspring."

Aunt Agatha's gaze narrowed. Her mouth turned down into a set frown, the sort the aged take on when they are certain the young are too foolish to protect themselves. "Be careful, *Barón*. Lady Wright is not a mare to be culled away from the herd by some randy, less-than-to-be-admired stallion."

Gillian was mortified by her aunt's statement. She started to protest but Andres's hand on her arm stayed her. "Your concern is understandable, my lady," he said. "But I assure you, Lady Kensett, my intentions toward the lovely Lady Wright are most honorable."

If Gillian wasn't already in love with him, she would have fallen so in that moment. Turning to him, she leaned close, her shoulder touching his. She smiled. Their faces were inches away from each other and it was as if the rest of the world, including her disapproving aunt, faded away.

It hadn't been easy for Gillian to face her desire. She'd wanted to honor her wedding vows and, truthfully, her pain over years of being ignored was so great that when she'd first arrived at Huntleigh, a liaison of any sort would have been out of the question.

But Andres's presence had breathed new life, new hopes and dreams into her. And he loved her. She could see it in his eyes.

Life was too short to live without love.

She'd made a mistake in marrying Wright, but a mistake could always be corrected —

One of the stable lads gave a shout that a rider approached. Gillian glanced over her shoulder in the direction of the drive. As her cousin's hostess when he and his wife weren't in residence, it would be her responsibility to welcome this new guest.

However, any welcoming words died in her throat as she realized who the tall rider on the broad-chested bay was.

Aunt Agatha recognized who he was as well. "Thank God," she said fervently. "It's Wright."

She turned to Gillian with a look of triumph. "See, he does care. He's come to take you in hand at last."

CHAPTER TWO

By the look of the mud splattered on his horse and his boots, Wright had ridden hard to reach Huntleigh. He'd also traveled alone.

Gillian took a step back, uncertain what this could mean. Her experiences traveling with his family had always meant a contingent of servants, outriders, and hangers-on. The marquess and his marchioness never went anywhere alone . . . unless it was for a romantic assignation.

Wright dismounted, throwing the reins to a stable lad, but taking a moment to loosen the horse's girth himself. He gave the animal a pat on his neck, a gesture the horse returned by turning his head for a nuzzle.

Gillian could barely breathe, let alone think. It had been four years since she'd last seen her husband, and yet he'd figured large in her life for almost every day of them.

Gone was the uniform he'd so proudly

worn. He now wore boots and leather breeches beneath a wool watchcoat, its military cut flattering to his physique. His wide brimmed hat had been pulled down low over his eyes. He took it off and pushed his dark hair back as he gave instructions for the care of his horse to the stable lad.

Gillian's impulse was to pick up her skirts and run up to the house, but that would have been the coward's way, and she was no coward. Not any longer. So, she stood her ground, Andres at her side, and studied her husband with a critical eye.

Wright needed a haircut. The hair at the nape of his neck brushed the back of his coat. And he seemed to have grown taller over the years, if that were possible, and harder.

Then again, there were some things about her husband that were very familiar, such as his square jaw line, his strong nose, and his startling blue, deep-set eyes. His brows were straight and humorless, his lower lip full and sensuous, and he moved with restless energy — until he noticed her.

For a long moment, he studied her with the same critical eye she had just given with him. What he thought was not reflected in his expression.

Gillian realized she held her breath and

released it.

He noticed even that small movement. He began walking straight for her.

Andres placed a protective hand in the small of her back. Gillian was thankful for that light touch. It kept her knees from buckling.

If Wright noticed the Spaniard by her side, he gave no indication. His gaze was honed in on her.

"Praise the Lord, he has arrived," Aunt Agatha said under her breath.

"You didn't write him, did you?" Gillian demanded without looking at her aunt.

"I should have," her aunt murmured.

Andres leaned close to her ear. "*Amor,* you needn't fear him. Not while I'm here."

"I don't fear him, my love. I dislike him." Years of being treated with indifference had left her cold, unfeeling — and yet, she was very aware of him.

That awareness made her uncertain. She'd thought she was over him.

There had been a time she had expected Wright to come for her.

He hadn't.

And now that she was happy, when she'd finally discovered a measure of peace and contentment, *that* would be the moment when he would arrive.

"My lady, I don't make threats," he answered.

Gillian shook her head. "Why?" she asked, puzzled. "You don't *desire* me, Wright. You barely knew I existed after our wedding and we haven't spoken for four years. Indeed, when you returned from the Continent six months ago, you didn't search me out. So, why are you doing this now? Why have you just remembered I'm your wife and decided to stake a claim?"

A shadow crossed his face, a moment of hesitation from a man she had never seen hesitate about anything. It caught her off guard, made her wonder . . . until he said, "I want you home."

Gillian drew back, every suspicious bone in her body sounding a warning. She no longer worried that they had an audience. "I *am* home, Wright. This is my home. We don't suit. We never have. Weren't you the one who told me as much years ago? So, let us be free of each other. Set me aside, do what you will, but I'm not leaving Huntleigh with you."

"And I say you will," he countered, one foot already on the path leading up to her. "By law you have no choice. No one can stop me from taking you —"

"*I* can," Andres answered, being so bold

35

as to grab Wright's arm and turning him around to face him. "I *will*."

Wright's eyes narrowed. "Leave it, Baron," he answered, not bothering to place a Spanish accent on the title. "This is not your fight."

"But it is, *amigo*," Andres said, addressing Wright as an equal. "Gillian does not have to go anywhere she does not wish to be."

Tears burned Gillian's eyes. No one had ever stood up for her before. Ever.

"Are you challenging me?" Wright asked, his voice deadly quiet.

"I am," Andres answered.

Gillian's tears evaporated, replaced by stunned horror as the meaning of their words sank in.

"Swords?" Wright asked without missing a beat. "I'm afraid it must be done now. I don't have time to waste. I wish to be back on the road as quickly as possible."

"Then you may leave now," Andres said amicably.

"Not without my *wife*," Wright answered.

Andres shrugged. "Swords, pistols, knives. They are all fine with me."

"Then swords it is."

They both sounded calm about the challenge and neither man had given her so much as a glance once they'd started speaking to each other.

Wright turned to Packy, the head groom who had helped him with his horse. "Send someone to the house for dueling swords. I'm certain His Grace has them."

Packy nodded his obedience and directed one of the lads to do Wright's bidding. Andres once again removed his greatcoat and jacket, preparing to duel. Wright threw off his heavy coat while the men in the stable yard began moving back into a circle for the men.

Of course, their preparations were moot because Gillian was not about to let a duel be fought. She caught the stable lad before he could run to the house. "Stand right there," she ordered the boy, holding up a finger in warning.

"Go fetch the swords," Wright countermanded without looking up. The lad raced away.

Gillian's temper snapped. She stormed forward into the center of the cleared ring. "This is absolute nonsense," she said.

"Actually," her husband said, rolling up his sleeves, "it is the easiest way to decide the matter."

"No, it is not," Gillian said. "There are many easier ways, such as discussion or respecting *my* rights to decide what *I* want."

Aunt Agatha came forward and put her hand in the crook of Gillian's arm, gently pulling her to the side. "Gillian, you are being a bit of a ninny," she whispered, strangely subdued. "This is the way men decide these matters. Besides, you have no rights. You are married. When you chose to defy your husband, what did you expect?"

Gillian dug in her heels. "Not a duel."

"You didn't?" her aunt asked with a skeptical lift of one eyebrow. "What sort of men do you think they are?"

"Not the sort who would kill each other." Gillian practically tossed the muff to the ground in exasperation. She turned to Andres. "You *mustn't* do this. It's *nonsense.*"

The tall Spaniard came over and placed his hands on her arms. It was the first time he'd publicly touched her. "I do it for you, *amor,*" he said quietly. "I love you, Gillian. From the moment I saw you, I have wanted you. You are kind and good." He reached for a strand of her hair beneath her velvet hat. "So lovely, so caring. When I entered Huntleigh's hall, I felt the warmth of a home, the warmth you created." He smiled. "Do not worry for me. All will be well. There isn't an Englishman who is a better swordsman than I."

"You *love* me," Gillian repeated, her voice

38

Wright came to a stop three feet from her. Since she stood on the path leading up the hillside to the house, they were almost at eye level. He seemed oblivious to anyone else but her.

She spoke first, pleased she sounded calm and in control of herself. "Hello, Wright."

"Hello, *Wife*," he answered, the set of his mouth grim.

His gaze flicked over to Andres. So, he *had* noticed the Spaniard. She wondered if he'd heard rumors and if the thought of her with another man had been what had finally roused him to seek her out. Of course, he'd traveled for naught. It was too late for them and now was as good a time as any to ask for a divorce.

Gillian opened her mouth to speak but Aunt Agatha must have sensed her mood because she quickly said, "Perhaps, Wright, you and my niece would like to go to the house where it is more *private*." She started to take a step off the path to clear the way for them but Gillian stopped her.

"There is no necessity for us to go to the house." She smiled at Wright. This was *her* home, *her* little piece of England. It felt good to be confident in front of him. "Wright won't be staying long."

An angry muscle in his jaw tightened —

31

and for a second, the memory of their last argument hit her full force. She'd been in so much pain, and he'd said he was powerless to help her because he loved another.

His jaw had tightened exactly this way, and then he'd left.

"I have no intention of returning to London," she informed him, raising her voice so all could hear her. "I will not go. And *you* are not welcome here, Wright. Not at all."

Wright's response was to turn to Andres. He scowled and bit out, "Who are you?"

"The barón de Vasconia," Andres said, his tone just as insolent. He didn't offer a bow and she felt the lightning thrill of triumph. *Good. Let him know how it feels to have your spouse choose another —*

"Do you always stand so close to other men's wives?" Wright drawled with deadly intent.

Gillian's exaltation vanished.

She moved between the two men. "You are out of line, Wright," she said, her heart beating rapidly. His presence was setting off emotions she didn't wish to investigate closely. What had Aunt Agatha suggested, that her talk of divorce was to humiliate him? To hurt him as he had hurt her . . .

Wright swung his sharp gaze from Andres

32

to herself. "We need to talk, Gillian."

"I have no desire to speak to you at all," she answered, and needing to put space between them, announced to no one in particular, "I'm going to the house." She started to turn.

"Very well," Wright said, "I will go with you."

"That is not necessary," Gillian stated flatly.

"It *is*," came the strong reply.

She wanted to argue. She wanted to lash out at him with her tongue until he bled.

But she wouldn't. For whatever reason, she couldn't. Words, angry, sad, broken, bitter — all clogged her throat. Instead, her muff on one hand, she picked up her skirts and started up the path.

He must have taken a step after her because she heard Andres say in his lovely rolling accent, "I am sorry, my lord, but she does not wish you to accompany her." She turned to see that her gallant Spaniard was blocking Wright's way up the path.

"And who does she want to accompany her?" Wright wondered, the words almost a snarl of frustration. *"You?"*

Andres did not flinch. "If I am so honored," he answered.

Gillian's feet were suddenly rooted to the

earth. She had not anticipated Andres doing battle for her. He was tall but Wright was taller, and more muscular. And far more threatening. "*Barón,* it is all right," she said.

He shot her a heart-stopping smile. "But it is not. If my Gillian wishes to be alone, then it is my pleasure to see it is so."

My Gillian. He had only called her that in their private conversations. Along with *amor.*

She could have kissed him for his chivalry in protecting her, but he should not have done so. Not in front of everyone. Wright had been correct. They should have spoken in private.

As it was, her husband chose to ignore the Spaniard. He looked up the path at her. "Gillian, we can do this one of two ways. I've written. I've been reasonable. I have been patient. I'm asking you politely and within my rights as a husband for you to come home with me."

"And my other choice?" she asked, her earlier confusion concerning him vanishing in the face of his high-handedness.

"I will resort to force."

Force? That would be unreasonable and Wright never did anything unreasonable — especially for her. Or so she had thought.

"You wouldn't dare," she informed him.

"My lady, I don't make threats," he answered.

Gillian shook her head. "Why?" she asked, puzzled. "You don't *desire* me, Wright. You barely knew I existed after our wedding and we haven't spoken for four years. Indeed, when you returned from the Continent six months ago, you didn't search me out. So, why are you doing this now? Why have you just remembered I'm your wife and decided to stake a claim?"

A shadow crossed his face, a moment of hesitation from a man she had never seen hesitate about anything. It caught her off guard, made her wonder . . . until he said, "I want you home."

Gillian drew back, every suspicious bone in her body sounding a warning. She no longer worried that they had an audience. "I *am* home, Wright. This is my home. We don't suit. We never have. Weren't you the one who told me as much years ago? So, let us be free of each other. Set me aside, do what you will, but I'm not leaving Huntleigh with you."

"And I say you will," he countered, one foot already on the path leading up to her. "By law you have no choice. No one can stop me from taking you —"

"*I* can," Andres answered, being so bold

as to grab Wright's arm and turning him around to face him. "I *will*."

Wright's eyes narrowed. "Leave it, Baron," he answered, not bothering to place a Spanish accent on the title. "This is not your fight."

"But it is, *amigo*," Andres said, addressing Wright as an equal. "Gillian does not have to go anywhere she does not wish to be."

Tears burned Gillian's eyes. No one had ever stood up for her before. Ever.

"Are you challenging me?" Wright asked, his voice deadly quiet.

"I am," Andres answered.

Gillian's tears evaporated, replaced by stunned horror as the meaning of their words sank in.

"Swords?" Wright asked without missing a beat. "I'm afraid it must be done now. I don't have time to waste. I wish to be back on the road as quickly as possible."

"Then you may leave now," Andres said amicably.

"Not without my *wife*," Wright answered.

Andres shrugged. "Swords, pistols, knives. They are all fine with me."

"Then swords it is."

They both sounded calm about the challenge and neither man had given her so much as a glance once they'd started speak-

wondrous at how easily he'd made his admission. "I love you, too, Andres. But what sort of a future will we have if you run my husband through?"

Andres laughed, the sound confident, carefree even.

Gillian wanted to pop him with her muffed hand to knock sense into him. "Or Wright could kill you," she said, wanting to be certain what was at stake. "Don't let his London clothes fool you. The man has been a military officer for years and even before that, he was a noted swordsman. I couldn't bear to have anything happen to you."

She couldn't bear to have anything happen to either of them. She had no desire to see Wright dead. "If you fight this duel, everyone will talk. We will have to leave England. You don't know my husband. He's a very powerful man in his own right, let alone with his father's influence."

"I don't care if I live in England," Andres told her. "Or what gossips may say. Our love will keep us safe."

Over the past hour, she had cavalierly made the same statement to Aunt Agatha. Now it sounded like madness, and she understood what her aunt had been trying to say to her.

She looked to the other side of the circle

of men. Wright stood, a solitary figure with his arms crossed. Andres was a great favorite amongst her relatives and the servants. They would be cheering for him. Wright had no one to champion his side. The irony, of course, was that he was all alone . . . much like she'd felt living under his father's roof.

"Do all men think themselves immortal?" she wondered softly before saying to Andres, "Please, don't do this."

His expression sobered. "You know the answer, *amor.*"

He wouldn't cry off. Not with his honor on the line.

Gillian turned away from him and walked over to where her husband stood, his face a stone mask. "Wright, you must not fight a duel. Not over me."

She could feel Andres watching her. Feel everyone watching her. Embarrassment brought heat to her cheeks. Gillian had never enjoyed being the center of attention.

"I take care of what is mine, Gillian."

She shook her head. "I am not some animal that you can buy and sell. Or some woman in a harem you can lock up. My decision not to return with you has nothing to do with the *barón.*"

Wright gave her a small, tired smile. "It doesn't matter, Gill. He has taken up your cause and as your husband, I am honor bound to exert my authority."

Gillian reached for her temper. It protected her from guilt. "A battle of honor? Wright, I matter very little to you."

Once again there was that stubborn set of his jaw returned. "Obviously you matter a great deal to me, my lady, or I wouldn't be here."

"Please, don't even attempt to portray the role of wounded husband," she said with exasperation. "Our marriage was a sham."

"It was legal and valid."

"But it was a union of convenience. Your father wanted my father's connections and their good will. Otherwise, you wouldn't have given me a second look."

He released a world-weary sigh. "Gillian, does it matter anymore? This is an old argument between us. So what if those were considerations when I asked for your hand? You could have refused. Why didn't you?"

Because she'd fallen in love with him.

It was one thing to admit it to her aunt or herself, another to reveal the depth of her foolishness to the man who had made her so foolish.

Besides, he was right — it no longer mattered. She had Andres . . . although, especially after Aunt Agatha's accusations, a portion of her feared her aunt might be correct in suggesting at least some of Andres's attraction was the opportunity for Gillian to defy her husband.

She immediately shut that stray thought away.

"We all make mistakes, Wright," she answered him.

His angry sharp eyes went to Andres and then back to her. "Yes," he drawled, "apparently we *all* do."

His criticism vanquished any remnant of guilt. "I hope he runs you through," she said. Turning, she walked away.

But she didn't go to Andres. The crowd around him had stepped back so that both he and Wright stood very much alone.

Instead, she marched up to her aunt. "You must talk sense into them."

"I don't waste my breath on men," Aunt Agatha answered. "Or goddaughters."

"You seem to have forgotten that rule earlier," Gillian said crossly. "You were offering me quite a bit of advice."

"A pity you didn't heed it."

The stable lad they'd sent for swords came running down the path carrying them followed by a number of relatives and other guests from the house who apparently wished to witness the duel. Huntleigh cause and as your husband, I am honor bound to exert my authority."

Gillian reached for her temper. It protected her from guilt. "A battle of honor? Wright, I matter very little to you."

Once again there was that stubborn set of his jaw returned. "Obviously you matter a great deal to me, my lady, or I wouldn't be here."

"Please, don't even attempt to portray the role of wounded husband," she said with exasperation. "Our marriage was a sham."

"It was legal and valid."

"But it was a union of convenience. Your father wanted my father's connections and their good will. Otherwise, you wouldn't have given me a second look."

He released a world-weary sigh. "Gillian, does it matter anymore? This is an old argument between us. So what if those were considerations when I asked for your hand? You could have refused. Why didn't you?"

Because she'd fallen in love with him.

It was one thing to admit it to her aunt or herself, another to reveal the depth of her foolishness to the man who had made her so foolish.

Besides, he was right — it no longer mattered. She had Andres . . . although, especially after Aunt Agatha's accusations, a por-

41

tion of her feared her aunt might be correct in suggesting at least some of Andres's attraction was the opportunity for Gillian to defy her husband.

She immediately shut that stray thought away.

"We all make mistakes, Wright," she answered him.

His angry sharp eyes went to Andres and then back to her. "Yes," he drawled, "apparently we *all* do."

His criticism vanquished any remnant of guilt. "I hope he runs you through," she said. Turning, she walked away.

But she didn't go to Andres. The crowd around him had stepped back so that both he and Wright stood very much alone.

Instead, she marched up to her aunt. "You must talk sense into them."

"I don't waste my breath on men," Aunt Agatha answered. "Or goddaughters."

"You seem to have forgotten that rule earlier," Gillian said crossly. "You were offering me quite a bit of advice."

"A pity you didn't heed it."

The stable lad they'd sent for swords came running down the path carrying them followed by a number of relatives and other guests from the house who apparently wished to witness the duel. Huntleigh always entertained a large number of guests for the Christmas holidays and many lingered on their visits for months. Now they would have a good story to tell when they returned home and Gillian wished the ground would open up and swallow her whole.

Her cousin Carter Lowrie straggled behind the others, appearing as if he'd just risen from bed. Charming, good-humored and a bit lazy, Carter came up to the women and asked, "Why is Andres in a duel?"

"Because Gillian's husband has come for her and wishes to run him through," Aunt Agatha said with a gusto that Gillian thought was quite unbecoming.

"Ah, Wright has finally arrived," Carter murmured. "Thought he would show himself sooner or later."

Gillian scowled at him, knowing his sentiment was probably shared by a good number of the men whether they liked Andres or not. Raising her voice so she could be overheard, she decided to let them know the truth. "The *barón* and I have not done anything that should warrant a duel. We are merely good friends. *Truly,*" she added in the face of her cousin's unconvinced look.

At that moment, Andres stepped into the center of the stable yard. He whipped the air with his sword, testing it.

Wright did the same. Pleased, he said, "Your terms, *Barón?*"

Gillian clasped her hands inside her velvet muff. She realized *she* was the one who didn't believe this was going to happen. Men didn't fight over her. Especially her husband.

"First blood wins," Andres said calmly.

"As you wish," Wright answered without any sign of emotion.

And then they raised their swords.

They were truly going to fight. Gillian began shaking. Wright was a bruising swordsman. She'd overheard an officer who had served with him on the Peninsula describe him that way. For the first time she realized her husband had killed men.

She didn't know Andres's experience but she knew his heart. He would fight to the death for her.

There was the slide of steel-on-steel and then both raised their arms —

Gillian found her voice. *"No."* She rushed forward, placing herself between the two men and their swords.

Both had been ready to deliver slicing blows. They pulled their weapons back just in time. Wright swore colorfully. "Do you realize you could have been killed?"

44

She shook off his complaint, unconcerned for her own safety. "This is nonsense," she informed them, speaking as if they were schoolboys. "I'm not worth fighting over."

"We disagree," Andres said.

Wright kept quiet, wary and impatient. Both men were anxious to continue their duel . . . and Gillian knew what she had to do.

Her husband would not give up. His pride was at stake.

And Andres . . . Andres so much wanted to be her champion. His love, his loyalty pierced her soul.

But she could not ask him to stake his life for her. Wright was ruthless. He was his father's son. The marquess didn't hesitate to mow down anyone who stood in his way.

There was one thing she could do to protect her beloved Andres. "I'll go with you, Wright. You've won. Have a coach readied. We'll leave as soon as I pack."

She did not wait for his response but started walking toward the house.

CHAPTER THREE

Brian Ranson, the recently named Lord Wright, watched his wife storm up the path toward the house. Her back was ramrod straight, her skirts swung with indignation — and he knew.

Gillian had taken a lover. A Spaniard, no less.

The realization flew in the face of every notion he'd held about his wife. He had expected the old Gillian, a mouse of a woman who'd been easily cowed by playing to her conscience.

Instead, he'd arrived to see her looking in good spirits and with a healthy measure of pride. She was confident, strong willed . . . and stunningly beautiful.

Of course, her looks had always been there. There were few men who wouldn't have admired her golden blond hair or her figure, which was round and full in all the right places. Brian had always found Gillian

attractive, even when he'd been in love with Jess, a slim brunette.

But there was something more here surrounding Gillian. Perhaps it was the laugh lines around blue eyes that snapped with intelligence. Or that she hadn't hesitated to make her opinion of him clear. From the moment he'd presented himself, she'd let him know her displeasure and he felt chastened. It was a novel experience for a man who'd once had the ability to make infantrymen, officers, and French alike quake in their boots.

And convinced him he was exactly correct in his instincts to bring Gillian by his side.

This new Gillian was the sort of woman he needed. She could face the challenges ahead . . . if he could bring her to London.

The Spaniard brushed by him, heading up the path after Gillian.

Brian caught his arm. "*My* wife," he said.

"That can change," the Spaniard answered.

"No, it won't," Brian said, feeling a bit smug at putting the rival in his place. "She's made her decision."

The Spaniard shook his head, unoffended. "You are a fool," he said softly. "That woman has more honor and dignity than you and I together could ever imagine.

47

She'll go with you because it is her duty but she'll find no joy in the task." He dropped his gaze to where Brian's hand still held his arm.

Brian released his hold, struck by the truth of his opponent's words.

This time when the Spaniard turned to go, he let him.

He turned and discovered everyone watched him, their disapproval clear in their expressions. He was the villain here, and he didn't know quite how that had happened.

Brian hid his doubts by taking charge. He nodded toward Packy. "Prepare a coach for my lady and bring it up to the house with all haste." He didn't wait to see his order followed but started up the path.

Lady Kensett's soft voice called to him to wait.

A stab of annoyance went up Brian's back. He'd been riding hard for the last five hours. His reception so far had not been pleasant. He didn't have time to go chasing his wife, let alone listen to the admonishments that he knew Lady Kensett wished to convey, and yet he would not be rude.

He tried to divert her by saying, "I know. You were right. You warned me. I should have come sooner."

She placed her hand on his arm, forcing

him to slow down to her aged pace as they walked up to the house. Impatience made him want to shake her off; manners forced him to obey. She smiled up at him as if knowing exactly what he was thinking.

"They aren't lovers," she confided. "Not yet, at least. Although I believe she was ready to capitulate. The *barón* cuts a very romantic figure."

"No wonder he is so angry," Brian responded. "I robbed him of his prize. Of course, perhaps I would be doing the men of England a service by running him through."

"Possibly, except I do believe he does love Gillian," Lady Kensett said. "This was no passing fancy for him."

That gave Brian pause. The sharp-eyed old lady noticed. She never missed a thing. "Good. It's nice to know you have some feelings for her, Wright, even if they are nothing more than proprietary. That duel was like watching two dogs with one bone, except that one of the dogs had true feelings for the bone. The other man just wanted it because it was his."

"Gillian is my wife," he answered as his defense. "Of course, I am concerned another man has *serious* feelings for her."

"And that is why you let her languish out

in the country for so long?"

He made an impatient gesture. "I came as soon as I could." Which was true. He couldn't really even afford the time here now but desperate men took desperate measures. His life was unraveling and Gillian was the only person left who might be able to help him. In his defense, he added, "And she hasn't wanted me to come for her. Or did you notice how welcoming she was when I arrived?"

"Gillian is a sensitive sort. I warned you when you asked for her hand. I said she was a country girl and used to country ways. You shouldn't have let her know you had a mistress, Wright. It was very careless of you."

"Or very honest."

Lady Kensett snorted her opinion. "What? Am I walking beside that rarity of rarities? An honest man? Please, Wright, you are a politician. You know that some things are best left unspoken."

"I'm *not* a politician," he insisted. "I'm a soldier."

"Not anymore. Not now that you are your father's heir. It was deuced bad luck for you that your brothers died. Before you could have done as you pleased. Now, you march to the marquess's tune."

"Is all of England about nothing but building power and social status?" he asked bitterly.

"Yes," Lady Kensett said without hesitation. "And it's always been thus. You've forgotten because you've been so busy fighting the French. There are expectations that go with a title. Responsibilities." She frowned. "I just had this discussion with Gillian."

He frowned. It was probably concerning him. He decided not to touch it. "What I find difficult," he murmured, "is how everyone thinks me odd to truly mourn the loss of my brothers. It is as if they feel I should be pleased with my good fortune over the title that came to me from their deaths." Even his parents seemed calloused. Not once had his mother shed a tear at their memories.

"It's good you've returned to England," Lady Kensett observed dryly. "Unfortunately, you've grown a heart and a conscience since you've been away. Get rid of them. They'll serve you no good purpose in London and Gillian has heart and conscience enough for the both of you."

Brian stopped. "Was I that jaded before I went to war?"

"Yes, and I'm not certain I didn't like

you better."

Lady Kensett's tart reply was unsettling.

They'd reached the top of the path. "Take that door, the garden door," she ordered, directing him with a point of her finger. "There is no need for you to go in the front entrance. The house is still full of relatives. Those that didn't go down for the duel will be waiting for you. I imagine there will be a flurry of letter-writing this night. The story may be all over London before your return. Remarkable how the post can be efficient when we least wish it to be." She was leaning heavily on his arm and he realized she was tired.

"Here, let me lead you to someplace where you can sit and rest," he said.

"The garden door will be fine enough," she responded, not refusing his offer. "There is a sitting room off to the side."

Brian had been to Huntleigh before. Holburn had invited him out for some hunting shortly after his betrothal to Gillian had been announced. It had been a good day and it had convinced Brian his parents had been right in insisting he marry her. It had also given him the opportunity to discuss with the duke a vote coming before the House of Lords that Brian's father had been keen to see go his way —

"She did love you, you know," Lady Kensett said, interrupting his thoughts.

Brian didn't comprehend at first. His mind was still in politics. Lady Kensett made a sound of frustration. "You are a fool, Wright."

"I am not trying to be," he said in his defense, opening the garden door to a wood-paneled hallway and allowing her to enter first. "And how could Gillian have loved me? We barely knew each other." In fact, they were still strangers, especially since she had changed so radically.

"Men just don't understand women," she said to the empty hallway.

For the first time in his life, Brian could agree with that statement. Certainly Jess had played him for a fool and now Gillian —

No, Gillian was coming back to London with him. The one person a man ought to be able to count on was his wife, or so Brian had told himself repeatedly on his way to Huntleigh. Gillian was a good sort. She knew her duties. She was just the person to be in his corner.

"You haven't been hearing a word I've been saying," Lady Kensett said. "Go on then. Find your wife. Let's see if you can keep her this time. Use the back stairs. Her room is on the second floor. A servant can guide you when you reach it."

Brian didn't argue but led her to the side room where there were a few chairs and a lovely view of the winter garden. Bowing over her hand, he assured her, "I was listening. And I'll try to heed your wisdom."

"I doubt you will," she disagreed with a tight smile. "After all, I'm nothing more than an old woman and you are, once things are said and done, your father's son. But I wish you well with Gillian. I like you, Wright. Always have. I had hoped the two of you would have made a good match. It pains me to see her this angry."

"She has some cause," he admitted.

"Oh, I have no doubt of that. What worries me is what you shall do about it. Happy hunting." She sank wearily into an upholstered chair and gave a soft sigh of relief. She waved for him to leave and he did so.

Brian walked down the hall. He'd known this wasn't going to be easy. And it wasn't over yet. He had to make some sort of amends with Gillian and win her over before they left or else she'd truly have a fit when they reached London.

The stairs were located off the main hall. The house was full of Holburn's relatives, and Brian ran into several as he made his way up two flights. On the first floor, three women had their heads together. As he came around the corner, they shot him looks that would have pierced right though his heart if they had been arrows.

Fortunately, the second floor wasn't as busy. At the top of the stairs, he found a maid who nodded in the direction of a half-open door at the other end of the hall.

He walked to the door, but before he could knock, he heard Gillian saying, "Yes, pack it all in this trunk, Rennie. However, I want the green day dress and my walking shoes in this bag along with my toiletries. I have no idea what Lord Wright has planned for this trip. If we stay at an inn, the bag will be easier to manage than the trunk."

A stay at an inn. That was a good idea. He'd thought to go hard and fast and reach London in the very late hours of the night. But one night would not hurt anything . . . and give him some time alone with his wife.

"Yes, my lady," the maid answered, her voice sounding stifled.

"Oh, Rennie, please don't cry . . . or you'll have me crying, too."

"I'll miss you, my lady. We all will on the staff. Everyone is most upset."

There was a beat of silence. Brian leaned his shoulder against the door sill. Gillian was still hidden from view but he could see the maid. She was dressed in Holburn's blue and cream livery and very pregnant.

"I'll be back," Gillian assured her. "Before you realize I'm gone, I'll be returning again. And when I do return, I want to hold your baby."

"Well, you'd best not be gone long, my lady," the teary-eyed maid said. "Because I feel as if I could have this child tomorrow."

Gillian laughed, the sound full of humor. Brian was transfixed. He remembered the first time he'd heard her laugh. There was no sound lighter or full of joy than Gillian's laughter. It was one of the reasons he'd decided to obey his father and offer for her.

Of course, shortly after they married, she stopped laughing.

"You aren't going to have that child for another two months, Rennie," Gillian said, moving into Brian's line of vision.

"Oh, my lady, you must be wrong. I don't believe I can go on much longer. I feel ready to hatch, I do."

"Don't worry," Gillian said, gently brushing back a curl that had escaped the maid's mobcap. "It will be over before you know it and when that happens, this pregnancy will have been worth the discomfort. You are going to have the sweetest, happiest baby."

She made babies sound wonderful, and Brian wanted to believe that was true, even though it hadn't been his experience. However, he congratulated himself. He'd made the right decision coming for her. Gillian would make things right. She'd repair the chaos that had become his life.

He rapped lightly on the door, wanting to let her know he was there.

Her manner changed. The smile left her eyes and her lips curled in disdain.

Brian tried not to retreat behind his own wall of feigned indifference. "I thought you could use my help," he said in explanation for why he was there.

Gillian's manner didn't soften. "I had imagined you would be on the road for London already."

"I have no intention of letting you travel alone," he responded. He'd meant to sound conciliatory. The words didn't come out that way. They were too stiff. He sounded offended by her attitude, which he was.

She folded a shawl, not bothering to look at him as she said briskly, "You needn't worry. I am very adept at taking care of myself."

He wondered if she enjoyed that jab. Certainly it had hit its mark. He glanced at the maid, who followed their conversation back and forth with wide eyes. "Let us have a moment alone," he said.

For the first time in his life, a servant wavered at his command. The pregnant maid stood between him and her mistress and appeared ready to tell him "no."

"It's all right, Rennie," Gillian said quietly. "In fact, would you see if the coach is ready yet?"

Rennie didn't hesitate to obey Gillian's command. She bobbed a curtsey to Gillian and then walked past Brian as if he were some rube on the street. She left the door open behind her.

He shut it.

"I believe we should clear the air between us," he said.

She continued folding clothes from a pile on the bed and packing them in the trunk, ignoring him.

"I know you are upset, Gillian. But we are man and wife. If we have differences we are bound by our vows before God to settle them."

Her response was a short bark of laughter. She turned to him. "You bring up our vows now? Wright, if you had wanted to 'settle' our differences, you wouldn't have chosen your mistress over your wife."

"You needn't worry yourself about her. She's dead to —"

"Dead?" Gillian's whole manner changed. "Jess is dead?" she repeated in disbelief.

That wasn't what Brian had planned to say. She'd interrupted before he could complete his sentence that Jess was dead to him, but he quickly realized the advantage to her assumption. Besides it would make no difference. Her path and Jess's would never cross. "Yes," he confirmed.

Her hard manner melted. She slowly sank to the edge of the bed. "That's sad," she said. "I never wished that on her. How did she die?"

A cause of death escaped him. In truth, he wasn't a good liar. "I'm not certain," he hedged. "I wasn't there."

"You don't know?" Gillian shook her head as if the idea troubled her. "You told me you loved her."

He had. "Death sometimes happens quickly. Jess was a large part of my life. I trusted her." The word "trusted" had almost stuck in his throat.

Gillian shook her head and then frowned as if he'd turned right before her eyes into the lowest form of worm. "And *now* you have come for me?"

Words failed him. His wife had a sharp

mind. Too late he saw the trap of his own making, and there was nothing he could do but stand before her, guilty as charged.

"I need you." Brian had not expected to say such words. They'd come out of him on their own.

They'd surprised her, too. The line of her mouth flattened. "*Need* me?" Her gaze shifted away from him going toward the hearth. Her fingers rubbed a crease into the shawl's material. With a small, self-deprecating half laugh, she said, "You've never needed anyone. At least not a woman."

"I'm not made of stone, Gillian. Nor am I perfect. I know I hurt you when we married."

She pressed her lips together, dropping her gaze to the crease she'd folded into her shawl.

He pushed on, sensing victory. "You have the right to be angry, Gillian, but I'm *here.* That should tell you something about my hopes for us."

"We are strangers who don't even like each other —"

"That is *not* true. I have always admired you."

"Admired?" she repeated softly to herself. "You *never* admired me."

In a sudden movement, she threw the shawl aside. The lines of her face tensed. He braced himself for tears. Instead, she met him with lightning in her eyes. "I am going with you to London because I want my freedom. I love Andres Ramigio. I never thought I would love again after the way you treated me. But now, I have a second chance for happiness and I'm going to take it. London is where the lawyers and clerics are who will help me be free of you. I will be no docile wife, Wright. I will resist you every step of the way and the only way you will find peace is if you divorce me."

He'd faced French cannons that packed less firepower than his wife at this moment.

But she was coming to London.

"Fair enough," he answered. "You've given me warning. Now the battle will begin."

"The battle?"

"The war I plan on waging to win your heart."

Now it was her turn to be speechless. Brian smiled. It was the first point he'd scored with his wife. "I'll leave you to pack."

He knew when it was time to retreat.

So he was gone.

Gillian slammed down the lid of the trunk in frustration. He thought to win her heart?

61

He should have thought of that four years ago.

And here he was thinking he was so clever, but she understood what he was doing. He was attempting to unsettle her. He'd badger her until she relented, and then he would revert to his old ways once he thought he had her in the palm of his hand again —

A knock on the door alerted her that Rennie had returned.

"Is the coach ready?" Gillian asked. "We must lock this trunk and then I will be ready . . ."

Her voice trailed off as she saw it wasn't Rennie who had knocked, but Andres. The expression on his face broke her heart.

"Don't go," he whispered.

She ran and threw herself into his arms. He hugged her as if he'd never let her go. All this time, they'd dared not touch and now this felt so very good. So *right.*

Gillian buried her face into the side of his neck, breathing in the scent of his skin. He was strong and solid.

"I don't want to go," she confessed. She tightened her hold around his neck to let him know exactly how much she meant those words.

Andres pulled away. His silver eyes were serious as he said, "We will run away. We'll leave. Now. I have friends in Belgium. And I'll take you to Italy and perhaps, Greece."

Gillian drew herself out of his arms. "*I* won't run. Our love deserves more than that. Trust me, please, Andres. I will see myself free of this marriage."

"It will not be easy."

"I know."

He gathered her close again, his gaze shifting from hers. He had his doubts. She did too. Divorce wasn't easy. It required an act of Parliament. But Gillian had to believe it could be done. She did not want to live her life trapped in a loveless marriage. "My husband's family is politically very powerful. If anyone could arrange for a divorce, they can. All I must do is convince them they don't want me in their lives any longer. After all, as his father's heir, Wright must have a wife willing to give him a son. I won't let him touch me."

"And what shall I do in the meantime?" Andres asked, bitter disappointment in his words. "How can I let you go by yourself with *him*."

"Please, *amor,* you must trust me. My plan is the best. If I can't convince Wright to ask for a divorce, then I will run away with you. We'll have no choice. We'll become vagabonds and wander from country to country." She smiled at the thought, reaching up and brushing her fingertips against his hair. He was so handsome it was almost hard to believe he was in love with her.

Nor did she doubt his love. A wiser man in Andres's circumstances would marry for money. Andres chose her, a woman with nothing to offer him save herself.

He placed his hands on her shoulders. "I will stay here. I will wait. But you must promise that if you need me, you will send word. I will ride the swiftest horse and do whatever I must to come to you, *amor.* And until the day you send for me, I shall not smile. It will be a challenge to even breathe."

His words tightened around her heart. She came up on her toes to give him their first kiss. Closing her eyes, she pressed her lips against his and would have pulled back except for Andres's arms coming around her.

Immediately, their mouths melded together and he kissed her as a woman should be kissed.

Gillian had dreamed of kissing Andres this way. She almost couldn't believe it was happening.

Too soon, the kiss ended. When Andres released her, she wobbled a second, befuddled. She couldn't remember her name let alone her purpose.

Andres steadied her with his hand, pleased with himself. "Remember, send one word, and I shall come to you."

He pressed another quick kiss to her forehead and left the room.

Gillian was tempted to chase after him for another kiss. That would set the servants' tongues wagging. Instead, she sank down upon the upholstered seat in front of her dressing table. She raised her fingertips to her lips, wanting to remember the feel of Andres's kiss —

"The coach is here, my lady," Rennie said, entering the room with only one knock on the door for warning. Gillian quickly dropped her hand. "And I have the footmen in the hall to carry your trunk," Rennie reported, pleased with her efficiency.

Gillian forced her mind away from Andres's kiss. "Yes, thank you," she murmured, conscious that her cheeks burned from the direction of her thoughts.

"Is something the matter, my lady?" Rennie asked, a worried frown between her brows.

"The matter?" Gillian repeated quickly as she slid her arms into the sleeves of her coat — and then realized she had nothing for which to be ashamed. She had fallen in love with a man worthy of her and so unlike her husband she could dance a jig. "Nothing is the matter," she said, setting her velvet hat on her head and picking up her muff. "In fact, there never has been a time when everything is so right."

"Really, my lady?" Rennie asked, uncertain.

"Yes, *really.* Now bring in those footmen and don't forget my travel bag."

Her relatives and the other guests waited downstairs to see her off. All made promises to visit her in London. After serving a year seeing to her cousin's estate, she'd grown quite close with many of them.

Aunt Agatha stood by the open door. "Are you certain you don't want my maid to travel with you?"

"I'm fine," Gillian said. "Atherton's household has servants for the servants. I'll choose a maid from one of them. But while I'm gone, please watch over Rennie and send me a letter the moment she has her baby."

"I will," her aunt promised.

Gillian glanced around the people in the hall to see her off. She didn't see Wright or Andres. "Has Wright gone on?" she wondered, going out onto the front step.

Wright's horse was nowhere to be seen either.

"I presume," her aunt said. "We haven't seen him." She leaned close to Gillian so that her next words would not be overheard. "I will admit to you I am disappointed in him. He should be here. I'm most vexed at the idea that he would travel on ahead."

"We had a short discussion upstairs," Gillian confessed. "We didn't part on good terms."

"Oh, well, then Wright probably took off in a pout. You know how men are," Aunt Agatha said. "But it is disappointing. I had expected better of him."

"Really? I didn't. But then, I'm his wife," Gillian couldn't resist saying tightly.

Aunt Agatha nodded, still troubled and then sighed. "By the by, offering to duel for you was very noble of your Spaniard. Perhaps you should have let them fight. Then you wouldn't be leaving."

"And what would that have solved?" Gillian wondered. "No, this is the best way." She kissed her aunt's cheek. "I shall see you in London. Or perhaps here if you don't leave before next week. I may be returned by then."

"Cheeky girl. You think to best your husband. Be wary of him, Gillian. Wright has fought the French. He probably has more than a few tricks up his sleeve."

"As have I," Gillian declared, feeling confident and certain of her plans.

All she had to work out were the details.

Waving again to everyone, Gillian walked down the step to the coach. James held the door open for her. "I'm glad you are traveling with me, James," she said. "With you for my protection and George handling the reins, I'm in good hands."

"That you are, my lady," James said.

Gillian started into the coach, her spirits high — until she was stunned to see she wouldn't be riding alone as planned.

Wright had taken off his greatcoat and was sitting in the seat, his broad shoulders and long legs taking up most of the room in the cab. He smiled as if reading her mind. "Surprised?"

CHAPTER FOUR

Gillian's good humor vanished. She leaned to glance at the back of the coach to double check what she already knew — there was no horse tied there.

She had happily assumed Wright had ridden ahead of her. She was wrong.

Conscious that James still held the door for her and that all of Huntleigh's guests were gathered waiting for her to leave, she forced herself to smile as she said, "I thought you hated riding in coaches."

"I do," Wright agreed cheerfully. "They are damned uncomfortable." He shifted his weight, bracing one booted foot on the opposite side of the coach. "However, I thought this would be a splendid opportunity to know each other better."

Gillian didn't want to know Wright better. She knew him well enough. "Wouldn't it be wise to bring your horse along in case you decide you'd prefer to ride later?" Or until they were out of sight of the house and she threw him out of her coach.

Wright grinned as if reading her mind. "No," he said pleasantly. "I'm going to be happy to be right here beside you." He patted the seat next to him for emphasis.

She could have cheerfully punched him in the nose for his impudence.

Gillian glanced back over her shoulder toward the house. Andres had come to the door. He stood there, a silent, brooding figure. It would be so easy to run to him . . . and yet there would still be the problem of her marriage.

No, the best thing to do would be to go to London. The answer to freeing herself of this marriage would be found there.

She sent Andres one last, sorrowful look and climbed into the coach. "Move over," she snapped at Wright, giving his leg a hard shove for emphasis.

"Ow," he said without true pain.

Gillian nodded to James to close the door, settling herself. "Come over to my side of the coach again and it will be worse," she threatened in a low voice. She smiled at the friends and relatives calling out their wishes for a safe journey.

"*Your* side of the coach? We're being a little petty, aren't we?"

Her smile turned genuine. *This was exactly the tone she wanted to set for the trip.* "Not petty. Territorial. What was it you said earlier? You keep what is yours? I feel that way, too. Starting with the coach seat." She stuffed her velvet muff between them and gave him her back while she leaned out the window to wave her farewells.

Andres had left the doorway. She didn't see him amongst the crowd.

In a few minutes, they would be off the estate's property and who knew when they'd be together again.

Tears threatened. She wasn't one to cry easily. No good came of crying. Still, she couldn't keep her old doubts and fears at bay. Watching the passing scenery, she couldn't help but wonder if Andres had meant the words he'd spoken, if he truly cared enough to wait for her. After all, her husband hadn't had any difficulty forgetting her.

And what if she was wrong about Andres? What if he wasn't worthy of her love? Her marriage to a man she'd thought she'd loved had taught her not to trust her judgment.

A folded kerchief was thrust at her.

She turned, following the hand holding it to Wright. "Go on. Take it," he said.

Gillian didn't move. She didn't want him to be kind. "I don't need it," she murmured, staring out the window again. The coach had reached the end of the drive and turned onto the road. They were on their way.

"My mistake," he answered. "I thought you were crying."

She kept silent, wishing the telltale tracks of tears didn't run down her cheeks.

"It's hard to leave places with people you like and admire," he said as if they were having a conversation.

Apparently not needing comment from her, he continued, "I remember when I was sent off to school. It was hard leaving my tutors and governess. Then, when I had to leave school, it was hard leaving there. I became accustomed to the way things were."

She didn't want to hear his stories. She didn't want him to make himself sound human or empathetic. The only way she could see her way through this was to think of him as the enemy.

"I'm not sad to leave, Wright," she said. "I'm sad to be leaving *with you*."

The moment the words left her lips, Gillian wished she could call them back. It was not in her nature to be deliberately cruel. And, yet, perhaps that was what was needed

72

to keep him at a distance.

She sat back in the seat, crossing her arms and warring with her conscience.

He was silent.

Gillian dared not look at him. They sat thus for what seemed an interminable amount of time. Finally, she said, "I'm sorry to speak rudely. But you should know you have no hold over me. I'm not the silly goose of a girl you married. Things had changed between us."

"I gathered that idea when I had to fight a duel with a Spaniard," Wright drawled out.

She slid a look in his direction, wondering if he was angry or if he mocked her. She was discovering she couldn't tell with him.

He didn't seem to be paying attention to her but looked out his window. His face in profile gave no clue to his inner thoughts.

Gillian closed her eyes and pretended to sleep. No one had to talk when they were asleep. She stayed quiet for a good long time, but eventually the silence became too much for her. She half opened her eyes a bit to see if he'd noticed she'd gone to sleep.

He appeared to be asleep, too.

No, he really *was* asleep. Here she sat, her every thought taken up with him and his outrageous behavior and he had the indecency to put her out of his mind and take a snooze.

She glared hard at him, willing him to wake.

Wright didn't move. In fact, it almost sounded as if he snored. Not awful, room vibrating snores but the soft sound of someone who was exhausted.

Gillian threw herself back into her corner of the coach, glad she'd met Andres. Wright had the disconcerting ability to upset her. He didn't have to do anything. Even sleeping he upset her . . . except it gave her a chance to be silently critical of him.

He needed a shave. The growth wasn't heavy but it was definitely out of character. Wright had often shaved two times a day all those years ago when she'd been close enough to him to notice these things. He appeared now as if he'd missed his morning shave, which wouldn't be surprising considering he'd been traveling, but it wouldn't explain his overlong hair.

Interestingly, there were other signs about him that his valet was not doing his job well. Four years ago, Wright had been meticulous about his dress and his person. His valet Hammond was infamous for being just as much a stickler. Either Hammond had left Wright's service or the valet was going a bit daft.

For example, Gillian remembered Hammond boasting that he used a special starch on neck cloths and had a secret method for applying it. However, right now, the ends of Wright's drooped like any other mortal man's. And one of the buttons on Wright's greatcoat hung by a thread.

Every female instinct inside her sensed there was a mystery here. Something was not as it should be.

Then again, hadn't that always been the case with her husband?

He snuggled closer to his door as if trying to make himself comfortable.

Gillian wished she had thought to bring along some needlework. Then perhaps she wouldn't be so distracted by Wright's presence that she was counting his whisker hairs.

She imagined he had not taken the marquess's orders for him to return to England well. Wright had always been a bit of a rebel in his family. Of course, as the youngest son, no one had cared much. There had been two other sons between him and the title. But that had all changed with their deaths.

Gillian had been living under Atherton's roof when they'd brought news that the oldest, Anthony, had died in a wild coaching accident. Supposedly he had bribed the mail's driver to give him the reins and that action had almost cost all the passengers their lives. The marquess didn't waste a beat but had ordered that his second son Thomas be sent to him.

And then Thomas had died in a misfortunate accident. He'd been walking along a narrow side street in a very disreputable area of town after losing a sinful amount of money at a gaming club. It was said a cat had jumped on a window ledge, knocking over a heavy clay flower pot. The pot had fallen on Thomas's head, killing him instantly.

When the marquess had ordered them to send for Wright, Gillian had known the time had come to leave. She'd hated living in that cold house where even the servants had treated her with disdain. She knew then that if she didn't attempt to escape, she'd have no chance once her husband returned.

And she wasn't about to suffer what she'd endured before he'd gone to war when he'd spent his time with his mistress and not with her. The marchioness had once alluded that Gillian was less of a woman because of Wright's preference for Jess. If that wasn't a reason to pack her bags and leave, Gillian didn't know of one.

Her gaze slid back to her husband. Questions crowded her mind about Jess's death.

She'd known very little about her. After he'd left for the Peninsula, there had been no reason to know anything. Gillian had spent many a restless night resenting the woman, but she hadn't wanted her to die. She'd never have wished that on anyone.

He shifted, turning toward her, his arms folded at his waist, and she caught the glint of gold on his ring finger.

Wright was wearing his wedding band.

She was shocked. She should have noticed it earlier when he'd removed his gloves to duel with Andres. She couldn't remember if he wore it after they were first married. She'd been too miserable to care.

Gillian glanced at her gloved left hand knowing she wasn't wearing her wedding band. She'd taken it off the moment she'd decided to leave him and hadn't missed it at all.

So why did she feel guilty now?

She glanced back at his ring. She'd purchased it herself. It was the one thing she'd done for her own wedding. His parents had taken over the planning of the event, and her father and stepmother had been thankful to them for doing so. As Aunt Agatha had explained, the marchioness understood what was expected by society for such a grand event better than Gillian and her parents did — and could afford what needed to be done.

Gillian had been swept along, a small player in the midst of a grand event. She'd barely known Wright before he'd asked her father for her hand . . . and didn't know him any better afterward.

The first time they had ever been alone had been on their wedding night.

She pushed back against the seat, closing her eyes tight, willing away the memories and failing.

That was the night Wright had told her about his mistress, the night he had confessed he'd loved this former dairy maid who had grown up with him. Of course, he'd made his confession *after* the marriage had been consummated.

And for that, she could never forgive him.

As if sensing her anger, Wright woke with a start. He glanced around, his eyes glassy. Realizing he was sprawled across the seat, he sat up. "Sorry. Didn't mean to take over."

"You're very tired," she observed.

He nodded and rubbed a hand over his face.

"Your valet is not doing you a service," she said. "The marvelous Hammond is growing lax in his duties."

"Hammond is fine," he replied. He

yawned. She realized he wasn't angry. He was trying to stay awake.

Again, she had a sense that all was not as it should be. "Wright, is something wrong?"

His head whipped around. "Why do you believe something is wrong?"

"I've never seen you sleep this hard." She could have mentioned the wedding band, or that after months of writing, his sudden appearance at Huntleigh could be seen as a concern.

"I haven't been sleeping well," he murmured. "It's nothing more."

"Jess's death has really saddened you, hasn't it?" she asked, curiosity making her probe for the truth.

His brows came up. He leaned back in his corner. Slowly he nodded his head. "I knew her all my life . . ." His voice trailed off as if he didn't wish to discuss the matter.

But Gillian had to ask questions. The man she knew as her husband was acting strangely. She remembered him as being almost as cold and indifferent as his father. This was a new Wright, and she didn't know if she trusted him.

"What is going on, Wright? Why did you come for me? Why did you put on your wedding band? And why this almost disregard for Jess's death?"

That gained his attention.

"I don't have disregard for Jess's death," he bit out.

"You seem remarkably —" She paused, searching her mind for the right word. "Sober. You are sober but not heartbroken over her death."

"I've adjusted to the idea," he mumbled, an idea Gillian found preposterous. But then he went for the attack before critical words could escape her mouth. "And I have a name," he insisted crossly. "Why do you insist on referring to me by my title as if we are mere acquaintances?"

"Because we are mere acquaintances."

He scowled at her, an expression so terrible it startled a laugh out of her. *That* wasn't what he'd wanted. "I might have liked you better when you were a mousy debutante," he muttered.

"I know you didn't," she countered.

For a second, he looked stunned, and then gave a bark of laughter. "You're right. I actually admire your spirit. You have bottom, Gillian," he said, referring to her courage, and then he smiled his approval, the expression completely transforming him into the man she'd tumbled into love with that night on the ballroom floor . . . and she couldn't help but smile back.

Wright seemed to have changed. This man was different than the one she'd married. They would not have had such a moment four years ago. She liked him better now.

He held up his left hand. "Is the ring what bothers you? I'll take it off if you wish, but mind you, Gillian, my not wearing this ring doesn't make us any less married. We are what we are. You might not like it. You might not like *me*. But *I* am your husband."

Perhaps it was Jess's death that had freed him to come for her? Perhaps he truly *did* want to be her husband.

Her expectations of him, her opinions all seemed to be turned upside down. Gillian knew she shouldn't trust him, but was surprised at how open she was to this new person he seemed to have become. Was it her imagination that he was gentler, kinder . . . more considerate? Such small things and yet they wore well over time.

"What is going on here, Wright? Why did you come for me?"

"I told you I needed you."

He said the words as if they were the explanation for everything.

"And I don't know that I have anything to give you. I fear it is too late for us. We aren't good for each other. We never were. And I want you to know, I will not go back to live under your father's roof. I can't live among such shallow people any longer. I refuse to do so."

Again, his reaction was not what she'd anticipated. He shrugged. "We won't be going to my father's house."

Gillian's mouth dropped open. She had to close it before she could ask, "You don't live there. And they let you?" She fell back against the seat. "I thought especially after your brothers' deaths and how hard they battled with you to return to London, they were going to keep you under lock and key."

"Come along, Gillian. I am more my own man than that."

She rolled her eyes. "I know the marquess. Everything must be his way."

The angry muscle in his jaw tightened. She wondered if he knew how easily he gave away what he was thinking with the tense reaction. "I know my family's faults, Gillian. I don't need instruction from you."

"Did you come for me because you need a housekeeper?" she guessed, ignoring his show of temper.

"I have a housekeeper," he returned levelly. "What I want is a wife."

"We've had this conversation," she said almost pleasantly. "I don't want to be your wife."

"I should have married a meeker woman," he grumbled, and she had to laugh.

"I will accept that as a compliment." She turned to face him. "Now, tell me why you *really* came for me."

Wright groaned and leaned his head against the back of the seat. "You are tenacious."

"Thank you," she said dryly.

He stared at the ceiling a moment and then said, "I want a position on Liverpool's personal staff. There are those in Parliament and the War Office that wish Wellington to return home. They believe we have no chance of defeating Napoleon. They are wrong. We are going to chase the bugger all the way back to Paris and put him in a cage. However, Wellington's enemies will do anything to stop the war, even to cutting off funds. I can help the army in the War Office. I can see that the men receive what they need to fight hard and fight well."

He turned to her. "My father doesn't want me there. He believes there is no political advantage and wants me to accept an ambassadorship to Holland. It doesn't carry the political costs of the position Liverpool is offering."

"And you don't want to be an ambassador?"

"Absolutely not. I'd rather count bullets and boots for our fighting men than sip tea with diplomats."

Gillian ran her fingers over the velvet muff between them, considering this information. "It helps that my father is one of Lord Liverpool's mentors."

"It does," he agreed, his voice carefully neutral.

"I know his lordship. He's always been kind to me."

"He has," her husband agreed.

Thoughtfully, Gillian brushed over the velvet before reaching a decision. She raised her gaze to his. "If I help you, what will you do for me?"

"So it has come to that between us. Tit for tat. Very well, Gillian, what is it you want?"

"My freedom, Wright. What I've always wanted."

"I won't give you a divorce," he insisted. "I can't."

"Yes, you can," she challenged. "If you take on a position as a member of Liverpool's staff, you will be able to do anything . . . quietly. So there's my price, Wright."

"What if I don't?"

She smiled. "Then I shall make such a

84

noise and fuss over our marriage that no one shall want you around them. I'll disgrace you, Wright, and I'll leave you anyway." Who would have thought four years ago that she'd have so much power?

His gaze narrowed. She braced herself for a broadside of anger.

Instead, he drew back into his corner of the coach on that observation. For a long moment, he was silent. "Very well," he said at last.

"Very well, what?" Gillian pressed.

He leaned toward her. "You help me succeed at gaining the position I want on Liverpool's staff, and I will give you your freedom."

He had agreed. She was stunned. She could be with Andres.

"But for now, you must play the adoring wife," Wright reminded her. "And you must do it convincingly."

"I'm a marvelous actress," she assured him, her spirits soaring with happiness.

"Then it is a pact," Wright said. He held out his hand.

"Yes, a pact," she agreed, taking his hand and giving it a firm shake.

Wright laughed and then brought her fingers to his lips. "You are a formidable opponent, my lady," he murmured before brushing a light kiss to the back of her hand. He released his hold before she could protest.

For a second, she sensed a trap. She hadn't anticipated his capitulation to her demands would be this easy. Then again, he believed in his cause. It meant more to him than her.

Wright lowered the window and leaned out. Gillian had not noticed how dark the day was growing until now. "Pull over at the next decent-looking inn," Wright ordered George. He sat back into the coach. "There should be someplace to rest our heads coming up here shortly."

She nodded. This had been a tiring day, one filled with highs and lows. Besides, she never liked traveling in the dark.

They didn't speak then, each lost in their own thoughts. Gillian's were on Andres. She could not wait to write and tell him the good news. Perhaps she could post a letter from the inn.

A few minutes later, the coach turned off the main road, stopping at the Bear's Hollow, a cozy inn located a half mile off the main road. George had known of the place. He told them it was clean and without frills, which was perfectly fine. Gillian was exhausted by the day's emotions. She longed

for nothing more than her dinner and a good night's sleep.

The innkeeper, Mr. Peters, had a nephew serving under Wellington. He had heard of the dashing Colonel Lord Wright and was honored to have them for guests.

Gillian waited in the coach while Wright made the arrangements. He came out to escort her inside. "You'll want some privacy. I'll wait for you downstairs." Mr. Peters led her upstairs.

The room he showed her was charming, and very clean. A four-poster bed covered in a white counterpane dominated most of the floor space beneath a window.

Mr. Peters lit the fire in the hearth's grate and left her to herself, saying, "If you and your lordship need anything, you have only to ask. I pray that the two of you are comfortable here."

Gillian was happy to see him bow out, desperately needing a moment to freshen up a bit. However, once she was relaxed, the implications of the innkeeper's kind remarks sank in.

She and Wright were expected to share a room — and that bed, which suddenly seemed very small.

This would not do.

Gillian went downstairs, a woman on a

mission. She found Wright in the taproom that also served for dining. He had claimed a small table over by the hearth. A rather large family with several lively children and an elderly parent were sitting at a table in the middle of the room enjoying their dinner.

"How is the room?" Wright asked, rising to his feet as she approached. "By the way, I ordered a glass of sherry for you. I remember it is what you like to sip before dinner."

"Thank you," she murmured, as she took a fortifying drink to approach the subject uppermost in her mind. "We must have separate rooms."

Her husband studied her a moment. He wasn't pleased.

She readied herself for a quarrel. Her foremost argument would be their pact, but then he said, "Very well. Let me see what I can do."

At that moment, Mr. Peters and his wife approached the table, carrying trays loaded with food. "I also took the liberty of ordering for you," Wright confessed and seemed to brace himself for her response.

"It's perfectly fine," she said, another topic on her mind more important than his high-handedness. Besides, she was hungry.

He waited until the majority of the dishes

had been placed on the table before raising his voice and saying, "Peters, we have a problem. I am going to need two rooms."

Caught in the act of placing warm bread on the table, the innkeeper's brows came together. "Two?"

Wright held up two fingers as confirmation. "Can that be arranged?"

"Yes, yes, my lord. Anything for you." He glanced over at the tableful of family who had stopped eating their meal to hear if this had anything to do with them. It did. "I'll tell that family they can't have the room. We'll move them out to the barn."

Shocked, Gillian asked, "Are you saying you only have two rooms in this inn?"

"Two rooms fit for guests," the innkeeper said. "There's one other room for my daughter. It's the tiniest of places. The wife and I sleep in the back parlor. If you will give me a moment?" He bowed and started toward the family.

Wright made no move to call him back. Gillian looked from her husband to the innkeeper who had reached the family's table. "You aren't going to stop him?" she asked her husband.

Reaching for bread, Wright said, "My lady wishes two rooms."

Gillian could have groaned aloud. He was

doing this on purpose.

The innkeeper was starting to make his request. The family had gone silent and frowns appeared on several faces. Gillian could not let him go on any longer. "Innkeeper, please, everything is fine."

"What do you say, my lady?" the innkeeper asked, turning his head as if he were slightly hard of hearing.

"I said, *one* room is fine," Gillian answered. "Please do not put those people out."

"Yes, my lady," Mr. Peters said with a huge smile of relief. A relief echoed by the family at the other table.

Gillian felt the worst sort of person for even giving them a concern until she glanced at Wright. He buttered his bread, a secret smile on his face.

Every suspicious nerve in her body went on alert. Without a doubt he had an ulterior motive in mind. Wright had plans to seduce her.

At that moment, his gaze met hers, and she knew she was right. He had the devil's own gleam in his eye. He meant to sleep with her and win her over. He truly thought that she was that simple.

So much for the pact.

But if he thought she was the same foolish

girl he'd married years ago, he was wrong.

A woman's will was much stronger than a man's . . . and her husband deserved the lesson she was going to happily teach him. Her heart belonged to Andres and there was no way to make the fact clearer than letting Wright know exactly where he stood in that most sensitive of marital battlegrounds — the bed.

"May I have another glass of sherry, my lord?" she asked sweetly.

"Certainly," he said, almost filling the glass to the brim. He lifted his in a toast. "To tonight."

Men could be such fools. Four years ago, she hadn't understood the power a woman could exercise over one of them. Now, she did.

"Yes, to tonight," she echoed.

Brian sensed a new ruthlessness to his wife, especially when she gave him such a sweet, "come hither" smile.

She was laying a trap. Years in the military gave him a sense of when to be wary.

And the problem was, the very male part of him didn't care if it was a trap or not. That part of his anatomy wanted to come to her "hither."

It had been a long time since he had made

love. Too long. Yes, he did want to share a bed with Gillian. Not only were they man and wife, but she had quickly become one of the most fascinating women he'd ever met.

Muscles that had been sore with exhaustion from weeks of sleepless nights now hummed with energy and he went lightheaded as blood flowed to another part of his body.

Gillian slid a look at him from beneath her dark lashes with a feminine knowledge as old as time. She knew she had him hard.

And he knew she couldn't wait to rebuff him.

It was suddenly a game of cat and mouse they were playing. The question was, which one of them was the cat?

Brian grinned, certain it would be him.

CHAPTER FIVE

Wright's arm came over to rest protectively on the back of her chair as he held up the sherry bottle. "More?"

Gillian had to swallow a smile. This was almost too easy. She knew his intentions. Fortunately she had a good head for drink, but she shook her head anyway. "I'm fine."

He frowned his disappointment as he set the bottle back on the table.

He did not remove his arm. A moment later, the innkeeper brought over a bottle of wine. Gillian did let Wright pour her a glass and his spirits seemed to be restored by that small allowance. It was actually a respectable vintage and went well with the chicken. Gillian felt herself start to relax.

The truth was, Wright could be a charming companion. Especially when he set his mind to the task.

He started telling her the tale of a Portuguese boy who had climbed to the highest boughs of a tree to save a cat. Both of them became too afraid to climb back down. Wright's soldiers managed to bring the boy out of the tree but the child was distraught until they agreed to save the cat. The smallest man under Wright's command had bravely climbed for the cat, only to have the animal hiss and claw at him.

In the end, Wright had gone up himself.

"You are adept at climbing trees?" she asked.

"I am one of the best," he answered.

Gillian frowned her disbelief and he laughed. "It's true," he assured her. "I like climbing them. The higher the better. I climbed almost every one of them at High Meadows." High Meadows was the Atherton country seat estate in Berkshire. "But I understand why you are laughing. My men weren't too certain of me either. I had arrived only a few weeks before. I was an untested officer, the worst sort."

"So what happened?" Gillian asked.

"I proceeded to climb the tree," Wright said, cutting a slice of his chicken. "Unfortunately, the cat kept moving — upward."

"Perhaps he didn't want to be rescued," she suggested, drawing a parallel with her own circumstance.

He indicated with a lift of his brow he

94

knew what she was thinking. "Sometimes, the sensible course is out of our hands." She didn't know if this was part of the tale, or if he was responding to her own unspoken thoughts.

"The thought did strike me," he admitted, "that if we all left, kitty would have come down on her own. Unfortunately, that course was closed to me. We'd attracted a great deal of attention. I looked down from my perch in the tree to see I was surrounded by every villager for miles around, infantrymen from other companies as well as my own, and Wellington."

"He was there?" Gillian widened her eyes at the mention of the famous general.

"Yes, watching to see if I would make a fool of myself. It appeared as if I would."

She leaned toward him, her distrust evaporating in the face of a good story. "So what did you do?" She knew that Wright would not let the cat best him.

He smiled as if acknowledging her thought. "I followed that cat out onto the highest, thinnest limb."

"Could it hold your weight?"

"No."

"Did it break?"

Wright grinned. "You know it did. First it bent under my weight. The cat was not pleased. He dug his claws into the limb and made great yowling sounds at me. My men said they could be heard all over the valley."

"And then what happened?"

"I heard a cracking noise behind me. I knew the limb was about to break. The cat heard it, too."

"And?" she prompted when he paused for dramatic effect.

"The cat was no fool. He jumped right into my arms and I leapt for the tree's trunk. We made it just as the limb started to give way under my feet." He laughed at the memory. "The frightened cat, who didn't want to have anything to do with me only moments before, scrambled to the top of my head."

Gillian started laughing at the picture that formed in her mind.

"I grabbed hold of the tree trunk and scaled down it wearing the cat on my head," Wright continued. "He'd balance this way and that while digging his claws in for good measure as I brought the two of us down to the ground."

"Were you given a hero's welcome?" she teased.

"Only by the men who had placed their bets that I would make it," he answered. "The majority of them were not pleased to lose a quid or two on what they'd thought would be easy money." He sat back in his chair, smiling at the memory. "Wellington commended me on my foolhardiness and then he rode off. The next day, I received orders to join his staff. He told me that any man who would go that far to accomplish his mission was a good one to keep close."

Wright's expression sobered. He looked into the flames in the hearth. "Saving that cat opened many doors for me. It may even have been the best thing I've done in my life. I learned a great deal from the general." He reached for the wine. "Do you care for more?"

"Are you going to have more stories to tell?" she asked, quite liking him when he was this way.

He smiled. "You aren't bored?"

She shook her head. "I've always wondered what it would be like to be somewhere else beyond England. I can read books but it isn't the same as talking to someone who has been there."

"Well, if that is the case," he said, topping off her glass, "let me tell you of the time my men decided to make goat cheese that exploded and sent everyone running for shelter."

It was a delightful story as was the next

one and the next.

Gillian found she actually liked Wright. She'd forgotten he was different from his father. The two of them had the same mannerisms but experience separated them.

Wright's stories about the Portuguese, the peasants, and the soldiers he obviously admired brimmed with good humor and kindness — but she knew he had other stories to tell as well. Her husband had seen battle. There was a small scar over his lip and another larger one across the back of his hand.

She used to follow the reports of the battles in the papers wondering if he'd been in them. She knew the fighting was often desperate. She'd prayed for his safety and well-being.

Now, sitting here by the fire after a good meal, she realized those prayers had been answered. He had returned in one piece and, thankfully, with no more damage than those few scars and with his spirit intact.

In fact, she was so involved in the stories he told that she hadn't noticed how late the hour had grown. The fire in the grate was low. A chill was creeping into the air and the family who had dined at the table beside theirs had long gone to their beds. Mr. Peters sat in a chair by the door, his arms folded across his chest, his eyes closed. It was one of his snores that finally interrupted their conversation and made them realize they'd talked most of the evening.

Wright smiled at the innkeeper. "Shall we let him go to his bed?" he asked her.

"I think it would be kind," she agreed. She lifted the wine bottle. It was empty. No wonder she felt mellow and pleased with the world.

His fingers brushed the side of her cheek. She turned to him in surprise.

"I'm sorry. I had to touch you, that's all. I wanted to know if your skin is really as smooth and soft as it appears." His gaze seemed to stroke where his fingers had touched. "It is."

Gillian felt a stirring deep inside, a stirring she'd felt for him before. She shook her head. "This is not what I had expected."

"What isn't?" he asked.

"You." She tried to explain without committing herself. "When we first set down, I expected this meal to be one of verbal sparring. Instead, it was quite enjoyable."

He moved his empty wineglass away from the edge of the table. "You expected me to ravish you at the first opportunity," he suggested.

"I had thought that was your intention,"

she admitted, feeling a bubble of laughter at his description.

"Would I have succeeded?"

"Absolutely not. I didn't like you."

"And now?"

Gillian hesitated and then confessed, "You are not what I remembered."

He sat back in his chair. His gaze shifted away from her. "War changes a person. What I once valued no longer seems to matter. You talk about how ill at ease you felt under my father's roof. Imagine how I felt returning home from the war to be surrounded by talk of inconsequential things like gossip and blathering on about who uses what tailor. Men are dying, giving their lives to the honor and protection of their country, and here at home . . ." His voice trailed off as he studied the walls, the chairs, the peacefulness. He finished his words with a wave of his hand. "It's as if the war doesn't exist."

"People can't always relate to what they don't see or what doesn't affect them immediately," she said, not as an excuse but in an effort to help him understand. She placed her hand on his arm. "You mustn't judge them too harshly."

His lips pressed together as if he disagreed but then he conceded her point. "And perhaps that is the reason men seem to need war. They haven't experienced it. Don't know it. It seems simple on the surface, especially when one is far away from the battlegrounds. But up close, it's a different matter." He looked down at her hand, reached for it, held it as if feeling its weight, and then raised it to his lips. He pressed a kiss into her palm.

Where his mouth touched, her skin tingled.

Gillian pulled her hand away. "What was that for?" she asked, embarrassed at the chord of alarm in her voice. She had not anticipated his gesture, or her reaction.

"It was for your kindness," he said, making no move toward. "For understanding. I've not been able to speak to anyone as I did just now with you. It is a gift, my lady."

She raised her hand to her temple, feeling a bit foolish. She was on guard against his advances and so, of course, had overreacted.

Even now, he didn't seem to take offense at her confusion.

He rose from the table. "Come. We are both tired. Let us go to our room."

She noticed he didn't say "our bed."

Wright pulled out her chair, but made no move to take her hand or touch her. Gillian was thankful. Once she stood, she realized the wine had more of an effect on her than she had anticipated. Or she wanted to believe that this swimming dizziness was the wine. She refused to believe it was Wright, especially since now was the time when she needed to gird herself against him. She hadn't decided how to handle the room situation, but she knew what the outcome would be.

He indicated with his hand for her to lead the way. As they walked out of the dining room, he gently woke the sleeping inn-keeper, slipping a coin into his palm for his good service.

Mr. Peters's eyes opened the second he felt the metal. "Thank you, my lord. Thank you."

Wright held up a hand as if to quiet the man, but Mr. Peters was anxious to be of service. "Do you need help going up the stairs? My Mary turned down the covers in your room and made a fire."

"You have done more than enough," Wright said, trying to leave the dining room, but Mr. Peters followed him.

"There is a lamp on the table at the foot of the back stairs. Take it to light your way. Oh, here, perhaps I should go with you?"

He would have charged ahead of them

except for Wright catching him by the collar. "We can see to ourselves, Peters. Clean the table and find your bed. You've worked hard this night."

"Yes, my lord. Of course, my lord," the innkeeper said.

Wright made an impatient sound before issuing a stern, "Good night," and coming out into the hall to join Gillian. Wright indicated with a wave of his hand the direction of the back stairs where a lamp burned on a side table.

"That was kind of you," Gillian said over her shoulder as she walked toward the table.

"What was?" he asked, truly puzzled.

"Giving the man a vail for his service."

"He earned it," Wright answered.

"Yes, but most wouldn't have given it to him," she said. In fact, she'd overheard more than one servant in the marquess's household complain over their employer's tightfisted tendencies as well as those of his friends. Generosity, a quality Gillian greatly admired, was not a common virtue amongst the *ton.*

Wright shook his head as if her praise embarrassed him. "You'd better be careful, Gillian, or you'll be thinking me a better man than I am."

A sharp rejoinder was on the tip of her

tongue to say that could never happen, but the words didn't come out because he *was* different than anyone she'd come across in London. Perhaps the war had changed him or perhaps her instincts all those years ago in a crowded ballroom had not been completely wrong . . .

She was such a fool. Even after years of his neglect, she was willing to give him the benefit of a doubt. She shook her head. It wasn't all her fault. He was trying to be charming and it had been a long, stressful day. The sherry had mixed with the wine and she was not as alert as she should be.

There was also still the matter of her sharing a room with him. Experience had taught her that Wright would do what was necessary to gain what he wanted.

Gillian wasn't worried about the room. She was certain she could set Wright in his place. In spite of what had turned out to be an enjoyable evening, she had not fallen under his spell. She knew a trick or two to keep him at bay.

They had reached the staircase leading up to their room. She placed her hand on the solid sturdy stair post, leaving the lamp for Wright to pick up.

She'd gone up one step, when she heard him say her name so softly she could have imagined it.

"Yes?" she answered, turning to him — and that is when he caught her off guard.

Before she realized what he was about, he swept her up into his arms and kissed her.

For a stunned moment, Gillian couldn't think, she couldn't move. His kiss was an onslaught of her senses.

Memories of her wedding night came rushing back to her. She'd been so enamored of him. So silly, silly in love. Kissing him had been as natural to her as breathing — and it still was.

She attempted to think of Andres but his face wouldn't form a picture in her mind. Instead, all she could see was Wright. Damnable, irritating, annoying Wright. How she wished their lips didn't fit together.

Gillian leaned against the banister for support as if to avoid him. His arms came around her, his hands gripped the rail, trapping her. Not that he needed to do so. With a will of their own, her arms went around his neck, flattening her breasts against his chest.

Their hips fitted together as if pulled by two magnets. He deepened the kiss and, God help her, she followed him.

A footfall sounded behind them as if someone approached.

Her first thought was of Mr. Peters. She should not be seen smooching like a dairy maid on the staircase of a public house. She started to break away, but then Wright bit her bottom lip, soothing it with the tip of his tongue and she could have melted into his arms.

Dear God. Who would have thought after all that lay between them, all he had to do was kiss her to make her forget pride and common sense?

He'd performed this same trick on their wedding night. It had thrilled her, frightened her . . . tempted her, just as it did right now.

What little sanity she had left shouted *no* through her mind. She must not let him kiss her this way. She must not let him seduce her. She had to remember how he'd been able to walk away from her. How he'd not had so much as an hour for her before he left to join Wellington.

She had to remember the mistress he'd chosen over her.

But that mistress was gone, the devil of temptation whispered to her. There was no one else but herself. Even the earlier footfalls threatening discovery had vanished from her doubts.

Gillian tried to think of Andres, but couldn't. Wright's kiss obliterated all thought of her beloved Spaniard.

His lips made their way up to her ear. "Let's go to our room."

The brush of his breath against her skin almost sent her through the ceiling. Fortunately, his arms now held her fast. He smiled. She could feel his lips curve —

The spell he wove was broken.

He'd had her until he smiled.

Wright left the lamp behind as he half carried, half backed her up the stairs, his lips barely leaving hers. In the upstairs hallway, he backed her against the door to their room. His arousal was hard and bold between them. He cupped her breast and she could have cried out because it felt good to be touched this way.

She'd been wrong when she'd thought his kisses would remind her of their wedding night. Back then she'd been shy and he hesitant and slightly uninvolved.

There was nothing uninvolved about him right now. He kissed her with a raw, urgent need.

And she wanted him, too. She wanted to taste him, to feel him, to take him inside her. She barely remembered their joining. There had been nights when she'd tried to remember and had failed.

Andres. She had to think of Andres. Noble, kindhearted Andres. Andres who waited for her.

Gillian reached behind her for the door handle.

The door opened and she practically fell inside — effectively breaking the kiss.

"I need a moment of privacy," she managed to mutter, her heart racing. She shut the door and leaned back against it, thankful to have escaped. The only light in the room was the warm glow from the hearth. The white counterpane on the bed seemed to take on an unholy glow in the firelight.

There was no time to rest. She had to pull herself together. She could not, *must not* let him kiss her like that again. She had no defenses against him.

All he had to do was touch her and she reverted back to the silly chit who had been so dovey eyed for him when they'd first married.

"Gillian?" He rapped light on the door. His voice took on warmth as he said, "May I come in?"

She couldn't let him in. She'd worked too hard to be free of him to give it all up now. She raised a distracted hand to her head and knew what she was going to have to do.

It's what she should have done from the very beginning.

CHAPTER SIX

Brian leaned against the door. He swore he could smell her light floral scent through the wood.

Who had known Gillian could kiss the way she did? She was passionate, giving, and yet innocent. There was a hint of chasteness in the way she approached kissing. The Spaniard had not had her yet. Brian would have staked his inheritance on it.

Memories of their wedding night came flooding back to him. He'd only been unfaithful to Jess once, and it had been that night.

Of course, he'd been so angry at his father for forcing the marriage and so determined to keep his beloved Jess in mind, he'd done little more than was necessary with Gillian. He'd been young, full of brass, and arrogant.

He'd also had the ill grace to tell her of his love for another.

His callousness stunned him. No wonder Gillian wanted nothing to do with him.

Dear God, he was seven kinds of fool, especially since Gillian was worth twenty-five of Jess. Time had proven his father right. Jess would not have been a worthy wife. The disappointment of the shallowness of her love still burned like an acid on his heart. He had wanted to offer Jess the world and she'd tossed it aside.

But Gillian was different. She was quality. She had intelligence, grace, and the courage of her convictions. She was also educated. She'd make an honorable mother to his children.

For the first time since his brothers' deaths, since he'd been ordered home and discovered everyone he had trusted had betrayed him, Brian felt hope. His instincts had been to send for Gillian. He was now overjoyed that he'd taken matters into his hands and come for her.

She was a jewel beyond price. A blessing!

Brian leaned against the door, anxious to claim his wife. If he could reach through the door, he would. No woman had ever taken him to this level of arousal.

"Gillian," he whispered against the door. "Let me in. I'm ready for you." He was also very aware that the door to the other room,

the one the family was using, was right across the hall. He didn't want to wake them.

But instead of the sound of the door handle being turned, instead of a whispered, "Come hither," he heard the sound of something being dragged on the other side of the door.

He frowned and listened again. He wasn't mistaken.

Alarmed, Brian decided being gentlemanly and polite could be damned. Something was wrong on the other side of this door. Gillian might need his help. He grabbed the handle, opened the door, leading with his shoulder — and came to a halt.

The door wouldn't open more than a few inches of the way.

Brian frowned and tried to shove it open, realizing something was blocking the doorway. *Furniture.* A big piece of furniture like a wardrobe had been placed in front of the door. "Gillian? What's this?"

Her voice came from the other side of the door. "It's protection, Wright. I've pushed the wardrobe in front of the door. I'm not sleeping with you. Go make your bed someplace else."

"You've thrown me out of my own room?" he asked in disbelief.

There was a moment's hesitation and then she said, "Yes, yes, I *have*."

At first, he was confused, but as her words sank in, a red haze fell over his eyes. Had she played him for a fool? Was this some sort of scheme to exact revenge for their years apart?

And he was furious that she was now hiding behind a wardrobe like some spinster when only moments before she'd been panting in his arms.

"Open this door," he said in a voice that brooked no disagreement.

There was no reply.

There was also no compliance.

He threw his weight against the door. It slammed against the wardrobe but didn't move it. He pushed against the door with all his weight. "You'd best move, Gillian. I'm going to knock the thing over."

"You'll damage it," she warned.

"I'll pay for damages later." Right now, he wanted his *wife* to know who was in charge. Matters had gone out of hand long enough.

But the wardrobe didn't move. He made another attempt. It didn't budge, not even an inch.

"Gillian," he said, not bothering to keep his voice down. "Move that wardrobe or I shall take it apart in splinters."

"You haven't been too successful so far," came her prim reply.

Brian roared his frustration. He shoved at the door again and when that time wasn't any more successful than his first attempt, he pounded the door with his fist, needing some sort of release before he exploded.

The door opened across the hallway. Wearing his night cap, the father of the family peeked out into the hall. Targeting him as a focus for his anger, Brian all but growled before ordering, "Back in your room."

But when the wide-eyed man pulled back to obey, Brian had a new idea and stopped his neighbor's door from closing with one hand. "Let me have a look in there."

"In here, my lord?"

"Yes," Brian answered absently as he took charge and shoved the door wider to take a look around the room. He knew he was being rude but this was war. A war between a man and a woman. Not even the French could be as formidable opponents. And he was not going to let Gillian best him.

In the glowing light coming from the hearth he could see the family huddled in the room's two beds and a few cots. Brian wasn't interested in them. Instead, he noticed the two windows on the far wall. He'd wager his room was laid out much the same way.

A chubby toddler came suddenly awake. The child stared at Brian as if he were a mad man, which right now he probably was, and then opened his mouth to cry. His mother scooped him up into her arms, trying to shush him — a scene that finally made Brian snap to his senses.

"So sorry," Brian said to the child's mother. He backed out of the room, nodding to the father. "Again, beg pardon. But thank you for your indulgence."

The door was slammed behind him. That slam was echoed from his room across the hall. Gillian had repositioned the wardrobe so that he couldn't push open the door at all.

He narrowed his gaze, wishing he could see right through his door. She probably thought she had him beat. He wondered why she'd run so hot and then cold . . . and decided it was because the intensity between them had frightened her off. He'd upset her avowed dedication to her Spaniard. He'd made her question herself and Gillian didn't like questions. He understood that about her now. She wasn't one to flirt easily or to be jaded about morals. That was the reason she'd left his father's house. He would have staked his career on it.

She'd said she wanted a divorce. Brian almost laughed. There would be no divorce. Not in his marriage.

Besides, he couldn't lose her. She was all he had left.

He went down the back stairs of the inn. Not bothering with the still-burning lamp, he walked toward the front door where he paused only long enough to remove his jacket and hang it on a peg in the wall before going outside.

Four windows to the taproom lined the front of the inn. Besides the dying fire in the grate, two candles were still burning. Peter must still be up doing chores.

Not wanting to be discovered slinking around outside, Brian hunched over so he couldn't be seen and ran past the windows.

At the corner of the inn, he stopped to study the side of the house. There were two windows on the first floor, exactly as there had been in the family's room. However, he decided to try the window over the taproom. There was a tall oak at this corner whose branches came close to those windows. Brian could have danced a jig. He was going to enjoy the look on Gillian's face when he climbed through one of them. And the irony was he'd shared the story of his tree-climbing abilities with her. It seemed poetic justice.

He jerked off his boots and socks, hiding them against the house. The ground was cold and damp beneath his bare toes but he'd need them to help him scale the oak.

Removing his neck cloth, he used it as a strap. Throwing it round the tree and holding each end, he began his ascent.

Some ten feet over his head was a good, steady limb that should hold his weight. If he stood on it, he'd be able to reach the first window.

As he passed the taproom windows, Peters came out and blew out the candles. Although his arms screamed in agony, Brian held still, not wanting his movement to draw the innkeeper's attention toward him.

When all was dark, he started up again.

The climb actually went better than he had anticipated. His muscles hadn't had a good stretch or challenge for months and his night vision, something he'd always prided himself on, was coming back.

Gillian had lit a candle. The lead and glass window was covered with curtains but he could see the glow of the candle flame and occasionally, her shadow as she moved around in the room. He was surprised she hadn't gone to bed. Perhaps she was nervous about where he'd gone?

She should be.

He grinned in anticipation of her reaction when he surprised her.

However, when he reached the limb, he realized it wasn't as steady as he had estimated. He pulled himself up, holding the tree trunk by one arm while he debated his next move, realizing he had another problem. In the dark, it wasn't easy to tell if there was a way to open the window on the outside or not. Chances were there wasn't, and he hadn't brought a knife with him to attempt to pry them open.

Well, he hadn't climbed up here for nothing. He was going to take a chance there was a way in.

Balancing himself by holding his arms out, Brian gingerly stepped out on the limb, moving toward the window. One step, two, three —

He reached out and grabbed the decorative brick over the window with his fingers. He was just able to sit his left hip on the narrow ledge. The stance gave him a better sense of balance — and he could breathe again. The worst part was over.

Not wanting to alarm Gillian until he was ready for his surprise, he began inspecting the window with his fingers, searching for a catch. Nothing.

He pressed on the panes, testing them. What if he popped one of the leaded glass diamonds out? Then he would be able to reach in and let himself in cool as you please.

That seemed the best plan but as he shifted his weight so he could start to wiggle the glass free, he heard an ominous crack.

He glanced down at the tree limb where he still rested one bare foot for balance. He'd had to put more weight on it for leverage to work on the window. The majority of his weight was still in his hip on the window ledge, but it was a precarious position. He needed to work fast.

At that moment, Gillian blew out the candle. Here was his moment. It was all or nothing.

Brian pushed on the windowpane. It was loose but he was going to have to apply more pressure to pop it out. He took the risk, placed more of his weight on the limb and pushed —

The limb gave out another crack.

The time had come for rash action. Meaning to just break the window and pay the innkeeper for the damage on the morrow, Brian put his shoulder into it. He had to draw back to gain some momentum, but at that moment, the limb broke and he felt himself start to fall.

Fortunately, his hands caught the ledge and he saved himself from a nasty tumble that could have broken a bone or two.

It also left him dangling against the side of the inn outside Gillian's window.

"This is not a good plan," he muttered to himself and wondered if he could pull his body weight back up onto the ledge. It was worth a try . . . except the window started to open.

CHAPTER SEVEN

Gillian had heard the tree crack.

She'd known immediately it was Wright. After she'd moved the wardrobe, she'd glanced out the window and taken stock of her surroundings. She'd known better than to think he would meekly walk away. Not after those kisses.

So, she'd checked to be certain the window was locked, blown out the candle, and waited.

Minutes later, his shadow had crossed the window.

Gillian had been confident he wouldn't be able to come in this way until he started pressing on one of the lead glass panes. She hadn't imagined that he would break it. She immediately began scrambling around the room, looking for something to use to fend him off when there had been the awful sound of wood splintering — and then silence.

Her intention had never been to harm him. In a panic she ran to the window and opened it, not knowing what to expect — and not expecting what she saw.

Wright hung by his fingertips from the window ledge.

Alarm flooded through her. He wasn't dead — yet.

"What do you think you are doing?" she demanded, relief making her voice sharp.

"Attempting to enter my room," he replied as if hanging from a window ledge was the most commonplace thing to do. "I would have used the door but it was blocked . . . or had you noticed?"

She couldn't help but admire his nonchalance. Anyone else would be screaming. He acted as if he didn't mind hanging outside her window. Intrigued, she couldn't help playing with him a bit.

"I'd noticed," she admitted. "I'm glad to see you are alive. Good night," she said and started to close the window.

"*Wait,* Gillian." He reached up and blocked the window with one hand, his body dangling dangerously free. "You can't leave me out here. What will the innkeeper say when he sees my body in the morning?"

"It's not that long a fall, Wright."

"But surely I will break both legs and then

you will still be stuck with me." He gave as charming a look as a dangling man can give and said, "Please, Gillian, help. The innkeeper has children. What if I look a terrible mess on the ground?"

When he saw her hesitate, he added slyly, "If I injure myself, you'll be forced to stay here and care for me. As attractive as that sounds to me, I don't believe you will be as happy."

"You're right. I have no desire to wait on you hand and foot."

"And you'd be forced to," he assured her. "Your conscience would weigh heavy until you did."

Did he know her that well? He was completely correct.

He was holding the ledge with both hands now. Gillian leaned out the window and took his wrist with her hands. "I'll help you in, Wright, but don't think that this means I am pleased with you. I'm not. And I won't kiss you. Not once more."

"I wouldn't think of asking for another, Gillian," he replied too readily. "Not after your kindness."

"It's not that you ask, Wright. You take," she replied archly and he laughed, the sound almost joyful.

She didn't want to think of him as happy

or attractive. She needed him to be a complete villain, and he wasn't. If she wasn't careful, he'd worm his way into her heart.

"I'm waiting for your promise," she said, sounding as strict as she possibly could. "I want your word of honor. No more kissing or I will let you dangle there until kingdom come."

There was a beat of silence. "Perhaps you should let me drop."

That wasn't the answer she wanted. But before she could frame a reply, he sighed heavily. "Have it as you will. No more kisses." He snorted. "That sounded silly."

It did. And made her feel petty, but it was the way matters had to be. She had to keep some distance between them.

She didn't want him to break his neck either . . . although it would solve her problems.

Pushing aside her dark thoughts, Gillian pulled his arm, giving him the leverage he needed to heft his weight up so that he could sit on the edge. He leaned back against the window and flexed his arms to relieve strained muscles.

"You pulled me up just in time," he said. The firelight reached his features. He was relaxed, smiling even.

"You weren't that much in fear of your

life," she murmured, and drew back — but then his large hand wrapped around her wrist.

Before she knew what was happening, he draped her over his lap, hanging her head out the window, her hair releasing from its pins. For a moment, she feared he would drop her until she realized exactly how strong the arms were that held her. He had his balance. He was athletic enough to know exactly what he was doing.

She met his eye, refusing to be cowed. "Well?"

His teeth flashed white in his grin. "You are a bold one, Wife. There are few women who have your courage."

He released her and she stood, pushing her hair back with one hand. "Was that meant to frighten me?" she asked, proud her voice didn't waver.

"No," he answered, coming in through the window. "My kisses are what frighten you. I didn't expect you to be afraid just then."

"Why did you do it?"

"It was a test," he murmured. "You think well on your feet. I respect that." He didn't wait for her answer but walked around the bed to the wardrobe. Taking in its size and breadth, he asked, "You moved this yourself?" He sounded impressed.

"I was angry," Gillian confessed. "There's no telling what I will do when angered."

That easy smile returned to his face. "Remind me not to anger you, Wife," he remarked, his voice low, teasing.

"You are already a master at it," she said, moving away from him and the bed. She didn't like being in such close quarters with him. He was too tall, too strong, too vital.

Earlier today, there had been a darkness about him. He'd been somber and had appeared and acted exhausted.

However, now he was completely revitalized. He had the energy and strength she'd remembered about him.

"I should have let you fall," she said, not realizing she'd spoken her thoughts aloud until he laughed.

"I'm glad you didn't."

He threw himself upon the bed, testing it. Gillian took another step back into the corner. He shook his head. "Don't worry, Wife. I'll honor my promises. No kissing."

"Or anything else," she added, wanting her distrust to be clear. "Starting with not calling me 'wife.' I don't like it."

He considered her request a second, and then said, "Yes, dear."

Gillian thought she would scream. Whereas he seemed to be full of energy, she was tired and cross. "I don't like 'dear' either. Call me Gillian," she said before he could open his mouth with new suggestions.

"Yes, Gillian," he said dutifully and ran his hand across his face. "Is that my shaving kit on the wash basin? I had James bring it up." He rose from the bed and walked toward where she stood next to the wash basin.

Gillian didn't want to skitter out of his way and yet had little choice. She walked to the other side of the room, pretending she needed to sit in the chair located in the corner. Wright and the bed blocked her way to the door, although there was no way she'd be able to move the wardrobe without help.

If Wright noticed her discomfort, he didn't say anything. Instead, he began doing the things a person does to ready for bed. He polished his teeth, gave his face a quick wash, and then yawned loudly. "I'm tired," he said, stretching his arms. "It's been a long day."

It had been. Without meaning to, Gillian echoed his yawn.

He smiled at her. "Aren't you going to prepare for bed?"

"I'm not tired." Her eyes watered, she was

so anxious to close them.

"Well, I am." He walked over to the bed and threw back the covers.

For the first time, his bare feet registered in her mind. "Where are your boots?"

"Downstairs," he said. "I hid them in some bushes. They'll be fine for tonight." He picked up the feather pillow and tossed it in the middle of the bed. "There, that side is your half, this side is mine. Or one of us can sleep in the covers and the other on the outside."

She didn't say anything. If he thought she trusted him enough to lie next to him in bed, he was wrong.

"Don't be this way, Gillian. You're tired. Come along. It *is* possible for a man and woman to be in such quarters and not kiss or ravage each other."

"I'm well aware of that," she responded primly, focusing as much as she could on the floorboards and not on him.

He gave a heavy sigh. "I'm attempting to be accommodating here, Gillian," he pointed out.

"I realize that." She also realized he was mocking her. She couldn't wait to be rid of him. He seemed to know exactly the right thing to do to goad her —

Her complaints broke off as he lifted the

hem of his shirt and pulled it off over his head.

Gillian's first instinct was to look away, but she didn't. Their wedding night came roaring back to her. There had been no light in the room then. Not a candle or even a fire in the grate like there was now because they'd married in summer. It had been pitch black, or had she closed her eyes?

She remembered the sound of him entering her room, crossing to the bed, and then disrobing. She could still recall the give of the bed as he'd joined her and her sense of anticipation in discovering he was naked beneath the sheets. Her heart must have beat double time that night.

Modesty had made her shy, but curiosity had made her bold. She'd been raised in the country and had six siblings all much younger than herself. She understood where babies came from and had a vague notion of how.

But she'd not seen her husband naked that night because by the time morning came, he was gone from her bed.

Now, she almost *had* to look. She'd always wondered what the only man she'd ever bedded looked like. She'd had imaginings but never confirmation.

Pretending to try to be comfortable in her

chair, she let her gaze drift toward him — and then stared.

His chest was all flat planes. There was no pudge to him at all, even over the waist of his breeches. No wonder he moved with such grace. His muscles were lean and long, his bone structure strong. Not even the Greeks could have sculpted such a perfect man —

"Enjoying yourself?" he asked.

Gillian blinked, heat flooding her cheeks at having been caught staring.

He laughed, again. She didn't know if she'd ever become accustomed to the sound. It defied the picture she'd spent years building of him. It made him human.

"Gillian, don't be so embarrassed. You have a right to look. If you started undressing, I'd stare."

The heated image such a statement conjured in her mind brought her to her feet in a mixture of outrage and yearning. "You are deliberately provoking me."

"No, I'm teasing you, or attempting to do so. I know you are uncomfortable, but, Gillian, be reasonable. I won't ravage you or even offer a peck on the cheek. I'm tired. You've worn me thin." He climbed under the covers, stretching out. "Come to bed, Gillian. You will only make yourself angrier with lack of sleep."

But Gillian wasn't ready to give up her anger, not when he looked so good in that bed. Instead, she girded herself with impotent rage. It was the only defense left to her.

"Have it your way then," he said with equanimity and rolled over, giving her his back.

Gillian stood ready to smite him down if he should rise out of the bed and seize her. Long minutes drew out between them.

Just as she was ready to relax her guard, he said, "Thank you, Gillian."

"For what?"

"For coming with me. It's all going to be good now. It will be all right." He didn't look at her but stayed on his side.

"I don't know that I can help your desire for a place on Liverpool's staff," she confessed.

He shrugged. "It is enough that you are here. A wife is important to a man in government. She gives him character." He leaned onto his back. "It's also nice to have someone close who is invested in whether a man succeeds or not."

She could have pointed out he'd had a wife all these years . . . but then decided that it had been said enough. In fact, she was finding it hard to stay angry at him.

She was forced to overreact and behave in ways not becoming to herself.

He smiled sleepily and curled back over. "I really could have killed myself in that tree," he muttered, his eyes closing.

"You didn't have to climb it," she reminded him.

"Yes I did. I did it for you."

Gillian was quick to jump on his claim. "How did you do it for me?"

He sighed. "I needed to prove to you how far I would go for you. Hadn't done that before."

That was true.

"And I had to have another kiss," he said. "You are a good kisser. I hadn't realized that."

"Does it make a difference if I can kiss or I can't?" she asked, uncertain what to think.

"In all the best ways," he mumbled, drifting off to sleep.

Gillian experienced a vague disappointment. Wright obviously had the ability to fall asleep at any time and in any place. Perhaps it was a skill he'd acquired in the military.

Perhaps he didn't find her as interesting as she found him.

But to make an intriguing comment about her kissing and then nod off — ? She didn't

131

know what to think.

No, she did know, she reminded herself. She was in love with Andres Ramigio.

"Andres. Andres Ramigio. I love Andres," she repeated as she walked over to the washbasin. She poured more water into the basin, her gaze meeting her reflection in the mirror and then drifting past her reflected shoulder to where Wright slept peacefully in the bed.

Gillian set down the water pitcher and raised a hand to her forehead. Dealing with Wright was giving her a headache. Her life had been simpler and happier without him.

She would not think of him.

She would not trust him.

She would not give one quarter of an ounce of care and concern to him.

Her resolve firmly in hand, Gillian splashed water on her face, dried it off, and returned to the chair. Crossing her arms, she resolved to stay there all night. It wouldn't hurt her. She'd slept in more uncomfortable situations before. Many nights she'd sat up nursing one of her many, much younger siblings when her stepmother was unable to do so. She'd also taken care of Holburn's crofters.

No, a night sitting in a chair wouldn't hurt her.

She just wished Wright didn't look so comfortable.

It had been a long, challenging day. Her mind felt numb. Her bones began to ache with the desire to rest and her eyes were getting that itchy, red feeling.

What had Wright suggested? That one of them sleep outside the covers while the other slept on top?

Was that truly such a bad idea?

In the end, she didn't know that she ever made a decision. Instead, she woke to morning light coming through the windows where the curtains had been thrown back. The wardrobe had been moved back in place, a toasty fire burned in the grate, and her husband stood half naked at the washbasin shaving.

He caught her eye in the looking glass. "Good morning," he said. He looked remarkably handsome and in good spirits whereas she felt as if she'd been dragged under the coach for a mile.

" 'Morning." She lifted the covers, ready to pull them over her head — when she realized that she was wearing nothing but her petticoats.

And she didn't remember climbing into bed or under the covers.

Gillian sat bolt upright. Her dress was

133

neatly hung over the chair she'd thought she'd fallen asleep in last night. Why, even her stockings were there. Someone had undressed her in the night.

Thank the Lord, that person had stopped at her petticoats or she could have found herself completely naked.

Her gaze went immediately to Wright.

He stood by the washbasin watching her, one hand cleaning off his razor in the soapy water. "Should I surmise you are not happy with me?"

CHAPTER EIGHT

"Not happy? I'm *furious* with you," Gillian said, clutching the bedcovers with her fists lest she set them loose on her husband. "How dare you undress me? How *dare* you take advantage of me in that shameful manner?"

Wright set down the razor. He wiped his face with a linen towel. "What do you believe I did?"

"I believe you took shocking advantage," Gillian said, her voice shaking with her anger.

He looked heavenward a moment as if searching for divine guidance. "Gillian, I woke to find you slumped over in that chair to the point your chin all but touched your knees. That's not the way to sleep, especially when you are that exhausted."

"I did not ask for help from you," she replied stiffly.

Wright swore to the heavens. He came to

the foot of the bed. "We're not strangers, Gillian. And I meant no harm. I helped you to bed. You are my wife. I took a vow before God to honor and protect you. No matter what you think of our marriage, I always managed to see to your needs."

"Financially," she shot back, still disgruntled.

"Yes, financially." He made an impatient sound as if wondering what else she wanted from him. "Well, last night, I went a step further. I saw you in that chair and realized that if you slept all night in that position, your back and neck would ache. We have four more hours travel to London. I can't imagine the trip would be any easier if you hurt."

He had a point.

"The fire was dying," he continued. "The room was cold and I worried about your comfort. Is that such a bad thing? I helped you into bed to be kind, Gillian, and for no other reason than that."

"But you took off my dress."

Wright closed his eyes as if their argument pained him. "I did. I also took off your shoes and stockings. I didn't know if you had another dress you planned to wear this morning or if you were wearing this one." He waved to the dress carefully laid out on the chair. "It would have been hopelessly wrinkled if I'd put you to bed in it. As for the shoes and stockings —" He frowned. "I thought you'd be more comfortable with your shoes off."

Gillian rubbed the toes of her feet together beneath the covers. He was right. "It's just so intimate," she murmured.

"They are feet, Gillian. Nothing more. I have them, too."

Wright took a step around toward her side of the bed. "I know we have a complicated history between us. I know I haven't been a good husband. I didn't want to be a husband when we married. But I'm different now. Circumstances have changed me. I'm trying to make amends — and don't tell me it is too late. I'm no fool, Gillian. You haven't known the Spaniard that long, and even if you did, you still have feelings for me. You wouldn't be so outraged at our close quarters or feel threatened by a simple kiss if you didn't."

He was right.

"What I'm asking," he continued, "is for a second chance. Yes, I've tried to maneuver matters to my advantage. But last night, I only sought your comfort. I put you under the covers and I slept on top. I wanted to protect you, Gillian. That's what

137

husbands do."

That's what husbands do.

Tears welled in her eyes. How often had she longed for someone who cared enough for her to see to the little things? The small kindnesses that let a woman know her husband cared?

She lowered her head to wipe away those damning tears before he saw them. "I'm sorry," she whispered around the tightening in her throat. "I may have overreacted. It's just that . . ." She let her voice trail off, knowing whatever she said could be taken in the wrong vein.

"It's just that you don't trust me. I understand that, Gillian. I wouldn't trust me either based upon matters between us in the past. But I'm here now. I want this marriage. I want you for my wife. It's up to you to decide what you want."

"And if I don't want you?" she asked in a small voice, humbled by his straightforward and very honest speech.

"Then I can't have what you won't give, can I?"

Gillian didn't know what to say. And he was right. He had been charming and kind and not at all the monster she'd been building him up to be in her mind all these years.

There had been a time she hadn't thought

him a monster at all, a time when hurt hadn't colored her opinion of him.

"I'll let you have some privacy to dress," he said, taking a clean neck cloth from his shaving kit and quickly tying it into a respectable knot.

She sat on the bed, her arms around her legs and watched him, surprised by the limpness of the linen in his neck cloth. "I'm surprised Hammond let you out of the house with that one," she observed.

Wright flashed her a smile in the looking glass. "It's not such a big thing. Besides, Hammond has other things to do beyond the starch in my clothes."

The comment surprised Gillian more than anything he'd said. When she'd last been around him, Hammond had behaved as if the only thing of importance in the world was the starch in Wright's clothing, and the cut and the shoe blacking, and a hundred other details to a fashionable man's dress.

"Perhaps the war has changed him, too?" she suggested.

Wright's smile faded, but only slightly — she had to be watching him closely to notice. However, his manner was good-humored as he agreed. "We've both come back wiser. Here, let me go. I'll have to sneak outside for my boots and grab my jacket from the front hall. When next you see me, I shall be respectably outfitted." He tossed his water in the bowl out the window before leaving.

Gillian sat still in the quiet room, wondering at this new Wright. It was almost as if her husband was a different man, not that there was anything wrong with that. She liked this new one better. He was kinder and more attentive.

Perhaps she had been hasty in her assessment of him?

One thing she was learning, the early infatuation she had once labeled love was dead. He had her heart racing again, and she didn't know whether to be happy or alarmed. His treatment of her when they'd first married had taught her not to trust her emotions. She needed to be wise and tread carefully.

With that warning in her head, she rose and started dressing. It didn't take her long. She wasn't fussy. However, she lingered over styling her hair. She'd salvaged most of the pins in her hair last night so she could twist it into a neat chignon, but she didn't pull her hair as tightly as usual. She also loosened a few tendrils around her face to soften the style. She also bit her lips a few times and pinched her cheeks to bring color to them.

She picked up her coat, gloves, the velvet muff and hat, and went downstairs to join Wright.

The family she'd almost displaced the night before was spread out through the dining room enjoying their breakfast.

Wright was seated at a table in the far corner under a window. He had on his coat and boots.

He didn't notice Gillian's entrance. Instead, he was concentrating on the act of peeling an apple while a young girl of around the age of seven, her hair in two braids, watched him closely — and for a moment, Gillian couldn't move she was so taken with the picture of him and the child.

She'd not connected the thought of Wright and children before. When she'd married him, she'd supposed they would have them, but she'd been so anxious about her marriage, she hadn't fully fleshed out the idea. Then again, she'd spent so much time taking care of her siblings, she hadn't been anxious for motherhood.

But now, seeing him being so gentle with the child, an almost overwhelming desire for children settled inside her.

He noticed her and beckoned her over

with a nod of his head before he returned to his apple peeling.

She crossed the room, reaching the table just as he finished his task. He held the curled peel up in the air. "Is this right?" he asked the girl.

"That's perfect, my lord," she said in a soft northern brogue. "You are very good at peeling."

Wright rose and pulled out a chair for Gillian. "This is Miss Amy Doward. Those are her parents at the next table. They are traveling home from London. Miss Doward, this is my wife, Lady Wright."

He said "my wife" with a proprietarial air. Gillian couldn't correct him, not in front of everyone . . . and she discovered she truly didn't have the will to do so. Wright was winning her over.

Miss Amy's brow furrowed with concern. She motioned for Wright to bend down so that she could whisper in his ear in a voice Gillian could overhear, "Should I curtsey? I am sometimes confused."

"Amy," her mother said, in that tone mothers used to excuse the precociousness of their children. She held a squirming toddler on her lap.

Wright waved her concerns aside before pretending to consider the matter. Gillian

decided to speak for herself, "No, it's not necessary. I've never been comfortable with it." She sat down so that she was on Miss Amy's level. "And all the rules confuse me, too. So many rules. I prefer saying hello with a shake of the hand." She held out her hand. "Hello, I'm Gillian."

A huge smile spread across Amy's face at the attention. Her two front teeth were missing and she was absolutely adorable. She shyly gave Gillian her hand. "I'm-Amy-Doward," she answered, her words running together in her excitement. She glanced at her parents, smiling her happiness.

"Miss Amy Doward was showing me a trick with an apple peel," Wright said, "that she assures me works every time."

"And what is that?" Gillian asked.

"If he holds the peel over his right shoulder and drops it to the floor," Amy said, "it will tell him who his true love is."

"Yes, the peel will spell out the first letter of my love's name," Wright chimed in.

Gillian shook her head, marveling that here was another side to this man she'd not imagined. She'd never considered him fanciful. "The first letter?"

Wright nodded. "Miss Doward assures me it is accurate every time." He turned his back to them and held the apple peel over his right shoulder. "Do I hold it like this?"

"Yes," Amy said with complete seriousness. "Now drop it."

He let go and then immediately turned to see what letter was formed.

Amy beamed up at him. "It's an S," she announced.

" 'Tis not," Wright countered. "It's a G."

"A G?" Amy scrunched her face in confusion.

Her three older siblings had to see for themselves. Even her parents looked over and Gillian was no less curious.

"I don't see a G, my lord," Amy's older brother, a lad of about ten, said.

"It's there," Wright argued. "A small g. See how it curls up."

Gillian had to look — and was surprised that he was right.

Amy decided he was, too. "It is a g," she said, obviously pleased for him.

"Of course it is," Wright said and beamed a smile at Gillian that stole her breath. He seemed to know his effect on her because he reached over and brushed one of the curls from her face. "My true love's name starts with g."

And that is when Gillian gave in. He had been working hard to win her over, and he had succeeded. In one fell swoop, the past between them evaporated, replaced by the present. The things he should have done, the vows that should have been made — all vanished. What mattered was from this moment on.

He seemed to know her change of heart. His gaze went straight to her heart. "Gillian," he said, her name sounding like a benediction on his lips. "My true love's name is Gillian."

"Is your name spelled with a g?" Amy asked, breaking the moment between them.

Gillian laughed and said, "Yes, it is. How lucky I am that the apple peel didn't form a 'p' or an 'm.'"

"You are lucky," the child agreed ingenuously before her parents informed her the time had come to put on her coat and hat. They were ready to leave.

There followed goodbyes and well wishes for a safe trip. Amy's parents almost had her herded out the door with the others when the child abruptly turned with a small gasp of alarm.

She slipped past her parents, ran up to Gillian, and curtseyed. "I almost forgot."

"You performed a lovely curtsey."

Amy gave her a toothless smile, one last wave goodbye, and then joined her parents.

Gillian waited until they left to pick up

the cup of tea Wright had ordered for her. "The apple peel really is shaped like an S."

"Or an eight," he agreed easily, meeting her eye with that smile that had far too devastating an effect on her.

She set down her teacup.

"What is the matter?" he asked, immediately attuned to her distress.

"This isn't right," she murmured. She glanced out the window. The family was climbing into their coach. The toddler had started crying. He didn't want to be cooped up for hours of travel.

She wanted to cry too, but for a different reason.

"Gillian, what is it?"

Turning back to Wright, she whispered, "I don't want to love you. I don't want to even like you. I loved you once before, Wright, and you crushed me."

The smile faded from his face. For a long moment, she waited, wanting him to say something and not knowing what he could say. It hurt to look at him this way. He was undeniably handsome but it wasn't his looks that drew her to him. It was something more, a sense from the first moment she'd met him that she belonged with him.

And yet that proved to be a lie.

In fact, there wasn't anything he could say

146

that would make her trust him. She was being a fool for even sitting there —

Wright slowly reached for her hand, which rested on the table. He laced his fingers with hers. His gaze dropped to their joined hands. A frown formed on his brow. His jaw hardened. And then almost reverently he brought her hand up to his lips and kissed the back of it, and she discovered *that* was what she'd wanted. She'd needed to have this contact with him.

Words wouldn't have served. Words were too simple.

He raised his gaze. His eyes were coldly sober.

Could he care that much? Did she dare hope?

"I don't want you to leave me, Gillian. You are all that I have."

The walls she'd struggled to keep around her heart against him crumbled.

She squeezed his hand, not wanting to let go of this moment. She ached for Andres, for the promises she'd made to him . . . promises she'd be unable to honor.

Right or wrong, as silly and foolish as it was — she loved Brian Ranson, the Earl of Wright. *Brian.* The name sounded right.

The innkeeper's wife approached with their breakfasts. She gave them an approving smile as she set their plates in front of them. "There you are, my lord. Good hearty breakfasts for you and your lady." She paused, one foot ready to leave and the other staying. "I have to say this, and I know Mr. Peters would *not* approve my speaking, but I was watching the two of you. It's a treat to see a young couple like you who are so handsome together and who obviously care very much for each other." She bobbed an awkward curtsey, her face flooding with color as if she'd said too much. She made a hasty retreat.

"See?" he said, quietly. "We must be doing something right if others can see it, too."

He smiled at her then . . . and she smiled back.

Over breakfast, they made their first tentative partnership as man and wife. It was a very companionable breakfast and all that Gillian had once imagined her life would be with him.

Brian dominated the conversation. He had big plans for his future. He was determined to join Liverpool's staff. He knew it would be a challenge since his father had set himself against the idea. Gillian had several suggestions based upon advice she'd overheard her father make to other ambitious young men like her husband over the years.

Her father and stepmother would be pleased when they heard she and Brian were together again. Her father had not been happy when she'd left her husband.

"I'm anxious to show you your new home," he said, pushing his chair away from the table.

"I'm anxious to see it," she answered, setting her napkin down beside her plate.

While Brian settled with the innkeeper, Gillian collected her things. James and George had already seen to her valise. They waited with the coach by the front door.

Brian joined her, taking her arm and leading her out to the coach.

The day was damp and breezy. The sun appeared ready to play hide-and-seek all day. It was a good day for travel. They were approximately four hours outside of London and would easily arrive before dark.

A basket had been set on the floor inside the coach. "What is that?" Gillian asked.

"I had the innkeeper prepare a basket in case we grew hungry," Brian answered.

"After that breakfast?" Gillian shook her head. "Not likely."

"Either case, we'll be prepared," he said helping her into the vehicle.

"Yes, Colonel," she said, gently mocking his military planning and was rewarded with one of his quick smiles.

The basket actually took up a good amount of room on the floor, forcing her to lean against her husband to be comfortable.

Brian didn't appear to mind. He shut the door and pulled down the shade over the window, plunging them into a murky twilight. His arm came around her waist with easy affection. "Awkward having the basket there, isn't it?" he said, his lips close to her ear.

"Difficult," she murmured, but didn't make a move away from him other than to remove her velvet cap. She set it and the muff on top of Brian's greatcoat, which he had folded and placed on the seat next to her.

He knocked on the roof, signaling James they were ready to go.

With a shout of, "hey" to the horses, James set the coach on the road. Brian and Gillian jerked forward with the movement. His free arm came protectively in front of her. His hand around her waist didn't move. He didn't move it.

They rode in silence.

Gillian rested her head on his shoulder. She liked the clean, masculine scent of his shaving soap and tried to guess what it was as a way of taking her mind off how neatly she fit against his body.

She no longer doubted that he was as aware of her as she was of him. It seemed the coach echoed with the pounding beat of their hearts.

The coach leaned to one side as it rounded a corner, bringing her and Brian even closer.

He turned to her. She looked up. Their lips were mere inches apart.

"I was wrong," he said.

"About what?"

"It isn't possible for a man and a woman to be in close quarters and not kiss."

"You are right," she agreed and placing her hand over his heart, reached up and kissed him full on the mouth.

CHAPTER NINE

She was kissing him.

Brian could not believe his luck. He'd breeched Gillian's defenses. He'd laid siege and in less time than he had anticipated she had surrendered.

And she was so sweet in his arms. So giving.

He blamed youth and his own misguided bullheadedness for not realizing years ago what a remarkable, precious woman Gillian was.

He would make up for that now. *She was his.* He'd never let her go. Not now that he had her.

But it wasn't just how attractive she was or her intelligence that drew him to her. No, she made him feel good about himself. He'd never felt more alive in months, perhaps years, than he did being with Gillian.

Brian pulled her up into his lap so that he

could kiss her properly . . . and she kissed him back. The frightened bride he had to be so careful of was gone and in her place was a woman who didn't shy from his touch or his passion.

His fingers unbuttoned her jacket. The wool was soft beneath his touch. He kissed her mouth, her chin, her neck. "Sweet Gillian," he whispered and felt her muscles stretch into a smile as she pressed her lips against his forehead, her fingers in his hair.

Making love in the coach had not been his intent. He'd wanted privacy with his wife. He'd imagined kisses, but had not let his mind wander to something more.

Now, he wanted nothing more than to be deep inside her. He wanted to claim her, to keep her.

He forced himself away from the sweet scent of her skin where her shoulder and neck met. Leaning his head back against the seat, he had to close his eyes against the sight of his wife smiling at him, her lips swollen and full from his kisses. Otherwise, he wouldn't have been able to say, "I think we'd best stop this."

Dear God, the words hurt to speak.

There was a beat of silence. "Why?"

Brian opened his eyes. She was so beautiful to him. His Gillian had gone from being attractive to being the most graceful, lovely woman he'd ever met. He touched a lock of her hair the color of rich, golden ale. "Because if we keep this up, you will be ravaged."

A look of such unholy delight came to her eyes, it robbed him of breath. "I believe that is what I want, Brian."

His name had never sounded sweeter than when spoken from her lips. Her bold honesty set his senses afire.

"Well then, my lady, that is exactly what is going to happen," he assured her before setting down to business.

He kissed her ear, her nose, her eyes, her forehead . . . her mouth. Gillian didn't think she could ever have enough of his kisses or that she'd ever stop kissing him.

Time ceased to have meaning. Her world narrowed down to this coach, the leather seat, and this man. Her senses were alive with him.

His arousal strained his breeches. She remembered having him inside her. Remembered the alien feeling and the disquieting yearning for something she didn't understand. She'd spent years thinking long and hard about their joining.

She lowered her hand, finding the buttons

to his breeches. She undid one, then another —

"*No.* Not yet." His hands came down to her wrists. Brian turned, bringing her down onto the leather seat. He looked into her eyes. "It has to mean more, Gillian," he said. He braced an arm against the seat close to her head. "I *want* it to mean more."

Gillian leaned back into the corner. One leg was still across his lap, the other bent against his hip. "You don't want me?" Her mind was having trouble understanding.

"*I want you,*" he said fervently. "But I want us to start afresh. I don't want to drag the past with us. We have the opportunity right now to change everything."

"What do you want us to do?" she asked, uncertain.

"I want to repeat my vows. I didn't mean them the first time, Gillian. I was too involved in my own life but I need you to *trust* and believe in me."

"I do," Gillian murmured, and it was true.

"Then let this be the first day of our marriage — a marriage built upon all that is fine and good."

She reached out and placed her hand over his heart, deeply touched by his words. A new beginning. It sounded like heaven.

Brian took her left hand in his. His thumb

stroked the back of her hand as he said somberly, "I, Brian Anthony Ranson, earl of Wright, take you Gillian —"

He paused, and she knew he didn't know her full name. Instead of being offended, she offered quietly, "Bridie Hutchins."

His brows came together. "I don't deserve you." He started to sit up, to pull away. She reached out, laid her left hand on the side of his jaw, and brought him back around to face her. "I don't even know your name," Brian said to her unspoken question, his eyes troubled. "You could do so much better, even with that Spaniard."

"But you are the one who is my husband," she replied. She drew breath and released it before confessing, "You are the only one I want to be my husband."

He turned and pressed a kiss into the palm of her hand. Where his lips touched, her skin burned. He lingered there, unmoving, his body tense with pent-up emotion.

"Brian?"

"I'm fine, Gillian," he said, but when he looked at her, she saw the suspicious redness around his eyes. He'd been that moved by her words? It touched her deeply, banishing the last traces of doubt in her heart.

He reclaimed her left hand. This time when he spoke, there was no hesitation. "I,

Brian, wilt take Gillian Bridie Hutchins to be my wedded wife, to live together after God's ordinance in the holy estate of matrimony. I promise I wilt love her, comfort her, honor and keep her in sickness and health; forsaking all others, keeping her only unto me, so long as we both shall live."

"You remember the words," she said, surprised.

"I've had time to think about them," he answered. "I've reread them several times thinking about us and about what I've done wrong. I mean them this time, Gillian. I'm older and, hopefully, wiser. I want our marriage."

There it was. Proof that he'd not come for her because she'd left him and his pride demanded obedience, but because he now valued what she'd *always* wanted — a marriage based upon mutual esteem, respect, and love.

Oh, he didn't love her yet. She was not that naïve. But he would someday. The attraction between them was strong. They weren't afraid of speaking their minds or locking horns . . . or listening when the other person was right.

And Jess was gone.

It was unkind to be thankful a woman was dead. Gillian had a second of contrition until she absolved herself with her own happiness. Brian was hers, not Jess's or any other woman's.

What was hers, she kept.

Her vows were easy to recite. She'd never forgotten them, even when she had made the decision to not honor them. "I, Gillian, take you Brian Anthony Ranson to be my wedded husband, to live together after God's ordinance in the holy estate of matrimony. I wilt love him, comfort him, obey him —"

He stopped her by pressing his fingers against her lips. "That list isn't necessary, Gillian. I know you will honor it. All I ask is for your trust."

"I do trust you," she protested.

Brian shook his head. "You shouldn't. I haven't earned it. But I'm going to ask it of you now. Please, Gillian, vow that you will trust me, even when you are angry or hurt or perhaps afraid."

She leaned back in her corner. Was this because she'd left him? If so, he certainly was wise to ask it of her. She tightened her hold on their joined hands as she said, "I wilt love, honor, obey, and *trust* you; forsaking all others, keeping only you unto me so long as we both shall live."

There, she'd made her vow. Andres rose

in her conscience. She felt a stab of guilt but she would write him, would explain. As Aunt Agatha had pointed out, a wife belonged with her husband.

Brian leaned forward, pressing his lips to hers. The fire that had burned between them quickly caught fire.

It had been an unconventional ceremony. Promises exchanged in a rolling coach with both bride and groom half undressed, but to Gillian it could not have been more sacred.

She put her arms around his neck pulling him closer. The seat was narrow, the space confined and yet they fit together perfectly.

"I have my ring," she confessed. "I was going to throw it away, but I couldn't."

"The ring doesn't matter, Gillian. I shall always be here for you. You must believe that."

And she let herself believe.

This was the marriage she had once dreamed of. He was the man she wanted.

Their kisses deepened. Clothes were pulled off. They didn't attempt to remove Brian's boots. They were in too much of a hurry.

Brian entered her with one smooth stroke. It felt *good* to have him inside her.

"Are you all right?" he asked. "I haven't

hurt you — ?"

She kissed him. "I've never been better." She took a moment, allowing her body to heat his. "Now, make love to me, husband. I've been waiting years for you."

He was happy to comply.

This joining was so different from the first. There was no pain, no tension. She let him take the lead. He seemed to know what she wanted better than she did. His strokes became longer, went deeper. Was it her imagination or did he seem to be taking longer with her than on her wedding night?

His whole purpose appeared to be seeing to her pleasure. He whispered her name, urging her on, kissing her, loving her, pleasing her . . . calling her "Wife."

It was what she'd dreamed of hearing. What she'd wanted to be.

Had her husband known that when he'd come for her at Huntleigh? Or had something new and precious happened to their marriage? Had a change of heart occurred amidst the arguments and anger?

It no longer mattered. Gillian could forgive him anything as long as he held this way.

A yearning built inside her. A need she'd not known before. She could barely breathe, let alone think. Her blood beat in her veins, rushing to where they were joined.

"Brian?" she whispered, fearful.

He hushed her. "Relax into it. Let me take you there."

And exactly where was "there"?

"With me," he said, in answer to her unspoken question. "Come . . . with . . . me."

Suddenly, exquisite, sharp pleasure seared through her. She touched it, pulled back, and felt it radiate through her whole being.

She cried out his name. He thrust hard, deep . . . once, twice and sought his own release. For one blessed span of time, their bodies melded into one.

Life suddenly made sense.

She'd been destined to be right here, right now. She held onto him. He was the anchor in the middle of a turbulent storm.

And at the same time, love welled in her heart for him. It filled to overflowing.

How could she ever have doubted him?

Slowly, the world came back into focus. Gillian lay in his arms, her body well used and pleasantly exhausted.

The world beyond came back into focus. The smell of leather and horses mixed with that of his shaving soap and their lovemaking. James and George's muffled voices came through the coach walls. If they'd overheard any of what happened inside the coach, they gave no indication.

A chill went through the air, cooling her still-fevered skin.

He grabbed his greatcoat and rolled onto the seat so that she was on top, her head in the crook of his arm. He spread the coat over her. His arms banded around her as if he'd never let her go. He kissed the top of her head.

"You are wonderful," he whispered.

Gillian looked up at him. "I am?"

His gaze met hers. "You are so sweet, so giving."

"I liked you, too," she admitted — and he laughed, holding her closer still.

"I have been such a fool," he murmured. "You are a treasure. My precious, precious wife."

She liked the sound of that. She prayed he'd say that every day of their lives together. She also wondered if he'd ever said such to Jess.

As if reading her mind, he whispered, "It's never been like that before . . . with anyone." And Gillian grinned with happiness.

Silence stretched between them. She thought about telling him that she loved him. That she'd always loved him from the moment they'd met. But there was a boldness to such a statement. *Let him go first.*

After he'd said it, she would make her confession. And they would laugh about how long it had taken her to speak her heart, but he would understand.

Right now, she believed he understood everything.

"Liverpool would be a fool not to give you an appointment on his staff," she said, listening to the beat of his heart in his chest.

"He has no choice but to do so," Brian agreed. "Look at the beautiful woman I married."

Gillian lifted her head to see if he was joking. She'd not thought herself a beauty. She was attractive or as Aunt Agatha often said, "handsome enough." But beautiful? Especially right now? She was certain she appeared a mess.

And then he smiled at her and what she saw in her lover's eyes made her *feel* beautiful.

"I've hurt you so much in the past, Gillian. I understand that now. I've been selfish. I'm trying to change, but —" His voice broke off. "You are a gift. Please trust me, Gillian. Please trust me."

She came up on one arm to look into his face. "Brian, is something the matter?"

Gently, he brought her head back down

to his chest, combing her hair down her back with his fingers. The pins were long gone. She didn't care.

"Nothing is wrong, Gillian," he said. "In fact, if anything, all is right. It is as it should be."

That nagging seed of doubt attempted to unsettle her happiness. Gillian wouldn't let it. "Tell me about our house in London," she whispered, wanting to change the subject.

"It's small," he said. "There wasn't much available when I was looking, but it is in a good neighborhood. There are only two bedrooms upstairs and the furniture is not what I would choose. It came with the lease. We shall buy new. I'll let you manage that. And we shall need to hire more servants."

"What servants do you have?"

"Hammond, of course —"

She had to smile at the name of the always-present valet who went everywhere with Brian, even into the military. "I'm surprised he didn't make this trip with you."

"He's overseeing matters at the house for me."

"Why? Are you doing repairs?" she wondered.

"No," he was quick to say. "There are just . . ." He paused, smiled at her. "*Con-*

cerns he is handling while I'm gone."

"Are they concerns I should know about?" she asked, curious.

Brian gathered her closer in his arms. "You don't need to worry about them now."

Gillian happily snuggled deeper against the warmth of his body. She yawned, feeling drowsy.

"Well, then," she said, considering the matter. "We will need a housekeeper."

"I did hire one. Mrs. Vickery. I also hired a cook but her services were unsatisfactory. She's no longer with us."

She kissed his shoulder, liking the way he said "us."

"Well, you needn't worry about the staff any longer. I can manage all of that. I saw to those details in my parents' household and, of course, I managed Huntleigh for Holburn. His new wife Fiona didn't seem too upset with what I've done."

"I *knew* you would know what to do," he said. "Everything will be fine now. It will all be perfect."

Gillian raised her head to look up at him. "You sound so relieved," she said, half-teasing. "Have there been problems with the servants?"

"Gillian, I don't know how to set up a household. It's decidedly far more difficult than organizing an encampment for three thousand men."

She laughed, pleased that she would play an important role in his life. "The first guest we must invite once the house is in order is Lord Liverpool. I'll write my father for an introduction. He knows you, of course —"

Brian nodded.

"— but my father likes you and will be happy to write on your behalf."

"Your father likes me. Even after you left me?"

"He was furious I did so. I will have to write him when we reach London. He'll be pleased."

"That's good," Brian whispered. "Very good." He seemed to savor those thoughts before continuing, "We shall set ourselves up in society. We'll go everywhere. Hostesses will clamor for our company, and soon we'll be the talk of London."

Gillian laughed. "No one knows me. If you are counting on my name to draw invitations, you may be disappointed."

"They will want us," he said with assurance. "My argument with my father has been great fuel for gossips. All it will take is a word in the right places and we shall have invitations pouring in our door from those who would like to see what happens when my parents and I are in the same room."

"That doesn't sound comfortable."

"It will be." He smiled down at her. "I have no doubt of it. You have the poise to carry anything off, Gillian."

She prayed he was right. She had a tendency to be a homebody and had never truly felt comfortable amongst the *ton*. His mother, the marchioness, had been quite disdainful of Gillian's social skills.

But at that moment, if he'd asked her to walk through fire for him, she would have done it.

Wrapping her arms around his waist, she said, "The size of the house is unimportant to me, Brian. You know my circumstances growing up were modest. What matters is that our marriage means something to both of us. Whatever we do, let us work together."

"We will," he said, and sealed that vow with a kiss that grew heated. Within minutes, they were making love again.

There were other questions Gillian could have asked, but at this moment, they didn't matter.

And when they were done, when Brian had once more turned her inside out, she didn't care.

They reached the outskirts of London

shortly after two in the afternoon. Gillian and Brian had to finally let go of each other and dress. She didn't think they looked too bad. Brian helped her with finding her hair pins and redressing her hair.

Before they went further into the city, Brian had them stop for lunch. They shared their basket with the drivers. If James or George had heard any of what was going on in the coach, they didn't give an indication, and for that, Gillian was thankful.

She had mixed emotions about returning to the city. She preferred the clean air and the open countryside of the country. However, now, she had a purpose for returning to London. She thought about Brian's prediction that they could become a powerful couple in society and felt ready to face her future. She was a politician's wife. She'd sat at her parents' table enough evenings when they had entertained their political friends to know what it entailed . . . and she wasn't frightened of it. Not any longer. Her goal was to help her husband in any way possible. Her fears and doubts were secondary.

The coach headed into an older part of the city. Brian leaned out the window, directing James's driving. "We are almost there," he told her, his voice surprisingly subdued.

The neighborhood was respectable but not the best area for a man with Brian's aspirations. Gillian decided she would find a new house for them once he had secured a position with Liverpool.

They turned onto a charming street with a small park in the center of the circle. Gillian waited, excited about her new home.

"This is it," Brian shouted up to James, and Gillian had to sit back for a moment before she trusted herself to speak.

The row house they'd stopped in front of was the last one she would have chosen. It was of a drab brown stone with black shutters and a light blue door desperately in need of painting.

Brian helped Gillian out of the coach. He seemed anxious for her opinion . . . which she thought best to withhold for a moment.

Giving the house a critical eye, she noticed a cracked pane in one of the windows above the door. Even the simple things, such as sweeping off the front walk, had not been done.

She wondered what the new housekeeper was thinking. If she'd known the mistress of the house would be showing up any day, everything would be in order, even down to polishing the brass on the knocker.

Nor could she understand Hammond letting such details slide. The fastidious valet usually had his nose in every matter that involved Brian. Or so it had seemed years ago. Perhaps war had changed Hammond, too?

While George and James saw to her luggage, Brian took her hand. "Welcome to your new home, my lady."

Immediately, Gillian was ashamed of her critical assessment.

Brian looked to the servants. "There is a stable around the corner where I have an account. You can take the horses and vehicle there."

From the top of the coach, James said, "If it is as well with you and Lady Wright, my lord, we'll be driving back. Harris's wedding is on the morrow and we'd like to be there."

Harris was the head gardener at Huntleigh. In all the rush and surprise of seeing her husband, Gillian had forgotten the young man was marrying on the morrow.

"Please give him my good wishes," she said.

James nodded. "That we will, my lady."

She turned to her husband. "Shall we?" she asked.

But Brian didn't move. Instead, he said in

a low voice, "Don't forget your promise to trust me, Gillian. Things aren't always as we'd like them to be but I'm working to make them right."

"I do trust you," she said quietly . . . while old suspicions reared their ugly heads. A baby cried in the distance and it added to her sense of disquiet.

"Right then," Brian said and led her to the front door. James and George followed with her trunk and valise.

The muffled sound of the baby crying was stronger here.

Brian opened the door.

The crying — no, shrieking — grew louder.

Gillian stepped inside. The foyer was the size of a stamp with a staircase and narrow hallway off of it. There was a sitting room to her right and a dining room to her left. The drapes in both rooms were still closed, making them seem dark and the sparse furnishings shabby in the hazy light.

The baby's crying came from up the stairs.

Gillian knew there was a question she had to ask.

But before she could, Hammond came charging down the stairs so quickly she stepped back out of fear he would run right over her and almost tripped over a valise that someone had set there. Hammond was without his customary wig and his sparse hair flew out in every direction. He hadn't shaved and deep, dark circles swooped low under his eyes.

And in his arms was a red-faced, squalling baby with a head full of dark hair.

Hammond shoved the child unceremoniously toward Brian. "I can't take it any longer, my lord. I've had enough. My bags are packed and ready right here by the door. I shall not ask for references."

"But where is the wet nurse?" Brian asked, awkwardly holding the baby. "What happened to her?"

"Happened to her?" Hammond repeated incredulously. "What happened is what has happened with every servant you have hired save for that idiotic Mrs. Vickery. She quit. Couldn't calm the child and said she'd had enough of this." He looked to Gillian and the coachmen. "It makes your ears start to itch after awhile. He never stops, except to sleep and that is only for an hour or two before he starts again. Now excuse me, my lady." He took his hat and coat from the peg by the door, picked up his valise, and almost fell over James and George in his haste to escape.

So. Now she knew why Wright had been

traveling without his valet.

The babe had quit screaming but his little body was doubled with pain. He whimpered and began sucking furiously on his fist. Gillian knew colic when she saw it. This baby must have had a terrible case of it because he was frighteningly thin. Or perhaps something else was wrong.

She'd helped her stepmother with her six babies so she knew a thing or two about them.

Wright knew she knew too.

"Whose baby is it?" she asked, suspecting the answer he gave.

"He's Jess's," Wright said.

For a second, the world seemed to spin around Gillian. Wright had needed her all right . . . *to help with his mistress's child.*

Once again, he'd played her for a fool.

CHAPTER TEN

"It's not what you think, Gillian," Brian insisted quickly.

She appeared ready to faint. He should have told her sooner, but he'd feared she'd not come through the door with him if she knew.

Still, having Anthony dumped unceremoniously in his arms was not how he'd planned introducing her to him either and he could curse Hammond to hell for it.

"James," Brian ordered, "help her." As the footman set down his end of the trunk and moved forward, Brian shouldered the squalling baby on his shoulder. Anthony's belly was tight. His legs kicked with anger. Brian held him close, wishing he could do something, *anything* to relieve the baby's obvious pain.

Gillian held up a hand, warning the coachman back. "I'm not going to swoon. I *don't* swoon," she announced, her voice cold. "James and George, take my trunk back to the coach. I'm returning with you —"

"*No,*" Brian said, stepping between her and the door. He couldn't let her go. Not after he'd worked so hard to bring her here. "Let me explain —"

"There is *nothing* you can say I want to hear." Her voice was tight with tension, her face pale. She wouldn't look at him and he sensed she was close to tears.

"It's not what you think," he insisted.

Hard, cold eyes met his. She wasn't close to tears. She was angry. He'd stared down French bayonets and not made a move but it took all his courage to stand his place in front of his wife now.

"You don't know *what* I think," she informed him.

He could have told her he had a better idea than she imagined, but that wouldn't gain him any ground with his wife. It was far easier to turn his temper on the footmen.

"Put her luggage inside the door and leave," he said in a voice that brooked no disapproval.

To their credit, both did exactly as instructed and beat haste out the door.

Gillian's gloved hands curled into fists at

her side. She still wore her hat and coat.

Anthony settled down into a whimper, his only way of begging Brian for release from the pain he was feeling. Brian had never felt more powerless in his life — and of course that was the moment Mrs. Vickery, his housekeeper decided to make her appearance.

"Oh, I say, Lord Wright, you are home. I hadn't heard a thing." She was a plump, cherry-cheeked woman with impossibly blond hair under her mobcap and swabs of cotton stuck in her ears.

"Then unplug your ears," he said from between clenched teeth.

"The what?" she asked in her high reedy voice. "Oh, the cotton." She pulled it out of one ear. "I'm so sorry, my lord, but I can't hear myself think what with our little Lord Anthony carrying on the way he does. Did Mr. Hammond tell you? The wet nurse I hired yesterday morning up and quit. I tried to stop her. Told her you'd paid good wages for a week but she was out the door first thing before breakfast. Said she couldn't take screaming and the child's too weak to nurse. Said Lord Anthony's crying was drying up her milk." She looked to Gillian. "I don't know what is wrong with folks today. No one wants to work."

176

Again, Brian found it easier to confront a servant than his wife. "Why was Hammond minding this child? I hired *you* to oversee this matter."

"Good heavens, my lord. I can't be seeing to the cooking and the cleaning and minding the baby. I thought the nurse would be seeing to him and when she walked out, I didn't know what to do. It is hard for me to think with all that crying going on." She looked to Gillian. With a nod to the baby, she said, "He never lets up."

Brian looked down at the child he held in his arms and felt helpless. Anthony was going to die. Brian knew next to nothing about babies but he'd seen men die and already this child had faced more than most. He was skinny, his skin thin, loose, and pasty, and his poor little frame was wracked with pain. Brian's eyes burned with his frustration. To have worked so hard to save him, to have given up so much and then to lose him anyway —

"What are you feeding him?" Gillian asked.

"Whatever the wet nurse has," Mrs. Vickery said. "We've tried a pap feeder on him. He screams all the louder."

Brian nodded that was true.

"It's the colic," Mrs. Vickery said. "There's

177

naught you can do for it. Some babies grow out of it. Some don't. If he can't eat, he'll waste away."

Anthony raised his fist to his mouth and began sucking furiously.

"Except he is a fighter," Brian said. "He's suffered like this almost since birth and he hasn't given up yet. There has to be a way to save him, Gillian. I've had doctors in. They don't give a lot of hope. You are my last chance. Please, can you help me?"

Gillian stood in indecision. He sensed she wanted to go running out the door. He had no doubt she was furious with him. She probably thought he'd used sex to trick her into staying.

Later, he would explain his initial intention for coming for her had been to help Anthony . . . but making love to her had been for him.

They would work it all out. He would see that they did if he had to tie her up and make her listen to him, but first Anthony needed her help.

The baby started crying again. He looked pitiful, like a hatchling thrown out too soon from the nest. Every day he grew weaker.

Gillian bent down and pulled her trunk forward three inches so that she could close the door. "Now, Mrs. Vickery, I shall ask again. What have you been feeding this child?" She started taking off her gloves and hat.

The housekeeper scratched her head. "Well, if there is no wet nurse, and there hasn't been because they have been hard to find this time of year. The spring is the best time for finding a wet nurse and that's what I told his lordship here —"

"What have you been feeding this child?" Gillian's sharp voice cut through the air.

Mrs. Vickery glanced at Brian as if she felt he should do something. "I'd answer her if I were you," he suggested.

"Milk," Mrs. Vickery said, folding her hands against the apron tied at her waist.

"Cow's milk?" Gillian asked. She'd slipped off her coat and hung it on the peg by the door.

"Yes, my lady. But I always made certain it was fresh. Well, at least not more than a day or two old."

Gillian ignored her and stepped toward Brian. She held out her hands. "Let me see the child." He noticed she didn't look at him. He placed Anthony in her outstretched hands. Gillian walked into the sitting room, moving toward the window. "Please open the drapes," she ordered.

Brian hurried to do her bidding. Mrs.

Vickery hung back in the hallway. "It's the *colic,*" she repeated. "There's nothing you can do with the colic."

Gillian didn't answer but took a seat by the window and examined Anthony. Brian hovered close to her as she folded back the baby's dress and pinched his legs. She took off his wool knit booties and examined his feet.

Anthony's toes curled in the coldness of the room. Without looking up, Gillian said, "Mrs. Vickery, start the fire in this room."

"I'd have to go out for coal," was the answer.

From his vantage point, Brian could see Gillian's lips curl in disdain. She was not pleased with his housekeeper.

His opinion was confirmed when Gillian raised her gaze to the housekeeper and said, "You don't know very much about babies, do you, Mrs. Vickery?"

The lady started to say yes, but ended up saying, "No, I do not, never having any of my own."

"You told me you had experience," Brian accused her.

"I have . . . but not a great deal. My sister has children."

Brian was flabbergasted. He'd hired Mrs. Vickery because of the knowledge she'd claimed to have about babies. Of course, now, seeing the situation through Gillian, he realized he'd been so relieved to find anyone willing to work with a screaming baby, he'd happily overlooked the house-keeper's shortcomings.

Obviously Gillian wasn't going to be so forgiving.

She put the booties back on Anthony's feet. He was crying, but his flailing fists and kicking legs didn't deter her. She moved with cool efficiency. Standing, she turned Anthony over onto his belly and rested him on her arm. She began stroking his back as she paced the floor.

Her method appeared a very awkward way of holding a baby to Brian, yet Anthony liked it. His sobs grew quieter and farther apart until he fell into an exhausted sleep. Gillian had performed magic and she'd done it in less than five minutes.

"He will wake shortly," Gillian said briskly. "At that time, I want to feed him a mixture of very, very thin porridge and goat's milk."

"Goat's milk?" Mrs. Vickery repeated.

"Yes," Gillian said. She looked at Brian. "Your baby has colic but he's also starving to death. His crying may be his way of tell-ing us he's hungry. Most babies can't toler-ate cow's milk. However, goat's milk seems to be milder. Perhaps it will work on Anthony. I just pray we aren't too late."

"I'll fetch the milk myself," Brian said horrified at the thought the child could starve. He turned to Mrs. Vickery. "Where will I find it?"

The housekeeper made a face. "I wouldn't know. I don't like goats."

"Try the dairy barn at Vauxhall Gardens," Gillian said impatiently. "Where there are dairy cows, there should be goats. Tell them we are nursing a baby and you want far more than the customary cup. They will charge you a pretty penny for it but we have little choice."

"The expense is not a concern," Brian answered. "In fact I'm thankful to finally have a program to help Anthony. If need be, I'll buy a herd of goats and put them in the back garden and milk them myself." He reached for the hat he had removed and hung on one of the pegs by the door when they'd first entered the house.

"But look at the hour, my lady," Mrs. Vickery said. "There will be no milk now. We'd have to wait until morning."

"Vauxhall milks at noon," Gillian replied. To Brian she said, "Tell them we want milk delivered every day, and we want it fresh."

"I will," Brian said. "I should return in

the hour."

"You'll be hard pressed to do that," Gillian answered, jiggling her arm holding Anthony because he had started to rouse and begin crying again.

"I'll be back within the hour," Brian reiterated and pushed her trunk more out of the way to ease the opening of the door.

As he was leaving, he overheard Gillian say to the housekeeper, "I need to go to the kitchen and brew a cup of chamomile tea. I'll feed that to the baby while I wait for Wright to return."

"Chamomile tea?" Mrs. Vickery questioned. "Is that not a strange thing for a baby?" Her words echoed Brian's thoughts.

"It's a remedy for colic that sometimes works. Now where is the kitchen?"

Brian closed the door. He'd hire a hack to reach Vauxhall in all possible haste. But before he took the first step, he had to look heavenward and say a prayer of thanksgiving. His instincts had been right. Gillian with her numerous siblings and who helped with her father's parish work knew what to do to help Anthony.

He just prayed they weren't too late.

True to his word, Brian returned within the hour. He'd only had to grab two dairymen by the collar to find goat's milk.

The stuff had a strong gamey odor. He didn't think he'd ever tasted it before . . . and he didn't believe he would start. Nor did he quite believe Anthony would like it.

The front rooms were deserted when he came in. He called up the stairs, "Gillian?"

There was no answer. Thinking they might still be in the kitchen, he started down the narrow hallway. He'd been to the kitchen once when he'd first leased the house. As he went down the stairs, he could hear Anthony. His cries not as strong as they had been earlier but they were as painful. Usually this meant he was beyond exhaustion.

He also could hear Mrs. Vickery grumbling and the sound of dishes being moved.

Brian had to duck to enter the kitchen which itself was a spacious room with high windows to the street. There was a line of cupboards around the edge of the room and a huge working table in the center.

Gillian sat rocking in a chair before the hearth while Mrs. Vickery and a scullery maid scrubbed dishes. Gillian did not appear happy. Neither did the housekeeper and the maid.

"I have the milk," Brian said to introduce himself. At his arrival, Mrs. Vickery's strange

184

mutterings went silent. She and the scullery maid were in front of a big tub of water doing dishes.

"Excellent," Gillian answered. "Is it still warm or should we reheat it?"

Brian tested the milk in a crockery jar by sticking his little finger in it. "It's room temperature."

"All the better," Gillian said, rising. Still carrying Anthony over her arm, she pulled a pot cooling before the hearth and brought it with her free hand to the work table. A gravy bowl and the pap feeder were waiting there.

The pap feeder was a curved tube made of silver. It had a spout at one end and was open on the other. To feed the baby, milk or a flour and water mixture called pap was poured through the open end of the tube. It flowed into the baby's mouth through the spout. Brian did not admire the device. He'd seen it used only once before and didn't think it effective.

Gillian spooned some watery porridge into the gravy bowl. "Mix the milk in. We want it very runny. And please hurry. Anthony is preparing for another big bout of crying. We just settled him down."

Brian moved fast. When he was done, Gillian instructed him to pour the mixture into the pap feeder while she held the spout in Anthony's mouth.

The baby was so hungry for sustenance that he greedily tried to suck on the silver spout. When the milk first came out, he made a face. He smacked his lips as he tasted it and then opened his mouth for more.

"That's the way he always starts," Mrs. Vickery said discouragingly. "He acts as if he likes it and then his belly becomes hard and bloated and he's crying all night."

"You didn't tell me that earlier," Gillian said, her gaze never leaving Anthony.

"I said he wouldn't take food," Mrs. Vickery defended herself.

Gillian didn't bother to answer her but explained in a quiet voice for Brian, "If his stomach is hard and bloated, it means gas and that will make him sick. We mustn't give him a great deal more of this. Not at first. I'm hoping the porridge will tide him over until the next feeding. There, now, that is enough."

Brian put down the gravy bowl. Anthony had only taken in less than three quarters of a cup and a good portion of that had either been spilled or spit out of his mouth.

Gillian began cleaning the baby up, heedless of the damage to her own clothes. She cooed soft encouraging words to the baby and put him to her shoulder to burp.

For his part, Anthony started crying again but the cries lacked his usual conviction and Brian felt heartened. "What do we do now?" he asked.

"I hope he will go to sleep," Gillian said, "and then we'll have a real test of my theory. A full belly should help him sleep longer in the night. I dressed him in bedclothes and changed his nappy while you were gone."

Brian was surprised to see she was right. He also took stock of his surroundings and was stunned at how filthy the kitchen was. There were stacks of dirty plates and cups. A cat he'd never seen before licked a spoon.

Gillian noticed his shock. "Why don't we take Anthony up to his bed?" she suggested. "Mrs. Vickery and Ruby," she referred to the scullery maid whom Brian had only seen on two or three occasions, "will finish cleaning the kitchen. You might want some supper but personally, I am fine."

Any appetite he'd had evaporated at the sight of the kitchen. "I'll show you the bedroom and carry your trunk upstairs."

"Bring the baby's food and the feeder," she instructed.

Brian picked up both articles and followed her up the stairs. In the hallway, she stopped. "I'd advise you to let Mrs. Vickery go."

"After seeing the kitchen, I agree."

"She tried to blame it on the cook, who left last week."

Nodding, Brian explained, "The cook up and left because she couldn't stand Anthony's crying. Just like the five wet nurses and one valet."

Gillian looked down at the sleeping baby in her arms. "I imagine it was terrible. The sound of a colicky baby will grate on one's nerves. But if the kitchen was that nasty it should have been cleaned immediately and Mrs. Vickery knows it. I was also not happy when I saw the baby's crib."

"You've been upstairs already."

"He needed clean clothes and a new nappy," Gillian said. "Wright, I was disgusted at the state of the nursery. The laundry has not been done."

"I know. That's why I needed you." He almost hated saying the words, knowing she would not appreciate them.

She didn't. With an irritated sound, she started up the stairs.

Brian knew he'd lost ground on that one. He charged up after her.

In the nursery, Gillian carefully laid Anthony in the crib. A fire already burned in the grate.

"At least Mrs. Vickery started the fire up here," he said, setting down the pap feeder and food on a side table next to a rocking chair. He took a candle over to the fire to light it.

"I started the fire," Gillian said. She folded a blanket over the baby. "I hope this is warm enough for him. Wright, he's very sick —"

"I know."

"Do you?" she countered, her voice brittle. She turned to face him. "Do you realize that he will need to be fed almost every two hours? Small amounts so that his stomach can handle it. He's like a baby bird, Wright. He must be nursed and protected."

"I've been trying to do that, Gillian. It's been difficult because I haven't been able to find anyone who could help until now."

"He's not your child, is he?"

Her sudden, unerring conclusion caught him off guard.

They stood facing each other. "What makes you believe that?" Brian asked.

She crossed her arms, walking over to stand in front of the fire. "You haven't been in the country long enough to have fathered this child. How old is he? Six months or so? Unless, of course, you have been traveling back and forth across the Channel for clandestine meetings with your mistress. I don't believe you've been doing that."

"No."

"I also remember you saying, what is yours you keep. You might neglect a person, such as you did myself for years, but you wouldn't mistreat him or her, especially a baby. There would be the best of care. This child has been neglected."

Her accusation about his treatment of her annoyed him. He could argue that giving her all the rank and privilege that befitted his wife including the care and comfort she received under his parents' roof would not be considered neglect by the population of England. Perhaps even the world.

However, it was true he'd never neglect a child.

"So what is Anthony's story, Wright?" she demanded. "Be honest with me for once and tell me everything I need to know from the beginning."

Brian moved closer to the crib. The anxiousness that had marred most of Anthony's sleep had disappeared. In fact, he slept so soundly, one could wonder if he still lived. "I like to watch him sleep," he said, more to himself than Gillian. He looked up at her. "Jess isn't dead."

His words had the suspected impact. Gillian actually took a step back. "Why did you tell me she was?"

"Actually, what I had started to say was that Jess was dead to me. I no longer include her as a part of my life. Unfortunately you leapt to conclusions and I allowed it to continue. After all, would you have returned with me if you had thought differently?"

There was a moment of indecision, but Gillian recovered. "Of course I would. Did I have a choice?"

"We always have choices. And the truth is, as far as I'm concerned, she is dead. What love I felt for her is gone."

"Because this baby isn't yours?"

Brian frowned at Gillian. She was so uncompromising. So hard. But if Gillian kept Anthony alive, he could forgive all.

"Do you truly find me so shallow?" he asked. "Oh, wait." He held up a hand. "You are going to inform me that I have been that shallow with you. But the truth is, I've never lied to you, Gillian."

"You weren't completely forthcoming either."

"Guilty," he agreed. "But I've never lied."

"Then answer my questions now," she said, and actually had the audacity to tap her foot. She was letting him know that no matter what he said, her mind about him was made up — he was a scoundrel.

"Anthony is my father's child," he said, and enjoyed the moment as understanding dawned and took the starch out of her.

Her mouth dropped open, and for once Gillian appeared speechless.

"Yes," he said to her unspoken question. "My father was having an affair with my mistress. Yes, I did confront him. He had no apology other than to tell me he felt obligated to show me what sort of woman Jess truly was."

Gillian shut her mouth.

"They made this baby," Brian continued, "but neither wanted him. Jess likes her London life and my father apparently —" Brian shrugged. "Who knows what my father thought? When I asked, he rattled on about inferior breeding and lines of aristocracy. It was nonsense."

"What did they do with Anthony?" Gillian asked.

"I believe they farmed him out but as you could hear, Anthony is a difficult child and he was tossed away into a home for foundlings. It was some parish poorhouse. He was left in a corner to cry all he wished. I brought him here four weeks ago. Right before Christmas."

"Why did you go searching for him?"

That was not a question Brian anticipated her asking. "Would you rather I have ignored him?"

She moved toward the crib. "Of course not. But I am curious."

It was Brian's turn to move toward the fire. He was conscious that they circled each other, the crib the starting and stopping point.

So, how to explain why he would go on a quest to find the son his father had with his mistress. "It wasn't out of anger," he said, "although I did feel betrayed."

"You *were* betrayed," Gillian agreed readily. "I'm not surprised at your father though. He is the sort of man who must feel in control of everything."

"Did he ever make a move toward you?"

She shook her head. "If he did, I admit to being too naïve to notice. All I could think about was you."

It was an arresting comment but one he set aside to examine later. At this moment, he had some explaining to do. She deserved answers.

"War is hard." He crossed his arms against his chest. What he was about to say made him feel vulnerable, an emotion he did not like. "The dying men in battle still ring in my ears. I handled it. We all did. But it doesn't make it easy and changes the way one looks at life. Then I received word both of my brothers had died in a very close period of time, and for ridiculous reasons. Anthony breaks his neck in a coach and Thomas injures his head. Meanwhile, I'm being shot at on a regular basis and survive. It defies common sense."

Anthony stirred. Both of their gazes went immediately to him. He settled back to sleep with a worried sigh.

Brian brutally charged on, "I was ordered home and discovered that my mistress had been entertaining my father for most of the time I'd been gone. Meanwhile, my father blocked all attempts I make to help my fellow comrade-in-arms and my choice of careers and my mother indulges her passion for wine and spirits to the point she is completely indifferent to me. And finally, my wife had left with nothing more than a curt note stating, 'I've chosen to live elsewhere.' "

To her credit, Gillian turned her gaze away from his in embarrassment.

"Then I learned of the child. He didn't even have a name. Neither Jess nor my father had bothered." Brian shook his head

194

at the memory. He moved over to the crib. This time, Gillian didn't move away.

"Who named him?" she asked.

"I did." He placed a light hand on the baby's back, feeling his chest move with his breathing.

"You named him after your oldest brother."

Brian nodded. "Jess had just given birth when I returned. I'd already heard about the child. I was told that she hadn't even wanted to hold him. She gave him up the moment she birthed him. We parted company the moment she admitted the truth of the story to me. That's something you would have known if you had still been around."

She ignored his accusation. "Did you say anything to your father?" Gillian asked.

"It came up in conversation. He was not pleased with the child's presence, although he liked Jess very much. He had no desire to give her up. Oh, and he told me I needed to bring you home."

She made a face. She'd never liked his father. He didn't like him very much right now either.

"I didn't want her back," he informed Gillian. "I didn't feel jealous. It was by chance I discovered they'd farmed Anthony out," he said. "Hammond had heard through that mystical way servants have of knowing everything."

"And you went to go see Anthony?" Gillian asked.

"I had to," Brian confessed. "He's blood. It may sound strange right now, but at the time, finding him made perfect sense. Then, when I found him, I was shocked at how sick he was. They'd all written him off to die. They hated his screaming. But he has a strong will to live. I had to take him in."

Her voice gentled as she said, "He might not live, Wright. You may have been too late."

"At least I'm giving him a chance," Brian said, defending himself. "My instincts were right about bringing you to him. And he is my *son* now, Gillian. I am all he has. He's mine."

"And what is yours, you keep," she whispered.

"I curse myself for ever uttering those words," he countered.

"Do you curse yourself for repeating our wedding vows? I curse myself for once again falling under your spell. I am so gullible."

"I meant my vows in the coach —"

She snorted her disbelief in a decidedly unladylike manner.

It had been a hard two days. Brian couldn't keep the bitterness out of his tone when he said, "Fine, *choose* not to believe me. But Gillian, you can't fault a man for wanting his wife to be by his side."

"I can if that man has not been by *her* side."

"Your point is well taken. But it's done. I can't go back and relive it."

"You won't have to," she told him. She stepped away from the crib. "I'll help, Wright. I'll do everything I can to save this baby's life. But once it's done, I want my freedom."

"From me?"

She didn't answer. She didn't need to.

"Gillian, I know our marriage has not been what you would have wanted —"

"We have *no* marriage, Wright." She hugged her arms as if barring herself from him. "What were you thinking when you made love to me in the coach? That now you had me in the palm of your hand? That I'd do anything you wished?"

"I made love to *my wife,*" he stated.

She shook her head. "I won't be a wife to you. I can't. But I will help keep that baby alive if it is possible. And if you want my help in wooing Liverpool and others to give you a position in the War Office, well, then, *freedom* is my price. You must promise to let me go, along with an income for my living."

Jealousy raised its ugly head inside him. "Will you return to your Spaniard?"

"That will be none of your business," she informed him coolly, completely in control of her emotions now.

He was the one ready to fly into a rage.

"Gillian —" he started, but she cut him off with a raise of her hand.

"Those are my conditions, Wright. Do you accept them?"

Damn but she was as cool as any officer in the regiment. She had him, and she knew it.

"If I agree, what do I receive?" he demanded, deciding to play her game.

"I've already said I will help you in every way possible with the child."

"But what are the terms for the other?" he wondered.

A cynical smile crossed her face. "I will be your hostess as we attempt to win a position in the War Office for you. However, don't expect anything more than that from me, Wright. I'm tired of playing the fool over you. You see, there was a time I fancied myself in love with you. Today even, with the apple peel and how charming you were,

and then our time in the coach — you deceived me again into believing you cared. But no more. I'll be by your side for one month. At the end of it, whether you have what you want or not, I'm leaving. Ours is strictly what it should have been from the beginning, a business relationship. Do you understand?"

All too clearly. "I do."

"Good. Then I assume you accept my offer?"

She was so cold, so distant. "Do I have a choice?"

Gillian shrugged. "I could leave now."

He could call her bluff. She wouldn't leave the baby the way he was . . . but that would only lead to more resentments later.

No, he was going to let this run its course. "I accept. Anthony needs you." He deliberately mentioned the child, not wanting her to think he needed her. Did Gillian believe she was the only one with pride?

"Very well," she said without bravado. "We have an agreement." She took a step as if not knowing what to do next. "There are only two bedrooms on this floor."

"The upper floor is for servants. I told you it wasn't a large house."

"I shall sleep in here with the baby then."

"No," Brian said, "*I* will. What did you say

he needs? Feedings every two hours. I will do those. You take the room across the hall."

His decision was a good one. He could see that Gillian had been ready to martyr herself for Anthony, sleeping on a cot with the baby, and probably blaming him for every little thing that gave her discomfort. Mrs. Vickery was lazy but not dull-witted. The sheets in his room were clean and the bed comfortable.

"If that is how you would have it," she answered, her voice less certain. "Excuse me while I unpack my things." She didn't wait for his response but left the room, closing the door after her.

For a long moment, Brian studied the closed door as if he could see through it.

Anthony stirred. The poor babe. After weeks and months of crying, he was exhausted. He was so bloody defenseless. It pulled at Brian's heart.

Just as the realization of how deeply he had hurt Gillian now made him reconsider all he'd once thought about himself.

He was changing. Perhaps it had been the years away at war. Perhaps he had always been destined to be the man he was slowly becoming.

One thing he did know, Gillian was part of that change. Even years ago, from the moment he'd met his wife, he'd recognized in her something pure, something powerful.

That was the reason he needed her back. The younger version of himself, the man who had married her had not appreciated what he'd found.

The man he was now did.

She'd admitted she had loved him from the moment they'd met.

Gillian was not one to give up love easily. He'd made a mistake and chosen the wrong woman once. It had taught him to appreciate the right one. Any doubts he might have harbored had been dispelled by their lovemaking.

No matter what she thought, he would never honor their agreement.

She was *his.*

He just had to convince her.

CHAPTER ELEVEN

Gillian marched across the hall into the other room and slammed the door with all her might. It felt good to manifest her anger into a loud, substantial sound — and then she realized she wasn't completely certain where she was.

The room was pitch black and cold. The drapes were probably pulled closed like they had been downstairs and in the baby's room. She *assumed* she was in Wright's room and that there was a bed around there someplace, but she didn't know where.

And of course, there was *no* fire in the grate because *nothing* was as it should be in this house. Not the housekeeper, the servants, or the *master.*

Worse, she'd just agreed to stay here.

Gillian swung her hand out in frustration and hit the footboard of the bed. It would have hurt except that she was so relieved to have some sort of bearing in the dark. She started following it around, thinking it would lead her to a night table and, hopefully, a lamp or candle.

A loud knock on the door startled her enough that she jumped.

"Who is it?" she asked.

"Brian."

"Go away."

"I have your trunk."

"Leave it outside the door."

"I have a candle."

"Stay right there." Gillian held out her hands and started walking in the direction of where she thought the door was. The dark was disorienting. "Talk to me," she ordered.

He chuckled. "I thought you could use some light. I don't know if Hammond was able to replace the old candles or do anything after the wet nurse ran out on us." There was a pause. "I'm fairly certain Mrs. Vickery was too busy cleaning the kitchen to see to your comfort."

She found the door handle. Opening the door, she found her husband standing in a blessed circle of candlelight. Her trunk was behind him in the hall.

"Thank you," she said, reaching for the candle, but he held it away.

"Let me check and be certain everything is as it should be."

"I'll be fine," she assured him.

He moved the candle even further away. "I know you will be fine but why stumble around when in a few minutes, I can show you what you need to know?"

She really did not like him.

Wright smiled as if reading her thoughts and enjoying them.

Gillian opened the door wider and stepped away, the permission he needed to enter. After all, the sooner he showed her what he thought she needed to know, the sooner he would go.

And if he thought he was going to receive another opportunity to seduce her, he was *wrong*. In fact, she almost hoped he'd try it. She wasn't afraid to double her fist and give him a punch.

Wright walked over the bedside table and lit an oil lamp. Its warm glow spread through the room, dispelling every shadow save one — Wright's. In his bedroom, he seemed larger than life. She moved away from him as he lit another lamp on a small desk by the window.

While he went to the door to bring her trunk in, she crossed to the window. As Gillian had suspected, the drapes were closed. She peeked outside. It was raining, a hard, pelting twilight rain that made the windows rattle. Funny but her emotions had been running so high, she'd not heard a thing.

"I'll start the fire and then move out of your way," Wright said quietly.

As in the nursery, a fire hadn't been laid out in the grate. However, the kindling and coal was by the hearth. Wright started laying out the kindling in a crisscross fashion.

Gillian watched him with one eye while she took stock of her new surroundings. The room's walls were white, the floor a dark wood. It struck her as a man's room. The bed was a simple four-posted one, much like they'd had in the inn the night before. A door leading to a dressing room was open. From her vantage point, she could see the cot Hammond must have slept on and a huge wardrobe with the doors wide open. Clothes and shoes had been tossed on a bench as if Hammond had been interrupted. Nor was there a pile of laundry waiting to be done as there had been in the nursery.

"I also had a word with Mrs. Vickery about the laundry," Gillian said, without looking at Wright. She crossed to the bed and turned down the covers. Thankfully the sheets were clean. "She was very lax about seeing to that chore as well. The baby's down to a few nappies. She tried to tell me

205

it was the upstairs maid's responsibility, but I don't think you have an upstairs maid, do you?"

"Mrs. Vickery hired a relative. The girl was lazy. She and Hammond had words and she left last week." Wright had the kindling going and had started laying coals on top of it. "I assumed Mrs. Vickery would manage it."

"What is it with men?" she asked the room in general, needing a release for the discomfort she felt being this close to him. His presence seemed to fill every corner, every nook. "They could let the house fall down around their ears and be oblivious to it."

"I have a wife," Wright said without looking up from his task.

"*Had.* You had a wife. But you will find another. You are adept at reeling women in like fish on a line."

That barb hit its target.

Wright rose in one fluid movement. "What do you want from me, Gillian? You say you want my honesty but when I tell you the truth, you throw it in my face. I made love to you in the coach because I find you beautiful. I admire you. I respect you. What kind of marriage will we have? I don't know. Probably the same sort my parents have — one of benign neglect — if you don't learn

to trust me."

"How can I trust you?" she lashed back.

"*I don't know,*" he practically roared at her, his frustration clear. "You will have to work that out yourself. After all, you've spent the past hours being certain I know how woefully inadequate I am."

He walked to the door. "I'm *not* letting that child die. I've had enough of death in my life. And if you can't see your way to either forgive or forget what has happened between us, then you are right, we are best apart. You don't have to wait a month. You can leave on the morrow. Because at this moment, Gillian, *you* are *not* the priority."

That's when she heard the baby crying and wondered if Wright had already heard it. He didn't even look back at her as he left the room.

Gillian stood still, hearing the nursery door shut. The crying persisted, grew shriller. Her goat milk remedy was obviously a temporary answer. The baby would have to be nursed consistently.

For a second, she was tempted to go to the nursery to see if she could help, but held back.

Wright would not welcome her there. His words stung. He'd cut her loose. Released her from any obligation.

It's what she'd wanted . . .

The baby's crying stopped.

Slowly she sank to sit on the edge of the bed. Common sense told her she should be relieved it was over between them. Wright was not good for her. She expected one thing from him, and he never gave it.

Her irrational side, the one that thought in pure emotion, wanted to break down and wail like Anthony that she could not have what she wanted from Wright.

They weren't good for each other. That was why she'd left him.

Then again, they barely knew each other.

A knock on the door had her on her feet. "Yes?" she asked, expecting Wright.

"I wanted to know if my lady and his lord-ship wish dinner?" Mrs. Vickery's voice asked in an overly formal voice. Apparently this cold shoulder was Gillian's punishment for making the woman carry out her duties properly.

Gillian couldn't give a care if the house-keeper was miffed. What upset her was the disappointment she felt that it was not Wright at her door. He had her in knots, and only she could free herself.

"I don't care for any. Thank you," she told the housekeeper.

"And his lordship?"

"He's in Master Anthony's room," Gillian said and could well imagine the housekeeper's eyebrows rising to her hairline. Once again, she'd find herself being gossiped about by the servants, just as she was in the marquess's household.

Tears began rolling down her cheeks. She swiped them away with her hand. She was being ridiculous. Of course, she didn't want to live with Wright. He was the worst sort of person.

But she didn't stop crying.

Instead, she kicked off her shoes and climbed into the bed fully dressed. She pulled the covers up over her head. The heat from the fire was spreading through the room, but she was cold. Very, very cold.

She must not be in love with Wright. She couldn't. She had to think of Andres. Uncomplicated Andres — who loved her.

And yet, as she drifted into an exhausted sleep, her last thoughts were of feeling Wright's weight upon her and his body moving within her.

The baby's crying woke her.

Gillian sat up, disoriented. For a second, she imagined herself back in her father's house.

The lamps had burned low. She couldn't

understand why she hadn't blown them out to save oil, and then remembered.

She was still dressed and her hair was an unruly tangle. She pushed it back with her hands and climbed out of bed. Crossing over to her trunk, she had every intention of opening it and pulling out a nightdress when Anthony's shrieking cry made her pause.

Where was Wright?

She didn't want to interfere but she knew how a colicky baby could drive a person to madness. Men weren't good with babies. They lacked the patience. Her father rarely touched them until they were at what he called a "reasonable age," which was someplace around five.

Or Wright could be sleeping soundly and not hear the crying.

Whichever way it was, she should check on Anthony.

Plaiting her hair into a quick braid, Gillian went out her door and crossed the hall. She cracked open the door to the nursery, not wanting to go barging and waking Wright if he was there.

However, what she saw gave her pause.

Wright hadn't deserted Anthony or slept through his needs.

He was walking the floor with the baby on

his shoulder trying to burp him and soothe him with soft words. Wright had removed his jacket and removed his neck cloth, but he still wore his boots. Gillian wondered if he'd slept at all.

It was obvious they had just had a feeding but Anthony was not satisfied. In fact, he seemed more angry than in pain.

Her husband sensed she was there. He looked to the door. "What?" he demanded.

Gillian pushed the door wider. "I heard him crying. I was just checking to see if everything is all right."

"It is." His voice was as formally offended as Mrs. Vickery's had been.

She should withdraw. He obviously did not wish her help . . . still, Gillian wasn't one to turn her back on a problem.

"You fed him?" she said, already knowing the answer.

"Yes." It was amazing how annoyed Wright could sound with one word.

"Did he eat well?"

"Yes."

"Do you believe he could still be hungry?"

Wright stopped his pacing. "I thought we wanted to feed him small meals until we were certain his body could handle the food?"

Gillian entered the room. She walked over

to where Wright stood and placed her hand on Anthony's back. The baby was furiously chewing his fist. "I believe he is hungry."

Wright shook his head. He was tired, but alert. She now understood how he could have fallen asleep so deeply in the coach the day before. "You said we should be careful, that his stomach can't hold too much. Small meals."

"It is a delicate balance," Gillian answered. She shook her head. "We must trust he will guide us. Let's try more food and see if that doesn't settle him."

It did. Anthony ate his fill and then fell fast asleep. Wright had fed him. He now sat still with the baby in his lap. He was so silent, Gillian started to wonder if he'd nodded off, too.

And then he spoke. "I don't know what I shall do if I lose him." He raised his eyes to hers. "He's such a defenseless, wee thing — and yet, he has a valiant heart. He's already overcome incredible odds to have lived this long."

Gillian sat on a stool beside Wright's chair. She did something she'd yearned to do from the moment she'd first met Anthony — she cupped his head with her hand, marveling at how downy soft his hair was. The newness of babies always amazed her. "He has quite a head of hair," she murmured, combing its short length with her fingers.

"My nanny used to say all of us boys did." He lifted Anthony's thin arm. "I never noticed babies all that much before. Now I see them everywhere, plump, laughing, healthy. I'll ask their mothers how old their baby is and they are all younger than Anthony . . ."

Glancing up, Gillian saw a tear in the corner of his eye. He blinked it away. She didn't know what to do. A part of her, the traitorous side, wanted to put her arms around him. She wanted to hold him close and vow that they would not lose this child.

But she wouldn't. She couldn't. To do so would open her up for more heartbreak —

"When I went to the foundling home, they'd almost forgotten he was there," Wright said, his voice low. "I demanded they find him. Someone had placed him in a closet because of his crying. No one knew how long he'd been in there. His clothes were filthy and he was just about as thin as he is now."

"That's a cruel way to treat a baby."

"That's life for those who have no one to protect them." He looked at Gillian. "But he survived them. And I realized that Fate had seen I'd be called home to find and keep him safe. I can't lose him. If I do, the world won't make sense."

Gillian closed her eyes. He was not going to chip away at her defenses, but it was going to be hard.

"Go to bed," he said. "You look tired."

"So do you."

He smiled. She wished he wouldn't. She liked him when he smiled.

"We are going to win," she suddenly promised him. "Someday, Anthony is going to be a chubby, happy baby. And a headstrong one," she added for good measure. "But we must be patient."

"I have patience," he answered.

"So have I."

And there it was, a truce between them. Built upon a mutual desire to help a baby fight for his life.

For right now, that was enough.

"You need to return to bed," Wright told her.

"Why don't you sleep and I'll take my turn watching him," she answered.

He shook his head. "He's going to sleep for a while. You were right. He was hungry. The tenseness seems to have left his body."

Gillian placed her hand on Anthony's abdomen. It didn't feel as full and tight. "The colic will be back."

"We'll beat it," Wright assured her.

She rose to her feet. "Well, good night."

"Good night again," he reminded her.

"Yes," she agreed, suddenly feeling awkward. She was accustomed to being the one having to do the extra duty. It pleased her that he wasn't like his parents and expected others to do for him.

The earlier angry words still rang in her ears . . . but they didn't seem to matter so much any longer. Not in the face of Anthony's battle for life.

She would keep her distance from Wright, and at the end of thirty days, she'd leave. She had to. She wanted a man in her life who loved her.

And what she'd just witnessed was that Brian Ranson was capable of love.

He just didn't love her.

Thirty days now seemed like an eternity.

CHAPTER TWELVE

The next week was a blur in Gillian's mind. There was always something to be done and Wright hired a host of workmen to do it.

She knew how to set up and run a household and didn't shy from doing so, in spite of Mrs. Vickery's dark mutterings.

Wright had an agency send her servants to be interviewed. She reasoned that in a household of this size, she needed a cook, a scullery maid, and two maids.

Surprisingly, Mrs. Vickery did not want to leave their employ and offered to serve as cook. After tasting a few of her meals, Gillian agreed to the change. The food Mrs. Vickery made wasn't fancy, but it was delicious and she was already wise to Anthony's many needs.

As for maids, the agency sent over Alice and Kate, a pair of sisters fresh from the country. They were good, hard-working girls, the sort Gillian liked. She would teach them what they needed to know.

It would be nice to hire a nurse for Anthony but until his feeding schedule became more routine, she and Wright agreed they would manage it.

She had to admit she was impressed with Wright. He didn't shirk from feedings or changing a nappy. He'd obviously been seeing to the bulk of Anthony's care before she arrived, but he assumed a partnership with her now.

The first day of their truce, she was on guard to his wrangling, but he didn't try anything other than to treat her with respect and consideration. Slowly, day after day, her guard came down and they fell into an easy pattern of living together — especially as Anthony started to improve.

He still had colicky moments, but he was gaining weight and the terrible hunger began to leave him. His body took on flesh and he could sleep longer between feedings.

Come Sunday, Gillian and Wright felt confident enough to leave the baby with Kate while they attended a church service. Gillian was absolutely certain Wright was not a regular churchgoer. She assumed he was attending for her. So she was surprised when the rector greeted him by name and the two of them had a good conversation.

Of course, she was introduced as his wife. If the rector wondered where she had been all this time, he kept his own counsel.

Standing beside her husband during the service, sharing a hymnal with him and hearing the conviction in his voice as he repeated the prayers, she felt humbled. Reflecting on her attitude and reactions to her husband, she could silently confess to God and herself, she'd been a bit shrewish at times. It was her only defense against a man who had proven himself unerringly kind over the last several days.

I mustn't care for him, she argued with God. *I will leave. I must.*

God's response was Divine Silence, Gillian's least favorite answer.

Mrs. Vickery served an early dinner that day since the servants customarily received a half day off. Gillian and Wright usually ate every meal together. They talked of Anthony or plans for the house or schemed of how they were going to curry Liverpool's favor. Then, they would go off to their separate rooms.

However, today was different. The meal was served and done and there was a good portion of the afternoon and the evening left.

Gillian found herself at loose ends.

Anthony was sleeping, there were no letters to write — the only chore she would allow herself on the Sabbath — and there was nothing to do save read a book of poetry that she wasn't truly enjoying.

"Would you like to play backgammon?"

Wright's question surprised and intrigued her. "What is backgammon?"

"A game of dice and strategy," he assured her.

"I've never played it."

"I played it on the Peninsula. It will challenge you, depending upon your luck. I'll set up the board and you may try your hand."

He set it up in the sitting room before the fire. A cold wind blew hard outside, but here, everything was cozy. While Wright was teaching her the game, Anthony did wake. They fed him and brought him down to be with them. Wright held the baby on his lap. Anthony was strong enough now to hold his head up or grasp a finger held out to him. He seemed to watch the proceedings of the game with interest. He knew them now. When they came to feed him, he would wave his fists and kick his legs.

Of course, Wright won the first game, but Gillian saw where she could have an advantage.

She won the second.

Her husband laughed at her. "Best two out of three," he challenged.

Gillian lost, but quickly said, "Best three out of five."

In that manner they passed the evening, and the next, and the next. Wright was a good competitor. He played to win and expected her to do the same. Usually Anthony was with them. Gillian liked to see babies on the floor where they could move around as they pleased. Anthony didn't move much but he was starting to investigate his fingers and his feet.

One evening, Gillian clapped her hands because she'd won a particularly close game against Wright. Anthony turned toward the sound and smiled at her.

It was the most charming smile. Stunned by the suddenness of it, Gillian said, "He smiled."

"Anthony?" Wright picked the baby up from his lap and turned him around to face him so he could see for himself. He started making the silliest noises to make Anthony smile at him.

But then their baby did something completely unexpected — he laughed.

For a second, neither Wright nor Gillian could breathe. No sound on earth could be closer to that of an angel's voice than Anthony's first laughter.

It brought tears to her eyes. She leaned across the backgammon board and kissed his forehead, and he smiled again.

Wright reached out his hand. "Thank you," he said. His jaw was tense but his eyes had gone soft and she knew he was as deeply touched by the sound as she was. "He wouldn't be this strong if it wasn't for you."

Gillian sat back. "He's blessed that you went in search of him." She didn't hide the admiration in her voice. "You saved his life. Few men would have defied someone like the marquess or tried to save another man's baby."

Wright lowered his eyes and a dull red rose up his neck over her compliment. "Others would have done the same."

"No, Wright. Anthony was a trial with his constant crying. Not everyone would have stood beside him as you have."

Her husband smiled, pleased with her compliment.

The laughter marked a new beginning for Anthony. A new awareness about his surroundings and his reactions to them. Day by day, he became more responsive and showed more personality.

Wright began making plans for wooing Lord Liverpool — a step Gillian found she was reluctant to take. She was enjoying their winter evenings spent by the warmth of the fire playing backgammon. They didn't talk about the argument they'd had when she'd first arrived, and sometimes she found herself imagining they could go on this way forever.

It was foolish of her, but there all the same.

She tried to focus on Andres, but even though it had only been two weeks, she found she could not completely recall his features.

Instead, her mind's eye pictured Wright's secret smile of pleasure as he moved a game piece to block hers. Or the way he held Anthony with such tender care it twisted her heart.

One night, she heard singing. She rose from her bed and tiptoed across the hall. The nursery door was slightly open and she could see Wright singing to Anthony. He stood in the middle of the room while his body rocked to the bawdy tune he was softly sharing with the baby.

She backed away from the door, not wanting to disturb the moment.

Andres would do these things, she repeatedly reminded herself. Andres was kind and good. He was heroic. He would have searched for an illegitimate half-brother and treated him like a son.

Except it wasn't Andres who had been called upon to accept this responsibility, but Wright, and Gillian couldn't help but admire him for it.

She also knew she should write Andres. She owed him a letter explaining the events of the past weeks and to give him re-assurance. She framed the letter in her mind. Once, she even took out paper and ink . . . but she hadn't written. The words in her mind didn't translate well on paper. Perhaps because what with the baby and the servants and all the cleaning and paint-ing she was organizing for the house, she didn't have time to give a letter her proper attention.

Or perhaps any reassurances or promises she would make to Andres in the letter wouldn't be honest.

The truth was that in spite of her best intentions, she had fallen in love with Wright — again. As often as he'd broken her heart, she still carried an infatuation for him, and probably always would, except this time was different. Seeing him with Anthony, watching him nurture the child while struggling to meet her expectations gave her a new measure of Wright as a man. Their years apart had brought a new maturity to him and seemed to have made him into all that was good and noble.

He just didn't love her . . . or not as much as she loved him.

There was a terrible danger in loving so much. It made a person a bit mad with wanting. And if it wasn't returned measure for measure, life could become a hell on earth.

Gillian knew. She'd almost been there before. In many ways, Wright's going off to war had saved her.

But now he was back. Bolder, handsomer, kinder, and more thoughtful than she could ever have imagined.

Yes, she had to write Andres . . . but not quite yet.

She blamed her decision on cowardice, fearing the truth.

Brian was falling in love with his wife.

His growing respect and admiration for her was coloring his understanding of love in ways he'd never imagined. He'd thought he had been "in love" with Jess, and he had been — but it had been the love of youth, of responsibility, or having no choice but to care for her.

He had not respected Jess's intellect or admired her courage. He'd known nothing of her personal resourcefulness because he'd managed to see to all her needs. She'd been a defenseless lamb in an uncaring world . . . much as Anthony was, and her willingness to toss Anthony aside was all the more puzzling to Brian.

In contrast, Gillian would fight for her children, just as she battled for Anthony's life.

What man could not fall in love with such a woman?

However he'd broken Gillian's trust not once, but twice, and if he wasn't careful, she'd be gone in two weeks' time. His backgammon games had gone a long way in laying siege to her defenses but he knew better than to grow complacent. The time had come to prove himself worthy of her.

With that thought, he set off for St. James Street and the gentleman's club called White's. Sooner or later, every man of importance in London graced the doors of either Brook's or White's.

Brook's was a Whig establishment and his father was one of its leading members. White's catered to a Tory clientele — and Lord Liverpool was a Tory.

When Brian had defied his father and

225

moved from under his roof, his father's first step had been to cut off all resources, including his club privileges. Brian had not been threatened by this. He did have an income of his own and acquaintances willing to bring him into any club he wished as a guest.

All he had to do was find one of them, which was easy enough to do. Within minutes of approaching White's, he saw Lord Harlan Royce, "Digger" to his friends. Digger was almost as round as he was tall, moved with exceeding haste in everything he did, spoke in abrupt sentences, and was one of the brightest minds Brian had ever met if one wished to discuss physics. He knew little on any other topic. He was hurrying up the street now, his head down against the wind, his coat flapping in the breeze as he headed for White's entrance.

Brian stepped in his path. "Digger?"

His friend paused just in time to keep from mowing Wright down. He squinted up at him. "Wright?"

"Yes, it is," Brian said with a surplus of male bonhomie. "How have you been?"

"Good. Married. Like it. You?"

"I'm back from the Peninsula. I commanded a regiment there."

Digger was impressed. "Worked for Wel-

226

lington?"

"I was on his staff at one time."

"Tell me about it over lunch," Digger demanded.

"I'm not a member."

Digger's head swiveled to him. "Not a member?"

"Been to war and all that. Not kept it up," Brian replied.

But his friend was too intelligent for that. His eyes narrowed thoughtfully. "Heard about you and your father," Digger said. "Impressed you had the bollocks to tell him what is what. I hear he is angry."

"Foaming at the mouth."

Digger laughed. "Is he now? He used to make your brothers dance to his tune. Didn't care how they looked in front of everyone. Would chew them right down to their boots in front of a crowd."

"He's learning I'm not so amenable. Even if he does cut off the funds. I have money of my own." Not a fortune, but he was keeping ahead of the game.

His friend nodded. "I barely speak to my father. Can't stand the man. Of course, he doesn't care because I've got three brothers ahead of me. Why couldn't I have been born a girl?"

"You wouldn't want that," Brian said,

knowing that Digger especially would be miserable.

His friend gave a sharp laugh. "You are right!" He waved Brian ahead through the door the doorman held open. "Come, let's have a good healthy drink and a hearty lunch while you tell me all of your adventures."

And in that manner, Brian gained entrance to White's.

He was greeted with warm respect by the staff and old acquaintances followed by an enjoyable lunch. Several other gentlemen, most friends of Digger's, curious about the war, joined them. They asked intelligent questions and Brian was happy to give them answers from his perspective — especially to Lord Taggert, who wondered if Napoleon could be defeated.

"He can and he will be by good British steel and bullets," Brian answered and could feel the mood of the gentlemen around him sway in favor of the war.

Brian also made a point of speaking highly of his wife, letting everyone know that Lady Wright was under his roof. Men were bigger gossips than women. By evening his marital happiness, appearance of obvious good spirits, and opinions on the war would be circulating through the *ton.*

Digger had another appointment. He apologized to Brian that he could not stay but left him in the capable hands of his comrades. By the end of a half hour's conversation, Brian had received three invitations to dinner and another to a ball. Everyone knew of his father's displeasure. Instead of making him an outcast, he was revered and respected as a bit of a rebel.

The hour approached two and Brian debated whether he should leave or not. He chose to linger and was rewarded for his patience by the appearance of no less a person than his quarry, Lord Liverpool.

Although Liverpool carried the cabinet title, "Secretary of State for War and the Colonies," he was of the same age as Brian and had also served in the military. However, their paths had never crossed.

Now was the time to be bold.

Excusing himself from the knot of men with whom he'd been discussing the war, Brian made ready to leave, using his approach on the door as his opportunity to have a word with Liverpool.

His lordship was of average height with a long nose and the dark eyes people attributed to his part-Indian mother. He was capable and competent, exactly the sort of man Brian liked working for.

Liverpool was accompanied by his secretary, a man named Robert Blount, who had also served under Wellington, and by Lord Chester, a personal friend.

Brian approached the door. As he came shoulder to shoulder with the great man himself, he stopped. "My lord, how fortunate it is to meet you."

Liverpool had been speaking to Chester. He turned to see who addressed him and his brows rose in a lack of recognition.

Brian bowed. "Brian Ranson, Lord Wright. We've met but I don't know that you recall the acquaintance."

His lordship frowned. "Know your father."

Damn the bad luck! Brian waited, not speaking.

"I heard you fought well. You were at Talavera?"

"I was, my lord."

"Bloody mess." He studied Brian a moment. "Wellington wrote me. He likes to hand-pick *my* staff." He didn't sound pleased.

"I wish only to serve my country, my lord."

"Your father has other plans. I've heard talk he wishes an ambassadorship for you."

"Based upon what experience? I know

little about the intricacies of diplomacy. I'm a military man, my lord. I understand warfare, supply routes, and what will keep an army marching. What good would such information do for anyone if I were posted to Holland to drink tea and share gossip?"

"Unfortunately, the gossip an ambassador shares could mean the protection of our country," Liverpool countered. "A wise man should not refuse such a post."

"A passionate one must go where he feels his comrades-in-arms need him," Brian dared to answer.

Liverpool conceded his opinion with a shrug of his shoulders. "How far do I dare to challenge your father?"

"It's a new order, my lord. My father is of the old. But we can discuss all of that later," Brian said, smoothly changing the subject. "You are familiar with my wife, Lady Wright? Her father is the Reverend Isaac Hutchins."

"And a good friend of mine," Lord Liverpool said, all reserve leaving his manner. "One of the best lecturers I had at Christ Church. Made me *think*. I haven't seen him in years but we correspond regularly. I knew you had married his daughter, but I have not had the pleasure of meeting her. Her father speaks highly of her."

"As well he should," Brian answered. "Indeed, I know my wife would be delighted to meet you. Her father has spoken of you often to her. Whenever she visits, one of his first questions is if your paths have crossed." Brian didn't know if this was true, but from his knowledge of Reverend Hutchins, it could be.

"Now that I am back from the Peninsula," Brian said, "and we have our household set up, we'd be honored if you and your wife would be our guests for dinner."

"I would be delighted," his lordship said. "Reverend Hutchins is the sort of man one could trust with his soul. I assume his daughter is of the same ilk."

"She is," Brian replied without hesitation.

"Robert," Lord Liverpool said to his secretary, "see that a dinner with Lord and Lady Wright is placed on my schedule. Make the arrangements with my wife."

"Yes, my lord," the secretary said dutifully.

Liverpool turned to Brian. "I'm glad our paths crossed, Wright. I shall give consideration to your request to be considered for a place on my staff."

"Thank you, my lord," Brian said with feeling.

"Now, if you will excuse us?" Liverpool

started to a table set up for his party.

Brian moved out of the way with a short bow. He'd thought himself done when Liverpool looked back at him. "Holland truly is a fascinating country."

"I have no doubt, my lord," Brian answered.

The cabinet minister smiled, and Brian knew he was dismissed. He left the dining room but took a moment in the club's vestibule to almost collapse. *He'd done it.* He'd stormed the War Office and had gained ground.

Of course there was no guarantee that Liverpool would name him to his staff, but over dinner Brian would do his best to convince him.

He went outside a happy man. The earlier threat of rain had turned out to be nothing. The wind was cold but nothing could dampen Brian's spirits. He couldn't wait to see Gillian and tell her what had happened. Together, they would make plans for the dinner party.

Brian had traveled about a half dozen steps when a small town coach pulled up at the curb beside him. He recognized the polished, burled wood vehicle without having to glance at the coat of arms proudly displayed on the door.

The door swung open and his father leaned out. "Climb in," he ordered.

CHAPTER THIRTEEN

Brian stood his ground. His father didn't respect anyone who jumped to his bidding.

His father frowned. At five and sixty, the marquess of Atherton was as tall and lean as Brian but with short cropped gray hair and an imperial attitude. They both shared the same light blue eyes. In fact, of any of his three sons, Brian was the one who resembled him the closest.

With a world-weary sigh, his father said, "Very well, would you do me the honor of joining me in this coach?" His words dripped irony.

Brian did so, shutting the door behind him.

The coach had bench seats on both sides of the cab so they could face each other. His father knocked on the side of the coach with the gold head of his walking stick, a signal for the driver. The vehicle jerked forward.

His father turned to him. It had been well over two months since they'd last seen each other. He stood his walking stick on the floor, resting his hands on top of it. "The last time we met in such a manner you refused to obey my wishes," his father said without a trace of humor. "Now I see you are still defying me."

"I'm not defying you, Father. I'm living my life. I'm doing what the future earl of Wright should do."

"And what is that?"

"Following my conscience."

"I did not want that child here."

Brian tapped down a surge of temper. His voice carefully neutral, he said, "Don't worry. You'll have nothing to do with him."

His father's lips curled into a sneer. "Why do you give a damn?"

"Because it is the right thing to do. The honorable thing."

"I see," his father said with the awareness of discovery. "You always were the stickler. Thinking to correct my wrongs?" He snorted his opinion. "Or do you imagine you can play the game better than I? You can't. My influence reaches every corner of this realm. Every rookery, every street, every cabinet office."

For a second, Brian wondered if he knew

236

of the meeting he'd just had with Liverpool. He couldn't. It had been a spontaneous meeting. Happenstance created from careful planning. In time he would know, but not yet.

"You are debating whether or not I know of your meeting with Liverpool inside White's," his father surmised. He laughed quietly at Brian's startled expression. "You believe you can defy me. I know everything you are doing. I receive reports before you can return home and take off your coat."

"What is the reason for this visit?" Brian asked, tired of being baited.

His father turned serious. "I am giving you another chance. I understand you are angry I sent the babe away. It was the expedient thing for me to do at the time. Perhaps it was hasty of me. Then again, I did not know you had such a soft heart."

"Expedient?" Brian shook his head. "He almost died. He still could die."

"Children die all the time," his father said without feeling.

"Especially when they are discarded as if they were baggage no longer wanted."

"Brian, this is becoming a tiresome argument. What do you wish me to do? Take the child in? Very well, I shall see it is fostered by a very good and reliable family. I didn't set up the matter anyway. Jess did."

"She wouldn't do that to her own child," Brian said. Even though Brian blamed Jess for her role in Anthony's abandonment, he'd assumed she'd done so at his father's insistence.

"She *did* do that to her own child. When I said I found children under foot tiresome, she took care of the matter. My son, she has played you for a fool since the day you laid eyes on her. All she had to do was heave her bosoms at you and you'd believe any story she told you."

The charge was true.

"What I find interesting," his father continued, "is the dogged perseverance of yours to always play the hero. You've always been this way — full of noble intentions and short on common sense."

"You are growing offensive, Father," Brian said, his temper starting to bubble.

"Of course I am, because I speak the truth."

Brian turned away from him, finding the air in the coach too close for this conversation.

"I did you a favor," his father said, changing the tone of his voice. "I know you thought you were in love but you had to see Jess for what she was."

238

"When did you climb into her bed, Father? How soon after I left for the war?"

His father shook his head as if it shouldn't matter. "She came after me —"

"How soon?" Brian repeated.

"A week, perhaps two."

"And in showing me what she was, the two of you have been together for how long . . . while I paid her bills?"

"You didn't pay *all* of them. She may have been born in a stable but she is an expensive piece of muslin. I paid more than my share."

Brian shook his head. "She wasn't that way until you put your hands on her."

"Damnation, son. She's a sly fox. She knew what she had and she wanted more. Still does. But what she didn't want was a brat." He leaned close to Brian. "Do you know why she had him? She was hoping to play on your sympathies again. The laugh's on her. You took the baby and tossed *her* away."

There was an element of truth in his words, a truth Brian didn't like. He'd loved Jess, been faithful to her . . . trusted her.

"I know it hurts," his father said with a definite lack of commiseration in his words. "But you had to be taught a lesson. You can't assume a title like mine and continue to be so naïve."

"Who is naïve, Father? You are still danc-ing to Jess's tune, aren't you?"

His father sat back. "She means nothing to me."

"But you haven't given her up, have you? You can't."

"I like her figure, her youth. Why should I give her up? You don't want her back, do you?"

There it was, what he'd spent his child-hood combating — a twist of words, a nudge or a push. His father would bludgeon everyone into letting him have his way. His mother wasn't much better. No wonder his brothers had been so aimless. They had been told when to think, what to believe, how to behave.

Brian would be eternally thankful that his parents' attitudes toward him had been one of benign neglect. It had allowed him to grow into a man.

"So, is this what you wanted to say to me?" Brian asked, wanting to bring the interview to a close.

"I hear you went to Huntleigh and brought back your wife."

Brian wasn't surprised he knew. It wasn't a secret. "Of course I have her with me."

His father's tone turned conciliatory. "Gil-lian has a practical head on her shoulders.

Her father has been invaluable to me on several occasions since your marriage. Keep her with you. The rift between you served no purpose." He made his heavy sighs before concluding, "However, I would give up the baby."

"Because?"

"He's a loose end. A messy one. You can't expect Gillian to raise another woman's child. She'll leave again and then where will you be?"

Brian sat back in stunned silence to hear his deepest fears spoken aloud.

"You like Gillian, don't you?" his father said, accurately reading his silence. "You've discovered you didn't make such a bad choice in a wife. She's a much better choice than Jess. I warned you time would tell, and so it has."

Brian found his voice. "How do you do that?"

"Do what?" his father asked, brushing an imaginary piece of lint from his coat sleeve.

"Know exactly your opponent's darkest doubts. How do you go unerringly to point?"

"I know my opponent," his father admitted, smiling freely.

Brian longed to wipe that smile from his face. "Well, you misjudged your mark this

241

time," he said. "Gillian is very happy. I'm happy. The only person unhappy is you. You can't control me and it annoys you, doesn't it? You keep thinking there must be a way to bring me under your thumb, to make me vote your way, dance to your tune. There isn't, Father. I might have done it out of respect at one time, but you killed that loyalty. You should have left Jess alone. She didn't have the strength to fight a man like yourself or the knowledge of the cost. You played with her like a cat does a mouse."

"No mouse, son. Women never lack resources, and most times they are the cat. That is what makes them so interesting. As for Gillian being happy, we shall see. What do you have? Thirty days and then she will be gone?"

How did he know that?

Brian smiled. "She is my wife. She'll not be gone in thirty days."

"Don't be so certain of that," his father advised him. "And you'd also best start to see to your attire. Your neck cloth needs more starch. Hammond has been doing a wonderful job for me."

"So he is in your employ," Brian observed, trying to sound disinterested. He and the valet had been together for well over a decade.

"He's *always* been in my employ," his father informed him.

The news shocked Brian. Hammond had been the one person he'd trusted.

"I've always known what you were doing. I've almost known what you were thinking. No matter where you were or how far you were from me."

Brian reached up and knocked on the roof of the coach. It was wiser than using his fist on his father's smiling mouth. "We'd best part company here," he said.

His father bowed his head. "As you wish, Wright." However as Brian opened the door, he couldn't resist one last salvo. "The ambassadorship to Holland will be offered to you, I suspect, within two weeks' time. I expect you to take it."

"I expect you will be disappointed." Brian smiled. "You see, Father, I won't be controlled. You may cut off funds, block invitations to soirees, toss babies aside, and I'll still be my own lead. Because, after everything is said and done, I'm still your heir. Not even the marquess of Atherton has the power to overturn the rules of noble succession. In the end, no matter what games you play, I will win."

The smile faded from his father's face. His expression could have been set in stone.

Reminding him of his mortality always had that impact. "You may leave now," his father said. "But don't forget, I always keep my aces close. There will come a day you will beg my forgiveness."

"I doubt that." Brian climbed out of the coach and shut the door. He watched the vehicle pull away before letting his temper consume him.

Mrs. Vickery was reporting to his father. There was no doubt in his mind. Why else would she be adamant about staying on as Cook when Gillian would have let her go?

Spying was a despicable act. Brian would not tolerate it. He couldn't wait to turn Mrs. Vickery out of his house and let his father know he'd found him out. With that thought in mind, he started for home.

Sitting in the back room that overlooked the garden, Gillian set her sewing aside. The hour had to be close to half past four. Kate usually brought Anthony to her by now, fresh from his nap and awake. This time of the day was becoming Gillian's favorite because usually she had him all to herself.

It was becoming far too easy to think of Anthony as hers. He was a delightful baby. Now that he'd figured out how it was done he was full of smiles . . . and there were

times she could almost dream she and
Wright were a family. It was a forbidden
dream. She'd always talk sense into herself
almost immediately — and yet, she couldn't
stop the yearning.

She must also write Andres. She had yet
to do so and she knew it wasn't fair to him.
It's just that she wasn't certain what she
should write although she was becoming
more certain that it would not be what he
wanted to hear.

Gillian didn't know if she would stay with
Wright, but her confused feelings were
signal enough that she could not give Andres what he wanted. It broke her heart to
think she might hurt him, and yet, she had
to be honest —

"My lady, my lady," Kate's shrill voice cried
from the hall.

Gillian reached the doorway, just as Kate
came running up, her face so pale her
freckles seemed to float on her skin. "It's
Master Anthony," the maid managed to
gasp out.

Not waiting for further explanation, Gillian picked up her skirts and went running
down the hall for the stairs. For once she
was thankful this was a small house. It took
her less than a minute to bound up the
staircase and charge into the baby's room

— where she pulled up short.

She had anticipated that Anthony was ill or choking or a dozen other terrible things that could happen to babies.

Instead, he was being held by the most gorgeous, elegant woman Gillian had ever laid eyes on — and she knew immediately that this was Jess, her husband's former mistress.

She was a brunette and shorter than Gillian by a head but her figure was absolute perfection. Every curve seemed to have been designed by God to show other women what they should look like. Her eyes were a deep, indigo blue and her lashes dark and full. Her skin was the color of cream and she smelled of June roses.

It was hard to believe this woman had ever been a milk maid. Gillian felt practically a drab cow patty in comparison. She wore her serviceable loden-green day dress, the one she threw on for seeing to household chores. And she hadn't bothered to style her hair other than to twist it into a chignon at the nape of her neck.

Uncaring of any damage to her soft blue muslin gown trimmed in rows of expensive lace, Jess held Anthony for Gillian to see. "Isn't he amazing?" she said. "So alive and alert."

Anthony reached for the white feathers in Jess's confection of a hat, trying to pull one out and stuff it into his mouth. She laughed, the sound light and airy and gratingly attractive. "No, no, no," she whispered and Anthony laughed, as charmed by his mother as every other man would be who crossed Jess's path.

No wonder Wright had been so enamored of her.

Jess's smile revealed she wasn't completely flawless. There was a gap between her two front teeth. However, instead of marring her looks, it made her appear charmingly appealing.

"This is my son," she said proudly to Gillian. "Isn't he handsome?" Her voice was surprising. It was cultured and almost musical. She had worked very hard to create a voice like that.

"What are you doing here?" Gillian demanded. "How did you enter this house?"

Finely arched eyebrows rose in offense at her tone. "I had to see him," Jess explained. "Brian won't mind. Brian doesn't deny me anything."

If the woman had found a lance and stabbed it straight into Gillian's heart, the pain could not be greater. Gillian placed a hand on the doorframe, willing herself to be

247

strong. She was Wright's *wife* . . . although she was alarmingly aware of her own imperfections. For that alone she could summon up enough anger for the woman to toss her into the street.

"I'm not Brian," Gillian said, proud that her voice was strong. "And I don't entertain women who toss their children aside. I consider them unfit to be referred to as mothers."

A bright spot of color appeared on each of Jess's cheeks. "I was warned you would be mean."

"Who warned you?" Gillian demanded, annoyed at being referred to as mean.

Jess smiled, pressing her lips closed and refusing to answer.

Forget the expensive clothes, the beauty, and the elegance. What Gillian could have hated the woman for, what raised jealousy's ugly head inside her, was that smile. Gillian didn't want to believe Wright had let her in . . . but she wasn't certain.

"Brian sleeps here, doesn't he?" Jess said, nodding her head to Wright's clothes hanging neatly on a peg. "He's not in your bed." She smiled again, pleased. "Of course he wouldn't be. He didn't want to marry you. He was displeased his father forced him."

Any sympathy Gillian might have felt for

the other woman's circumstances in life evaporated. Jess was a she-devil. Her words were poisoned-tipped barbs and knew exactly where to go for best effect.

"And now he's lost Hammond, too," Jess said. "Such a pity. Did you come between them?"

"I did not," Gillian denied, a bit too quickly.

Jess tilted her head in thought as if they were two good friends having a cozy chat. "Let me warn you, a man such as Brian can't go long without a woman. It's not in his nature. I'd be cautious if I were you."

"Thank you for the warning," Gillian answered. "Now leave." She stepped aside to give Jess complete access to the door.

Her movement brought her to Anthony's attention. He smiled and held out his hands to her.

Gillian walked right over and took him out of Jess's arms. "And he isn't *your* son," she said. "He's mine and Wright's. He would have died without us."

"But I am his rightful mother," Jess answered. "He came from my womb and no matter how you try, you will never replace me. Good day, Lady Wright. I hope you enjoy the rest of the afternoon and the evening."

She left, moving with a grace that would have been the envy of any duchess.

Gillian listened until she heard the sound of the front door opening and closing. She was gone.

For a second, a terrible rage consumed Gillian. How dare the woman walk into her home and lay claim to Anthony? How dare she accuse Gillian of not seeing to Wright's needs? Especially since *she* was the problem?

And then that rage broke into great, heaving sobs.

Anthony started crying with her.

Gillian sank on the edge of the cot Wright slept in every night. She hugged the baby back and forth, rocking him until they both calmed down.

"My lady?" an uncertain voice said from the doorway. It was Kate. Gillian wondered how long she'd been standing there.

Embarrassed to have been caught displaying such raw emotion, Gillian managed, "What is it?" as she pressed the back of her hand to her heated cheeks.

"I wanted to be certain all was as it should be," Kate said, her hands fidgeting nervously with her apron.

"It is. Thank you," Gillian said.

"Do you want me to take the baby?"

Gillian tightened her hold on Anthony, suddenly very possessive. He responded by laying his head on her shoulder — and her heart brimmed with love.

She'd cared for many babies, mostly her stepmother's, but Anthony was *hers*. He might not come from her womb, but she was the one who had saved his life. She and Wright had done it together.

She didn't want another woman to watch Anthony grow up.

She didn't want another woman in Wright's bed.

And she and Wright were going to secure a position for him on Liverpool's staff. She had no doubt they wouldn't do it. They were a formidable team when they chose to work together.

"My lady?" Kate repeated, a note of alarm in her voice. "Are you all right?"

Gillian forced herself to speak. "I am." She frowned. Her mind seemed scattered in a million different directions. She had to have a moment to think, to decide what to do.

"It's time for Anthony's dinner, isn't it?" she said to Kate, who watched her with concerned eyes. "Here, take him downstairs and feed him, please." She passed Anthony to the maid. She needed a moment alone so that she could think. "I'll be along in a few minutes."

"Yes, my lady."

Anthony readily went with Kate. As they left the room with him on the maid's shoulder, he gave Gillian another one of his happy smiles.

Gillian raised the back of her hand to her forehead. Tension and doubts were giving her a headache . . . and she knew what she had to do. A decision had to be made and there was only one direction she could honorably choose.

Downstairs, she sat at the writing desk in the sitting room and pulled ink and paper out. This was going to be the hardest letter she'd ever written.

She dipped pen in ink and started with:

Dear Andres,
I know I have been neglectful in writing you and I fear what I have to say will not be welcome news.

Gillian then confessed all. She told him that as deeply as she has cared for him, she is wed to Wright and cannot leave him. She chose not to admit her folly of loving her husband. Such a statement would only hurt the gallant Spaniard who had been so willing to champion her.

Her tears dropped on the paper as she wrote.

You are such a wonderful, noble man and deserve a woman who is free to love you without the taint of scandal. Unfortunately, it cannot be me. You are far too good a man to be involved in all this. But please know, my dearest Andres, I will always hold you in my heart.

There. She'd done it. For better or worse, she'd made her commitment to her husband, and she prayed she wasn't sorry. However, this was the best decision for Andres. He needed to find someone free to love him.

She sanded the paper and folded it into an envelope before she lost her courage. Her hand trembled as she addressed the envelope —

"Gillian?"

Wright's voice surprised her. She turned and saw him walk into the room. She'd been so involved in her task, she hadn't heard him come in.

Quickly, she slid the envelope into the desk drawer and closed it.

CHAPTER FOURTEEN

Gillian smiled in greeting, but Brian immediately sensed she was upset. It was there in her eyes and the way she all but jumped up from the desk as if he had caught her doing something she shouldn't.

"Oh, you are home," she said as if it was unexpected. "How is the weather outside? I haven't been out all day."

"It will snow tonight," he answered, distracted by her uneasiness. "Have you been crying?"

Her eyes widened. "No, I haven't —" she started and then changed her mind. "I mean, I was upset. But I'm better now."

He immediately advanced toward her. "Who upset you? Was it Mrs. Vickery?"

"No, why would she do that?" Gillian asked. She pressed her fingers against the desk drawer, ensuring it was closed before moving toward him. He'd noticed her slip something into it and now this small action was suspicious.

Of course, after his father's revelations that his hirelings had included the man closest to him, Brian was feeling more than a bit mistrustful.

He could ask her about what she'd placed in the drawer. She'd take whatever it was out and he would see it had been a shopping or menu list and he'd feel silly. Worse, she'd have another reason to nurse her grudge against him.

So, Brian kept quiet, although his curiosity knew no bounds.

"I had an interesting afternoon. I met Liverpool at White's and afterwards, ran into my father. Or rather, he hunted me down."

That captured Gillian's attention. "What did the marquess want?"

"Ultimately, for me to do as bid. He knows everything, Gillian, including our thirty-day pact. He finds it amusing."

Her face flooded with color. "How would he know that?"

"I have my suspicions," he started, but a footstep in the hall made him turn toward the door.

The maid Kate entered the room carrying Anthony. The moment the baby saw Brian, a smile lit his face and he started kicking his feet as if he could run through the air for Brian's arms.

In two long strides, Brian met the maid and took the baby from her. He held Anthony up in the air. The baby was putting on weight. In another week or so, he'd have healthy rolls on his legs and arms.

Anthony laughed at being so high.

"Careful, my lord," Kate warned, laughing with them. "He's just eaten."

Brian made a face, knowing exactly what she meant. He lowered the baby into his arms. "We'd best wait a bit before we play," he told Anthony and then said to Kate, "Please tell Mrs. Vickery I want to see her in the sitting room."

"Yes, my lord." The maid headed for the kitchen.

Holding Anthony, Brian turned toward Gillian, and then stopped. She watched him with large somber eyes. He sensed the tension in her. She was like a rope pulled to its snapping point.

"What is it?" he asked quietly.

"The baby truly adores you," she said. He waited, knowing there was more. There was a beat of silence and then, "I met Jess."

Of all the things she could have said, he'd not anticipated that one. He crossed to her, drawing her over to the settee, balancing Anthony with his other arm. Now he understood her peculiar behavior. Urging her to sit, he asked, "Where did you meet Jess?"

"Here." She raised a hand to her temple as if to stave off a headache. "Kate came running to tell me there was a strange woman in Anthony's bedroom. I went upstairs and there she was."

"Wasn't the front door locked?"

"I don't know," Gillian said. "It usually is."

"It was when I just came in." Anthony was investigating the knot in Brian's neck cloth while making a little cooing sound, which was his latest trick. "Someone must have let her in." And he suspected who had done so. "What was she doing up in the nursery?"

"Holding the baby. I arrived just as she'd picked him up. She knows he is hers. She's *proud* of him," Gillian added as if she couldn't believe a mother who had willingly abandoned her child would dare to be so.

"Did she say anything?"

Those solemn eyes rose to meet his. "She wants you back."

The suggestion was so ludicrous that Brian almost laughed. What stopped him was the grave expression on Gillian's face.

"Jess doesn't want me," he assured her. He sat next to her. "My father is the more lucrative catch of the two of us. Now, would she like to stir the pot up between the two of us? Absolutely."

She didn't return his smile. "She's very beautiful."

"*You* are beautiful," Brian countered.

Gillian made a sound of protest and would have risen, but he caught her arm and pulled her back down.

"You are," he insisted. Anthony gave one of his "coos" in agreement.

"Brian, the woman was elegance itself. Her dress was all lace and silk and I swear a cloud of roses follows her wherever she goes. The nursery still smells of her."

"Then we shall open a window and air it out. Gillian, you are far more interesting and intelligent than Jess ever could be. Your beauty surpasses hers. You don't need to spend hours pampering yourself and thinking about no one but yourself. Jess has no conversation. Or interests. Whereas, I will never tire of your intelligence or the wisdom of your mind."

"And yet, you loved her."

Was this what had her upset? Jealousy?

If she was jealous, then she must care for him.

Brian brought Anthony around to sit in his lap. "Jess was a part of my youth. She had a father who abused her and I felt drawn to protect her. She truly is as defenseless as a lamb. But *you*," he said, reaching for her hand and lacing his fingers with hers. "You are a part of my present and my future. You aren't afraid of life and haven't ever waited for someone to save you. You are as resilient as you are lovely. Your strength is in your faith." *How can I not help but be in love with you?*

He almost said the words aloud. He almost declared himself but caught himself. Gillian had to know he was in love with her . . . and if she didn't say anything, then it was because she didn't want him to be.

God knew he'd made so many mistakes with this woman. She'd be wise not to trust him.

But before they could resolve the issue, Mrs. Vickery presented herself. Her mobcap was slightly askew as if she'd been cooking like a whirling dervish down in his kitchen, something he knew was not true.

"My lord wished to see me? I must warn you, my bread needs to come out of the oven at any moment now."

"Then you'd best tell one of the others to take it out," Brian advised. Gillian was still pale and obviously upset. Perhaps it would be best if she wasn't here for this. "Why don't you take the baby?" he asked Gillian.

"And please pass on the word to the kitchen about the bread."

His statement brought Mrs. Vickery's eyebrows all the way to her hairline. "You needn't worry, my lady. I'll go tell someone —"

"You'll stay where you stand, Mrs. Vickery," Brian commanded, rising.

Such was his tone that the woman paused, one foot in mid-air.

Gillian gathered Anthony from him and held him close. Jess's visit had her rattled. For letting Jess into his house alone, Brian would have sacked Mrs. Vickery. But the reporting to his father was the deeper transgression.

"Is there a problem, my lord?" Mrs. Vickery asked.

Brian waited until Gillian and Anthony had left the room. "There is. You have been spying on me, Mrs. Vickery. You are in the employ of my father and have been sending him regular reports."

As bald as you pleased, she answered, "I'm not the first to do so."

"Do you mean Hammond?"

She appeared surprised he knew.

"Gather your things and be out the door in ten minutes," he instructed her.

Mrs. Vickery straightened her mobcap.

She appeared ready to say something in her defense, but then her expression turned as cagey as any common money grubber. "If you will pardon me for saying so, my lord, but you aren't thinking this matter through. If you wished me to do so, I could go to your father, tell him you gave me the boot, and then report back to you what happens over there under his roof. That way it wouldn't all be so one-sided."

"*What* is one-sided?" he asked.

"Oh, what everyone is saying about you," she said almost cheerfully. "The marquess takes my reports and creates rumors out of them. Of course, you didn't help yourself when you moved out from under his roof, if'n you ask me. Everyone thought that was not a good move. The marquess told folks the war had made you angry and a bit unreliable."

"You seem to be remarkably well informed, Mrs. Vickery," Brian observed.

"I have a bit of wit in my head," she answered. "And the curiosity of a cat. I wondered what the marquess would do with all this information. Then I overheard him speaking to his wife about what I'd said. That's how I know they are using my reports to make you appear a bit havey-cavey, my lord. Not that you weren't doing such a poor job of the matter yourself what with taking in that babe and all."

Brian heard echoes of his mother's voice in Mrs. Vickery's last words. His mother would never believe there was anything more important than her social life.

And he didn't know what offended him more — Mrs. Vickery's smug familiarity or that she thought him of the same ilk as his father.

"Your assistance isn't necessary to me, Mrs. Vickery. But I would say a word of caution. My father is notoriously fickle. Nor does he reward for loyal service."

"I shall remember that, my lord." She heaved a sigh as if to say what is done is done and turned toward the door but paused. "If I may make one last comment?"

With a nod, Brian bade her speak.

"I really do believe it is a miracle what you and Lady Wright have done for that child. And I told that woman so when she came in this afternoon."

"Who told you to let her in?" Brian had to ask, his curiosity having the better of him.

"The marquess sent a footman with her. They came in through the kitchen. He waited for her outside."

"Goodbye, Mrs. Vickery."

She bowed her head, for the first time acting truly ashamed of herself, and left the room. Since she'd taken on the role of cook, her quarters were off the kitchen below stairs. Brian would give her a few minutes and then check to see that she was gone.

He glanced out the window. It hadn't started snowing yet. If his father could use a footman to cart Jess around, then he could just as easily send one for Mrs. Vickery. With the thought of writing a message to that effect in mind, Brian crossed to the desk, opened the drawer, and saw the letter addressed to Andres Ramigio, *barón* de Vasconia.

This was what Gillian had been hiding from him. Ink and pen were still out on the desk. She'd just written this letter. No wonder she had seemed so agitated when he came in unexpectedly.

He picked the letter up and turned it in his hands. It was sealed shut. He was tempted to open it . . . but to what purpose?

Brian was glad now that he hadn't declared himself to her.

Or so he told himself.

He sat in the chair, holding the letter out, feeling the weight of it, debating what to do next. It would be so easy to tear it into a million pieces.

But that wouldn't change a thing.

Funny, but Brian had never thought that when poets wrote of a heavy heart, they meant the description literally. Right now, his heart felt the weight of ten stone in his chest.

He placed the letter back where he had found it.

Pulling out another sheet of paper, he penned his note to his father. He closed the drawer and went outside where he found a lad loitering on a corner willing to run the message for a coin.

By the time he returned, Gillian was waiting for him in the sitting room. She'd placed Anthony on a blanket on the floor and he was happily playing with his fingers.

She stood up from the settee upon his entrance. "Mrs. Vickery is packing."

"I sent a message to my father to send a footman for her."

"That is more than kind," Gillian assured him.

She was so very beautiful to him. It almost hurt to look at her right now.

He shifted his gaze to his son. Anthony smiled up at him and it healed some of the pain in his heart. He focused on what must be done next.

"We shall need to hire a new cook," Brian said. "And a valet. I also believe," he added thoughtfully, "that we should hire a nurse for Anthony." He reached down and picked up the child. "He's stronger now, isn't he? He's been sleeping through the night and he eats well."

"A nurse might be a good addition to the household," Gillian agreed. Almost timidly she suggested, "Then again, I believe Kate could serve the purpose. She's been doing so well the past week. We should move her from the servants' quarters to the nursery."

Where he slept.

Then again, once Gillian left him again, he'd return to his old bedroom.

"Brian, is everything all right?"

He glanced at her then. Her brows were drawn in concern. "That's the second time in the past hour you've used my given name. Be careful, Wife, or you might find yourself liking me." He'd meant for the words to sound lighter than they came out.

"I *do* like you," Gillian said. She sounded offended that he would doubt the fact.

But that wasn't what he wanted. He wanted something *more.* He wanted something Gillian obviously wasn't going to ever be able to give him.

"I'll need to find a valet," he said, changing the subject. "Then perhaps I'll have decent starch in my neck cloths again." He shook his head. He couldn't believe he was speaking of such mundane matters. Everything he'd thought he could accomplish, every goal he'd set seemed to have turned to dust. He really had believed Gillian would stay with him.

And he dealt with his shattered expectations by talking about starch and neck cloths.

"If you'll excuse me, Gillian, I'm going upstairs for a moment."

"Dinner will be served soon," she said as if uncertain he would return.

Brian attempted a smile. It didn't feel comfortable on his face. "I'll be down then."

He escaped.

Something was wrong with Brian. He wouldn't look at her and Gillian didn't know why.

He didn't return downstairs until Kate took the baby up for bed. Over dinner, his spirits seemed to have improved slightly or perhaps he was behaving that way to relieve her suspicions.

Kate's sister Alice and Ruby, the scullery maid, had done an admirable job of finishing the dinner preparations and the service was excellent. Of course, with Mrs. Vickery being asked to leave, everyone would be on their best behavior.

"I mentioned earlier I saw Lord Liverpool today," Brian said shortly after they'd sat down at the table. "He said he and his wife would be honored to come for dinner."

Gillian grabbed hold of the topic of conversation and gradually, the tension she'd sensed from him began to ease. She promised to pay a call on Lady Liverpool on the morrow and personally deliver the dinner invitation.

"You may not be able to pay calls tomorrow if the weather is bad," he said as if he, too, was willing to force conversation.

"You said you thought it would snow?"

"It may be already."

Gillian left her half-finished meal and rose from the table. She opened the heavy drapes to peer out. A full moon cast a silver light over every flat surface on the street outside. "You are right. It will snow. Already the world is hushing down."

"Hushing down?"

She smiled at him over her shoulder. He sat with his wine glass in hand, so incredibly handsome in the golden glow of candlelight it stole her breath. His good looks were enhanced by her knowledge of his character. She'd made the right choice between Brian and Andres.

"Hushing is my word," she explained. "I started using it when I was very young for those times when there is a stillness in the air. It's as if the world is preparing for what is to come, whether it is a storm or a harvest or snow. Everything seems to hush." She raised her fingers to feel the coldness of the windowpane. "And during a hushing, anything is possible. Like magic."

"Magic?" Brian laughed. "Are wishes granted?"

"Not that I know of," she admitted. "But they could be."

"Then what would be your wish during this time of 'hushing'?" he challenged.

Gillian decided to take him seriously. She thought a moment, looking around the room — and then discovered something. "I have nothing to wish for," she said quietly. "I *am* happy."

"With what?" he wondered.

"Everything. This house that I didn't think I would like so much is becoming a home. *My* home. Then there is Anthony. He's the sweetest child. I'm proud of what we've accomplished here . . . and what we *will* accomplish."

He sat forward, setting his empty wine glass on the table. "And what is that, Gillian? What do you see for *us?*"

His soft emphasis on the word "us" brought her focus to him.

She leaned back against the curtains, one hand holding the thick material for support. She wasn't certain *how* she wanted to answer that question.

And a part of her wanted *him* to take the first step.

For a long moment they faced each other. Gillian wanted to speak, and couldn't. She had no idea what she would say. What she felt, what she wanted had not fully formed into words yet — and the risk of saying the wrong thing was very great.

Brian broke the spell between them first. He shook his head. "That was unfair. I shouldn't have asked." He pushed his chair away from the table and came to his feet. "Perhaps there is only so much magic one can expect during a hushing. I'm up to bed. Are you ready?"

Gillian, too, found it easier to retreat.

"I will be in a moment. I need to have a few words with Alice and Kate about the morning."

"Kate has already brought up Anthony's pap if that is a concern," he said. They were having a mixture of goat's milk and porridge prepared each night for Anthony, although the baby had been sleeping for a good, steady six hours at a stretch and not waking for it. Gillian had also started him on mashed foods like peas and stewed dried apples.

"I need to leave instructions for breakfast," she said.

He nodded. "Well, then, good night."

"Yes, good night," she echoed.

Brian seemed to hesitate a moment. She waited, wanting more from him. He smiled, and then left the room . . . and she was alone.

Gillian sank into her chair at the table. For a long moment, she watched the reflection of the flickering candles on the table in the window panes. She had no one to blame for the state of affairs between herself and Brian but herself. He, who usually did exactly as he desired, was being respectful of the boundaries she'd established.

It was almost as if he'd let her go. He wasn't even waiting for the end of the thirty days.

As she sat in dark contemplation, snow began to fall. Small flakes at first that grew larger and heavier with each passing moment. An indescribable sadness settled over her. She fought it off by diverting herself with responsibilities.

Down in the kitchen, Kate, Alice, and

Ruby were rightfully proud of the dinner they'd served. Kate spoke up and let Gillian know that for the past week, it had been Alice who had been doing the cooking, not Mrs. Vickery.

"Are you saying you'd like the position of cook?" Gillian asked.

Alice, the shyer of the sisters, nodded.

Gillian debated for a moment. Their guests would expect wonderful food. The current rage was for French chefs but they cost a fortune. The meals Alice had been preparing had been simple but well seasoned.

"I shall give it some thought," Gillian conceded. "Let us talk in the morning." She gave the young women their instructions for breakfast and then, taking a candle, went in search of her bed.

Upstairs, the door to the nursery was closed. Gillian hesitated a moment in front of it. She could hear no sound of movement. She had no choice but to walk to her room.

When she'd been up earlier, she'd left the drapes pulled back. Now she watched the huge, damp snowflakes falling from the sky, hushing all sounds except the beating of her heart. The snowy light bathed her room in a silvery blue. It was the kind of night one wanted to spend cozying up under the covers.

On a night like this, one didn't want to be alone.

Gillian looked at her huge, empty bed. The covers had been turned down and a warming pan placed beneath them — but the bed looked cold. Lonely.

It was the time of the "hushing," when the world seemed ready for anything to happen.

This was her home. It had taken years to arrive here but now she knew, it was where she belonged.

And Brian was her husband.

She'd held back, fearful he would steal her heart — and he'd done so anyway.

Did pride matter any longer? She'd made her choice when she'd written Andres. If she was going to stay with Brian, she must be a wife to him in every way.

She *wanted* to be a wife to him in every way.

Gillian turned, threw open the door — and was startled to see Brian standing there. He wore his breeches and nothing else.

He was as surprised to see her as she him.

They stared at each other. Words Gillian could have said stuck in her throat.

And then he solved the problem of communication by reaching for her, pulling her to him, and bringing his lips down over hers.

CHAPTER FIFTEEN

Brian hadn't been able to sleep. Not with the letter Gillian had written to her lover down in his desk. He didn't need to read it. His imagination was having a fine time toying with all the possible things she could be saying to that silver-eyed Spanish bastard.

Over the past few weeks, she had become more precious to him than gold. She'd proven herself a helpmate. She'd honored him with the grace of her presence — and he wasn't going to let her go. Not without a fight.

And because he couldn't sleep, because he'd heard her footsteps out in the hall . . . because it was what she called the "hushing" when anything could happen, he'd risen from his bed and come after her.

Now, here she was in his arms.

It was his dream come to life and Brian had no desire to wake.

He kissed Gillian fully and deeply and she

kissed him back, all but melting into his arms. He could have drowned in that kiss. Instead, he swung her up, kicked the door shut, and carried her to the bed.

Gillian's hands came down on his shoulders. "Help me undress," she whispered.

Brian could have groaned with the pleasure of hearing those words. Setting her on her feet, he tore at the laces of her dress while he nibbled at her throat, kissed her ears, her eyes, her nose. His fingers became tangled and she laughingly grabbed his hands and pulled them forward.

"Let me."

He wasn't certain he'd heard her correctly until she gently pushed him down onto the bed. She removed the pins from her hair so that it fell in a shining curtain around her shoulders. Brian reached out to capture a lock of it but she stepped back, smiling at him.

She reached behind her back and quickly untied the laces that had been eluding him. She pulled the dress down over her shoulders. Whatever shyness Gillian had once possessed had disappeared.

Was it wrong to want a woman this much?

Every muscle, every fiber of his being was tense with desire.

She slipped the straps of her chemise

down over her shoulders, revealing first one bare breast and then another. Bold, firm, luscious . . . Brian could hold back no longer. He had to touch her. Coming up on the mattress, he greedily placed his hand over one as his lips sought hers.

He drew her back onto the mattress on top of him. After that, undressing was a speedy business, and once they were both gloriously naked, Brian didn't waste time making love to his wife.

Did it matter that she loved another? *Not if he could convince her to love him more.*

She was so graceful, so lovely, so giving. She met him stroke for stroke. He whispered all the things he feared saying in the daylight. He told her she was beautiful, that he worshipped her, that he needed her.

And she replied in kind, their words growing lost in their kisses.

He did not tell her he loved her. He showed instead, taking his time, deepening each stroke, watching the expressions on her face and experiencing her pleasure as his own.

She repeated his name, her fingers stroking his skin, his hair —

Her body tightened. She held him. Her legs came up around his waist. She gasped. Her arms hugged him close and he rode with her through the first turbulent, wonderful moments before thrusting himself deep and hard and finding his release. It was like being struck by lightning or being touched by the hand of God.

A sense of peace, of completion settled over Brian. This was where he belonged, where he wanted to be. He was with this woman, heart and soul.

Slowly, the world came back to what it was.

He reached for the bed covers and flipped them over their naked bodies. He cradled her close.

She smiled, a lazy, satisfied-as-a-cat-in-cream smile. Her hand stroked up and down his arm. Her eyes were shining in the dark.

Brian pressed his lips to her forehead. "Is this the magic of a hushing?"

"It's better," she answered and stretched herself out alongside him. "We do this well, don't we?"

"Very well," he agreed. He lifted her hand to his lips and kissed her fingertips.

She turned toward him. They were nose-to-nose, their bodies intertwined beneath the covers.

"Why did you come to me?" she asked.

Was now the time to speak what was in

his heart? Did he dare?

And then he thought of the letter.

"I couldn't sleep," he answered. "And there is nothing better to do on a snowy evening than make love."

Her eyes searched his. He could feel the questions in her mind. Could she read his as well?

"Is that all?" she asked, her voice edged with disappointment. "Did you really come to my room for lust alone?"

"I came out of desire, Gillian. There is a difference."

"And what is that difference?" she prodded. "Explain to me because I know no other than you."

He lifted her hand to his lips and pressed a kiss into her palm. "Lust drives all of us. But desire . . ." He rolled her over to his side. "Desire means that we don't want anyone other than the one we hold. It means only one person can satisfy us. One person we hold dear."

"And am *I* that person?" she asked.

Brian thought of the letter, of all the ways he could answer her that protected him — and said, "Yes."

"You no longer think of Jess?"

He had to laugh then. "Gillian, Gillian, Gillian — since you and I clashed in Holburn's stable yard, you have consumed all my thoughts and all my actions. I meant those vows I traded with you in the coach."

Her gaze lowered to his chest. She snuggled against him. "Good," she whispered.

And it was enough.

They made love again. This time, Brian took all the time in the world. He loved every inch of her, saying with his lips, his fingers, and even his toes, what he dared not speak aloud. He didn't quit until she was begging for release.

They did not leave the room the next day. London was covered with fresh, downy snow. It was not the sort of day to pay calls. And so, they stayed inside, enjoying their household, playing with the baby, and spending another night making love. He was beginning to know her body better than his own. Gillian was as unselfish in bed as she was in life, and for a span of time, he could pretend there was no world other than the one of their own making.

Gillian didn't speak of leaving.

He didn't mention the subject.

Gillian didn't say she loved him.

He didn't ask.

All too soon they had to join the rest of the

world. The snow covering the streets melted under the traffic of thousands of horses, of carts, of stomping feet. There was shopping that had to be done and arrangements to be made for the dinner parties they had lazed in bed and planned.

While Gillian saw to the house, Brian made his rounds again of White's and the War Office. He renewed more acquaintances and pressed his desire for a position on Liverpool's staff.

Knowing now that his own father had been gossiping about him, he made a point of being everything good a gentleman and officer should be.

Later, he returned home to find the silver salver by the front door full of calling cards and invitations. Brian discovered that a married man received different invitations than a single one did.

Before, when Gillian wasn't around and few seemed aware of her existence, he'd been invited to balls. Now, the invitations were for dinner parties and more private affairs. That was good. He was anxious for all of London to meet the beautiful woman he'd married. In that way, he'd stake his claim.

Handing his hat and coat to the new maid, he walked into the sitting room and called out his wife's name. Kate was the one who answered him. She held Anthony as she came down the stairs. As always, the baby reached for Brian who took him up in his arms.

"Lady Wright isn't here, my lord," Kate said. "She is out making calls. The house has been so busy with visitors coming and going and then she must respond. It makes me dizzy to think about it. She should be back shortly. Is there anything I can do for you?"

"I'm fine," Brian said. "Let me keep Anthony for a bit."

"Yes, my lord," Kate said. "I'll be up in the nursery tending to a few things. Call me when you wish me to take him back."

Brian nodded and she left.

"Come on, my fine man," he said to Anthony, whose face at the moment did resemble that of an old man beneath his head full of black, stick straight hair. "Let me write down a few of my thoughts from this afternoon." He spread a blanket on the floor before the hearth the way he'd seen Gillian do and placed the baby on his belly in the middle.

Anthony immediately lifted his head and looked around, his bright eyes a far cry from the defeated child of several weeks ago.

"When you do that, you remind me of a turtle," Brian said to his son. Anthony grinned at him and Brian was surprised to see a little white tooth. He'd not noticed it before.

"Every day you change," Brian said in admiration and crossed to the desk for writing paper.

It was a testimony to how intensely he and Gillian had been involved with each other that Brian had actually forgotten about the letter she'd written to Ramigio — until he pulled out the desk drawer and saw it missing.

He studied that empty space and thought about the woman who had slept so contentedly and peacefully in his arms that morning.

Perhaps she had torn it up. Certainly she wouldn't have mailed it.

Brian wanted to trust her. He told himself he did.

Still, a short while later when Kate came to take the baby, he couldn't stop himself from asking, "Did Lady Wright post that letter? The one to Huntleigh."

God, he hated himself for being so weak as to ask.

"To Huntleigh, my lord? Yes, she posted one a few days ago. I delivered it to the mail myself."

"Thank you," Brian said, dismissing her.

She bobbed a quick curtsey and went upstairs to feed Anthony.

Jealousy was an ugly emotion. It could run through a man with more heat and speed than the sharpest blade.

Brian stood as if rooted to the floor. He'd wanted to believe that Gillian was falling in love with him.

The truth was, his wife knew her own heart and the Spaniard had won it.

And what did Brian have left?

He began to move, pacing the perimeter of the room, turning, pacing it again. Jealousy built to anger. He'd never wanted anything in his life more than he had Gillian. She was his wife. She was *his* —

He stopped. What had she said to him when he'd first gone to Huntleigh for her? That she wasn't a possession?

Brian had gone to Huntleigh to make her honor her wedding vows to him. He'd won. She'd done so . . . and yet, it wasn't enough. He wanted her heart, free of any doubts. Obligation was no longer an acceptable reason for her to be with him. He wanted every last bit of her . . . and if he couldn't have it, then he'd rather she return to her Spaniard.

The realization rocked him back a step.

Was this love?

He'd thought himself in love with Gillian, but that "love" had too much pride to let him set her free.

And yet now, *now* he wanted what she wanted. Her happiness might mean more to him than his pride.

But he couldn't let her go. He didn't want to lose her.

Nor was he one to grovel.

The room's four walls seemed to close in on him. He was a man. If he set Gillian free to go to the Spaniard, what would that mean for him and the rest of his life? He'd be alone. There would be other women — but none of them would be Gillian. None of them would possess her resourcefulness, her resiliency, her ability to make him listen to what he didn't want to hear.

And she was to return shortly and he'd have to face her, knowing she'd sent the letter.

Brian wasn't certain he was in the mood to smile and pretend everything was all right. Gillian was obviously much better at that than he was.

The anger returned.

Going out into the hall, he took his coat from its peg, grabbed his hat, and went out the door. It would be best he didn't see Gillian right this moment.

His wife was going to leave him. He told himself he would see his way through this. He'd handle it. Distance was the best solution. He'd keep his distance and she'd never know how much he cared.

With that thought in mind, he headed to White's. There, he could hide in the company of men, drink himself into forgetting her, and no one would know he'd lost his heart to his wife.

Gillian hadn't meant to be gone from the house this long, especially since she had Alice with her. They'd left Ruby minding the baking Alice had done for dinner.

She had finally paid a call of introduction to Lady Liverpool who was everything kind and generous. Yes, her husband had mentioned Lord and Lady Wright.

The next step would be to send the invitations to dinner. She and Brian had been discussing who the other members of the dinner party would be. Tonight, over dinner, they'd have to reach a decision.

However, as she was riding home in the hack, she saw her cousin Holburn and his duchess Fiona walking down Oxford Street, shopping. She'd called for the driver to stop and what followed was a joyous reunion.

"I didn't know you were coming to town," Gillian said.

"We came to find you," Holburn answered. "I sent a messenger to Atherton's house, but he returned to say you weren't there."

"Wright and his father have had a severe falling out, which is fine with me. I prefer my own roof and my own servants," Gillian said.

"With Wright?" Holburn asked in disbelief.

Gillian laughed. "Yes. With Wright." She couldn't help but let her voice soften on his name.

"Didn't you leave him?" Holburn questioned in disbelief. "You sound happy."

"I am," Gillian admitted. Holburn frowned his confusion, but Fiona understood.

"Things are good between you?" Fiona asked in her lovely, lilting Scot's accent.

Gillian let all her happiness show. "He is the most wonderful, kind man in the world."

Fiona took her hands. "I am so pleased for you."

Before Gillian could answer her, Holburn said, "You left him, then you didn't want to go with him, and now you are *happy* with him?"

Gillian laughed. "I know, I know. I sound as if I'm the most fickle woman in the world. He's given up his mistress. It turns out he hasn't seen her in years. We've been doing so well and we have this wonderful child, Anthony —"

"You have a child?" Holburn interrupted. "I know you are a wizard at managing a household, Gillian, but you've only been gone from Huntleigh for a little under a month. Not even you can hatch a chick that fast."

"Not *my* child," Gillian said, correcting herself.

"*Wright's* child?" Fiona asked, sounding as confused as her husband.

"No, he's not." Quickly Gillian gave them a bit of Anthony's history. She trusted Holburn and Fiona with the truth. It helped that they didn't question the decision to keep Anthony.

"And so you have become a married couple and parents," Fiona said.

"Yes," Gillian answered, "and we've never been happier. Wright is wonderful. He's not as I had thought him. I don't know if the war has changed him or age or what — it doesn't matter. He is exactly what I want in

287

a husband."

"What of Andres?" Holburn asked.

Gillian sobered. "I wrote him a letter. I tried to explain. Wright *is* my husband. I pray he will understand."

Fiona placed her hand on Gillian's arm. "He will be upset."

"But he is a man. He'll shoulder it," Holburn assured her.

"Will you talk to him for me?" Gillian asked. "Please tell him how sorry I am."

Her cousin shook his head. "No matter what you say, it will not be good news for Andres. He fell at your feet the moment he set eyes on you. Still, you must be honest."

"That's how I felt," Gillian said quietly. "And yet, I don't want him hurt. I thought it best to tell him as soon as possible."

Fiona was the one to change the subject. "When will I have the opportunity to meet this paragon amongst husbands?"

"This evening, if you wish. Do you have plans for dinner?"

"We do not," Holburn said.

"Then join us. You will meet Anthony and see how deliriously happy I am."

"Deliriously?" Holburn teased.

"Yes," Gillian stated. "And you can tell me how your trip to Scotland was."

"That would be lovely," Fiona answered,

288

accepting the invitation.

Gillian gave them her address and they agreed to meet at eight. She climbed back in the hack, anxious to go home and tell Brian of her afternoon's adventures.

However, as the hack drove her to her doorstep, she noticed a blue enamel cabriolet with red wheels and yellow spokes waiting a few doors down. It was such a pretty vehicle it attracted attention, especially in this genteel but modest neighborhood.

Alice hurried to her kitchen while Gillian paid the driver. "Thank you," she said to the hack driver, who tipped his hat to her and climbed back in his box.

Gillian was readying to go into the house when the cabriolet started slowly rolling toward her. She was mildly surprised since she'd not seen anyone climb in it. The driver acted as if he'd been waiting for her arrival.

She doubted if she knew the vehicle's occupant. She'd not made the acquaintance of any of the neighbors on the street. Her life had been too busy taking care of Anthony.

However, as the cabriolet drove by, a window curtain was pulled back. Jess smiled at her. It wasn't just a friendly smile. Jess smiled as if she knew something Gillian would not like.

Gillian turned, giving the woman her back.

She went into the house, moving down the hall toward the back room Brian often used as a study at this hour of the day to go over papers and correspondence in private.

He wasn't there.

She went up to the bedroom. No Brian.

Kate was in the nursery with Anthony. Picking the baby up and giving him a kiss on his forehead, Gillian asked Kate, "Have you seen Lord Wright?"

"Earlier, my lady. He was in the sitting room and then I believe he left."

How odd that Brian would leave without telling anyone where he was going.

She didn't worry about it overmuch. She had to prepare for dinner guests.

However, by eight that evening, Brian still hadn't made an appearance. It was embarrassing to admit to Fiona and Holburn that she didn't know where her husband was. They sipped on drinks for an hour, making a fuss over the baby and catching up on news, and then Gillian had no choice but to serve dinner lest it be ruined.

Seeing how upset she was, Holburn asked, "Do you want me to send one of my men around town in search for him?"

"No, don't do that," Gillian said quickly

but Fiona overrode her.

"What if he is in trouble? Or has had an accident? Yesterday, we saw a coach that had slid on ice and gone off the road. It was terrible."

"He didn't take a coach," Gillian said. "We are still setting up our household and have been hiring hacks to take us around town." But Fiona's words did make her think of footpads and others who would hit a man over the head and rob him of his purse. Brian could take care of himself but what if he was in trouble. "Very well," she said to Holburn. "I appreciate your kind offer and will take advantage of it."

One of the sometimes convenient things about being a duke was having a host of servants at hand. Holburn sent several of his in search of word of Brian.

An hour later, when dinner was finished, the man returned and spoke to Holburn out in the foyer.

"Well?" Fiona demanded when her husband returned to the room.

"He found Wright," Holburn said.

"Where is he?" Gillian asked. Her first thought, her fear was that he was with Jess.

"White's. He's in a game and doesn't want to leave."

"In a game?" Gillian repeated.

"Faro."

"Brian is gambling?" Gillian questioned. "He has never shown signs that gaming held an appeal for him."

"He was in the military," Holburn said with a shrug. "If that isn't taking a risk, I don't know what is. Most military men of my acquaintance are hardened gamesters."

Gillian shook her head. "Did the servant tell him we'd sent for him?"

Holburn hesitated. He glanced over at his wife and then pursed his lips.

"Go on," Gillian said. "If there is more, I wish to hear it."

"My man told him that you were concerned. He did it discreetly, of course."

"And my husband answered?" Gillian prodded, determined to hear all."

"That he was happy at the tables. He was losing," Holburn continued. "And he was deeply in his cups."

"Wright was drunk? He has a good head for spirits," Gillian said to Fiona as if to convince her, or make sense out of this new behavior. "He doesn't overimbibe. Brian has been home every night since we've come to London."

"Perhaps he had plans you didn't know about," Holburn suggested gently.

Gillian nodded. Of course, this *was* as it

used to be between them. Back when they first married. Brian would go about his business and she'd find herself waiting for him to return home.

Usually, he didn't. Usually he lived with Jess.

No wonder Jess was smiling as she drove by Gillian earlier that afternoon.

Tears burned her eyes. She blinked them back. She wouldn't cry over him. At least he wasn't with Jess — she hoped.

"Gillian, Wright is a good man," Holburn was saying to her. "I'm certain he has an explanation."

"Of course," she said tightly. *She wished she hadn't slept with him. She wished she could go back to the day he arrived at Hunt-leigh.*

Thankfully, Fiona said, "Gillian, do you wish us to stay or to leave?"

"Don't go because of this," Gillian said, relieved her friend understood she wanted to be alone.

"We aren't," Fiona said. "It's been a lovely evening but the time has come to say good night." She walked to Gillian and put her arms around her. "Anthony is a brawny babe. You are right to be proud of him."

Gillian didn't speak. Her stomach was in knots.

"Please don't jump to conclusions," Fiona warned. "The servant could have misunderstood or Wright might have good reasons for his behavior this evening. Perhaps he heard Holburn was coming to dinner and wished to avoid him."

Holburn frowned. "That may be true. I had planned to have some hard words with him until I saw you happy. Of course, now I am not so pleased."

"Wait until he comes home," Fiona advised. "Listen to what he has to say."

If he came home.

"You are right," Gillian said, struggling to keep her voice light. However, the moment the door closed behind Fiona and Holburn, Gillian allowed all her doubts to return. She'd wait for Wright. He'd best come home this evening, and his story had better be good.

And then, she grew angry.

Anger was a good emotion. It made her feel strong. How dare he treat her this way?

She sat down to wait for him. As the minutes passed into hours, she finally had to go to bed . . . but the waiting only made her angrier.

She tossed and turned, unable to sleep and then lightly dozing — she heard the door open a short time after dawn.

Brian came in. He seemed to move with his usual steady grace but she could smell the liquor on him. He removed his jacket, taking it into the dressing room. A few minutes later, he came out, naked, and lay on the bed beside her.

For a long moment, Gillian was so stunned by his behavior, that he could stay out without any word of explanation or indication where he was, come home, and then climb into her bed as if her wishes had no merit, that she could barely think coherently.

This was not what she wanted in a marriage. This was not how she would let him treat her.

And then he did the unthinkable. He rolled on his side, turning his back to her, and with a heavy sigh, seemed to settle into sleep.

Well, she couldn't sleep. She *wouldn't* sleep. Not with him beside her.

With that thought in mind, Gillian took both her hands and shoved with all her might. He rolled off the bed like a log and onto the floor.

CHAPTER SIXTEEN

Brian came awake with a start, stunned to find himself facedown on the floor.

Admittedly, he'd been giving himself a steady dose of hot port all evening. Still, he'd never fallen out of his bed —

A pillow slapped him hard in the head.

"How dare you climb into my bed reeking of spirits?"

He turned to see Gillian standing on her knees on the mattress. Her hair tumbled around her shoulders. The burning coals in the grate highlighted the anger on her face and her billowing night dress made her appear an avenging angel — full of outrage and fury and completely, gorgeously luscious at the same time.

She hit him again with the pillow. "How dare you, Wright? How *dare* you?"

Brian wasn't one to allow himself to be plummeted, even with a pillow. He came to his feet, grabbing the pillow out of her hands and threw it across the room. "Dare I what?" he snapped. "Come to my own bed?"

In spite of the drink, his mind was clear. The only thing the port seemed to have done, now that he'd been bounced off the floor, was make him feel reckless. The potent wine certainly had not been able to dull the pain of her betrayal.

"You didn't tell me you were leaving, Wright," she said. "You walked out of this house without one consideration to me."

"*I* walked out?" He laughed at the irony. He'd laid his heart out for her to trample and destroy and here she was complaining because he'd gone to his club.

And yet, in spite of how angry her accusation made him, he still wanted her. She was so lovely. So brave, courageous, so everything a man could desire in a woman. "Why should I stay?" he whispered, speaking more to himself than her. "What keeps me here?"

Her response was to take her fist and hit him in the shoulder. She was crying. He thought that strange. For what reason did she have to cry? She was leaving him and there was nothing he could do.

"Holburn was here," she said, her words tense with emotion. "I met him and his wife while out on errands and invited them to

297

dinner. I told them everything was fine between us and then you didn't show. And I didn't know where you were and I've been worried that you'd been hurt and now I discover you made a fool of me, Wright. A fool —"

"Oh no, dear wife," he said, catching her arm by the wrist before she struck out at him again. "I made no more a fool of you than you have of me time and time again. And the curse is, I still want you. Damn you, Gillian, I *still* want you. I want to taste you and hold you and have you." Even more, he wanted her to believe in him. He wanted her to choose *him*.

She pulled back. "No." Her eyes were like ice shards. "You won't touch me. I won't let you."

Brian laughed with the bitterness of self-realization. "I won't take no. I can't." And he kissed her.

This was not a questing kiss, the gentle question between lovers. He wanted to own her, possess her. Keep her.

He'd steal her soul with his kiss if he could.

Gillian fought. She tried to resist, but she couldn't . . . any more than he could restrain himself against her. Her lips melded against his as she opened herself to him, and a surge of triumphant pride and blessed relief rose in him. Gillian could turn away from him but this part of her would never deny him. They had this.

Their kiss deepened, changed, grew. Through it, he beseeched for her to understand. She held his soul in her hands. He begged her to not crush him.

In turn, he tasted her forgiveness.

Her struggles ceased. He released her arms and they came around his neck.

Brian lifted the hem of her nightdress. Her naked skin was smooth and velvety soft. He didn't think he'd ever tire of touching her.

He pulled her nightdress over her head. He kissed her hair, her eyes, her mouth. His hands found her breasts, weighing them and caressing them. He knew what gave her pleasure. He now used that knowledge to make love to his wife using every skill available to him. He used his body to beg her to stay, to say what his pride would not let him speak aloud.

She loved another.

What should have been his was no longer — and yet, her hands soothed, encouraged, enabled. He brought them both to the mattress. Her skin glowed like alabaster in the room's early morning shadows. He rolled over, settling her weight upon him, her hips against his, their legs entwined.

The hurt and anger ceased to matter, vanquished by the magic of her skin against his. Her tongue tickled his ear. Her lips pressed against his throat. Her hand reached down to stroke him intimately.

At her touch, Brian groaned. What sweet madness was this? What *pleasure.*

He could hold out no longer. In one swift movement, he lifted her to sit upon him. Without hesitation, she rode him like some wild fairy queen. Magnificent, golden, demanding. And Brian gave. He grabbed her hips, burying himself deep, over and over again.

And then he felt her tighten, her body taking and holding his.

For a moment, they were suspended in time . . . and then he found sweet release. It drained him. Took all that he had and delivered it to her.

Here, Gillian. Here is the best of me, the essence of my soul. The gift that God has given us.

With a soft gasp, she collapsed on top of him. He put his arms around her and held her as if he'd never let her go.

Slowly, the room began to chill their overheated skin.

Brian brought the covers over them. His

body was still joined with hers . . . and he found himself making love to her again.

They made love three times those hours after dawn. It was as if he couldn't have his fill of her. They didn't speak. Brian no longer trusted words.

For him, this act of joining, this need was an exorcism of sorts. Soon, she would leave him. He didn't know what he would do after she was gone. She'd made a home out of a shell of a house. She'd given Anthony a mother and created herself into Brian's other half, his rib, his Eve.

Later he would deal with how he would go on. For right now, it was enough that she was here.

Gillian woke late in the day feeling as if her body had been well used.

Naked and wrapped in a tangle of sheets, she rolled over in the bed to discover herself alone. She sat up, pushing her hair back. The room smelled of sex and his shaving soap. The door to the dressing room was open, but she didn't hear a noise or see a shadow.

She rose from the bed. The first few steps brought out aches where she'd not known they could exist and the heat of a blush ran up her body. She'd attacked her husband.

She'd been so angry at him when she'd gone to bed and yet all he had to do was touch her and she'd thrown herself at him.

Or had she been so relieved he'd come home, she would have done anything to keep him there?

A glance in the mirror told her she looked a fright. Her cheeks were chafed from his beard. Her hair was a tangled mess and her lips were full and red from his kisses.

There was a knock on the door. "My lady?" Ruby the scullery maid's voice asked from the other side.

"Yes?" Her voice was hoarse. She couldn't help but blush again at the memory of what she'd done with her lips and tongue only hours before.

"His lordship sent me up with water for a bath. I've been heating it for you."

A bath would be heaven. "Thank you." She smiled, pleased that Brian had thought of her. "Is Lord Wright downstairs now?" If he was, she thought about quickly throwing on some clothes and going down to see him. Or of sending a note down inviting him to join her in her bath.

"No, my lady. He left the house already."

Gillian opened the door to see Ruby standing with two buckets of steaming water. "He left?"

"Yes, my lady. He spent time with Lord Anthony, kissed the baby, and then left the house."

"Did he leave word where he was going?"

"Not with me, my lady."

It turned out he hadn't left word with anyone. As he had done the day before, Brian had walked out without so much as a by-your-leave. He didn't return until very late.

Gillian had planned on waiting up for him. She couldn't. She finally had to go to her bed, only to be woken in the middle of the night to her husband making love to her.

She wanted to ask him where he'd been. She wanted to know why he was leaving so mysteriously. And yet, when he kissed her, his naked body against hers, she could not think to speak.

This next morning he didn't leave but stayed in the back parlor and worked with a secretary he'd just hired named Edmund Simon.

Gillian seethed at Brian's high-handed, extremely *rude* behavior. Her resentment built as the day continued and he seemed to be avoiding her.

Of course, she had a few tricks of her own. She made a point of having Anthony with her at all times. The baby was the bait. Eventually, Brian would be forced to confront her if he wished to see Anthony.

The enticement worked. At a quarter until seven, Brian walked into the sitting room where she sat on the floor before the hearth playing with an increasingly tired Anthony. Of course, the baby perked up at the sight of Brian.

"Hello, Gillian," he said pleasantly.

"Hello? That is all?" she demanded, bouncing Anthony in her arms.

Brian smiled and held out his hand for Anthony. The baby reached straight up for him. "Should there be more?" he asked, taking their child into his arms.

Gillian's temper flared, but along with it was resentment. "Are you playing some game with me?"

"A game?' he asked. "I don't believe so." He sounded perfectly relaxed.

She came to her feet. Certainly, he was toying with her. "Why?"

"Why what?"

"Why are you behaving this way?"

He brushed back Anthony's hair. "I'm not behaving in any way, Gillian. All is well between us. Don't fret over it."

Don't fret over it?

And then she knew. Of course. She was

always second to his Jess. No wonder the woman had been smiling at her as she'd driven past the house the other day.

"Have you been seeing *her?*" Gillian couldn't keep herself from asking. She hated how waspish she sounded. She shouldn't care.

Then again, she shouldn't have trusted him. To think that she'd written Andres, that she'd hurt him for this man . . .

"Seeing whom?" Brian asked. He frowned. "Jess? Of course not. Why would you imagine such a thing?"

"Perhaps you should," Gillian responded for no other reason than meanness. Something was going on with her husband, something he refused to discuss with her and that could only mean Jess. She hated her jealousy, felt eaten alive by it. "I don't feel well. I'm going to bed." She swept by him.

That night when he came to bed, she tried her best to keep her back to him and pretended to sleep. But that didn't protect her from him.

It was his touch. The anger he seemed to harbor against her during the day disappeared at night. He'd stroke her, his fingers so full of tenderness, of wanting, that she had no choice but to give in. They made

305

sweet, lingering love. He whispered in her ear how lovely she was, how much she pleased him — and she knew that if he was here with her now, he wasn't with another.

However, the next morning he was as distant as ever.

His actions made Gillian furious. Her anger kept her from crossing the divide between them. She considered leaving him again, and then realized she couldn't.

She loved Brian. It was as simple as that.

The truth was, if he was in bed with her, he was not with Jess. That was a victory of sorts. And after he accompanied her to church on Sunday, after he stood with her through the service and here and there placed a hand at the small of her back, she realized she was not willing to give up on her marriage. She'd seen the man he was. It was still there when he picked up Anthony and held him. She wanted that man for the father of her children . . . for the father of the child she felt she already did carry.

She wasn't certain yet, but she would be soon. For right now, her suspicion was nothing more than a woman's instinct.

But matters could not continue the way they were. Especially with Fiona calling upon her or sending a note every day to express her concern.

So Gillian was pleased when the evening arrived for their dinner with Lord and Lady Liverpool. They were delightful guests. Holburn and Fiona were also in attendance along with Lord and Lady Canning. Gillian thought she and Brian presented themselves and their cozy home very well. Lord Liverpool showed a decided favoritism toward her husband. Later, she overheard the cabinet minister remark to Lord Canning, "Do you see why we like him? Wellington says there isn't anything he can't do."

"Do you believe that is true?" Lord Canning drawled, sounding jaded.

"Yes. I believe he is the man we want for the position."

Gillian couldn't wait to relay this bit of conversation to Brian. Over a glass of wine, they discussed the evening before retiring and it all seemed to have been everything he wanted.

He took her hand. "Thank you, Gillian."

"For what?"

"For your help with all this." He waved his hand to encompass the sitting room where they enjoyed their drinks. "For settling Anthony. For being the person you are."

His comment deeply touched her, and gave her the courage to ask the question that had been so much on her mind.

"Brian, what has happened to us?"

Immediately, his face became shuttered. "What do you mean, Gillian?"

She regretted bringing up the subject. A hard lump formed in her chest. She'd carried it with her for days and now, she wanted to be done with it. "We were doing better," she said. "I thought you liked me."

He leaned back in his chair. "I admire you very much."

"Admire?" Gillian shook her head. "What does that mean, Brian? I don't know if I want to be admired."

"What would you rather have?"

Your love.

All she had to do was say the words and there she would be, completely vulnerable.

So, she chose silence.

Brian leaned forward, took her hand in his, laced their fingers together —

Gillian pulled it away. "I believe I'm best for bed. Are you coming?" It was an invitation. She kept her voice very neutral.

He didn't take it as such, and that was more humiliating. "I'll be up in a moment."

Upstairs, Gillian undressed in silence, wondering how long this would go on. Or had Wright decided he didn't need her?

She checked on the baby and then climbed

into bed.

Her husband came up several minutes later. This night, instead of waiting for him to make the first move, Gillian rolled toward him and put her arms around him. "I don't like the way things are between us," she whispered.

"How would you rather they be?" he asked.

"Like it was."

He came over on his back to face her. He combed her hair out of her face. "And how was it, Gillian? Have we really ever trusted each other?"

He didn't expect an answer. She wouldn't have given one. She would hate to admit to her jealousies.

So she did what seemed to suit them best. She made love to him. It was passionate, soul satisfying, and yet oddly distant. It was because she was afraid of what was in her heart.

She might love Brian, but she didn't trust him and she was discovering love couldn't exist without trust.

Fiona had insisted Gillian accompany her to interview an artist about her having her portrait done. The artist, rumored to be one of the best in London, was a petite man who smelled of oil paints and body odor and who wanted to dress Fiona up as a Scottish kelpie.

"And what does a Scottish kelpie wear?" Fiona asked.

"Very little," was the reply.

Fiona's eyes met Gillian's and they both burst out laughing. The artist was offended and all but threw them out of his studio. They could barely wait to climb into Fiona's coach before they doubled over into laughter.

"I am very resistant to having a portrait done at this point in my life," Fiona confessed. "I want babies in my picture and animals like my dog Tad." Tad was a gigantic wolfhound who lorded over Huntleigh now that his owner was mistress of the estate. "I know dressing up as some forgotten Greek is the fashion but I think it fussy and silly."

"And what does Holburn think of the idea?" Gillian asked.

"He thinks it is wonderful. He wants to see me as Aphrodite."

"You are beautiful enough to be so," Gillian said.

Fiona colored prettily. "You are talking nonsense like my husband. I don't want to wear draperies in my portrait."

"What would you wear?"

"The Lachlan plaid, of course. I wonder if I could coerce my husband into a kilt."

"For a portrait?" Gillian asked.

"And because I think he'd do a kilt justice," Fiona replied, wicked laughter in her eyes.

"Would he do it for you?"

"It would be worth the try to convince him."

"I'm certain he'll do it," Gillian assured her, "if you wear the Aphrodite garb. I can see the picture of the two of you now."

Both women laughed at the image they'd conjured and took some time for shopping at the small shops comprising the Exeter Exchange. Fiona happily linked her arm in Gillian's and for a moment, all Gillian's doubts and worries seemed to fall away until her friend brought her head close and said, "It is so good to hear you laugh. I've been worried about you. Is everything all right between yourself and Wright?"

Gillian pulled up short. What could she say? What *should* she say?

The truth would be a betrayal to her husband and a lie would betray a friendship.

"Matters are as they should be," she replied, hoping she sounded serene.

Fiona studied her a moment, her mouth

tight, and Gillian knew she didn't believe her. However, instead of more prying, Fiona said, "My husband has secured a box at the Royal Theatre tonight for a party. I have a friend who is performing *The Quaker* and we want to support her."

"You have a friend who is a singer?"

"She started off as a dancer. Grace MacEachin and I came to London together from Scotland. This is a golden opportunity for her. Holburn and I want to give her every ounce of support. So, if you join us this evening, after Grace sings, and I believe it is a very small part, you must join us in cheering and stamping our feet. Then she will receive much notice and move on to larger parts."

"I would be happy to do so," Gillian agreed. "It's unusual for a duchess and an opera singer to be such fast friends."

"In this day and age, it seems we can be anything we wish if we are bold enough to try for it — which is one of the reasons I want *you* to be completely happy," Fiona said.

Tears stung Gillian's eyes. It would be so easy to completely confide all of her troubles in Fiona. Instead, she said, "I shall speak to my husband and see if we have plans this evening. If we don't, I'm certain we would both enjoy being a part of your company and cheering and stamping our feet for your friend."

Before Fiona could answer, they heard someone shout her name.

They both turned and saw Holburn approaching. He waved as he dodged his way past other shoppers toward them.

He was also not alone.

Andres Ramigio accompanied him.

CHAPTER SEVENTEEN

To his credit, Holburn hadn't realized Gillian was with Fiona. However, once he laid eyes on her, his step slowed. He glanced at Andres . . . but it was too late. Gillian and the Spaniard had seen each other.

Andres appeared thinner than she remembered, but just as handsome.

There was hurt in the depths of his quicksilver eyes, a hurt she had caused. He offered her a short, somber bow of acknowledgment.

In return, she felt her face flush with heat. She wanted to run. She chose not to. This was a difficult meeting but it had to be seen through.

She sensed rather than saw Fiona and Holburn exchange worried glances. So for them, she put on a smile and held out her hand. "Barón, it is a pleasure to meet you again."

Andres didn't make a move for her offered

hand. His gaze slid away from hers. Her heart ached in the presence of his sadness.

"Lady Wright and I have finished our shopping," Fiona said in a too bright voice as she took Gillian's arm. "Here, my dear, let me walk you to the coach. Holburn, you and the barón wait here until I return and we shall go for tea."

Gratefully, Gillian started to leave with Fiona but Andres suddenly moved into their path. He shook his head as if coming to his senses. "Please, Gillian, I need a moment with you."

The shoppers, Holburn and Fiona, everyone and everything seemed to come to a halt. She struggled for common sense. "Now is not the time."

"When will there be a better one? Or a more innocent opportunity? Perhaps you wish to sneak around your husband?"

The disdain in his voice struck like a lash. "I said everything in the letter, Andres. I'm sorry. I didn't mean for this to happen — to you or to me." She didn't wait for his response but turned and hurried away knowing her maid Ruby would follow . . . knowing Ruby was a witness to everything.

Of course, the problem was she didn't have a vehicle of her own. She realized it the moment she reached the street. She turned to request the beadle guarding the entrance to hail a hack when Holburn caught up with her.

"What are you doing?" her cousin demanded.

"Running," she confessed, shooting a glance at the wide-eyed Ruby who waited no more than three feet from them.

Holburn took her arm. "First, you will take my coach." He looked to Ruby. "It is over there. You know where. Go wait for Lady Wright inside."

Ruby bobbed a curtsey and went flying.

"There will be rumors amongst the servants," Gillian muttered. Why hadn't she asked Kate to accompany her? Kate would have kept her silence.

"Not if you keep your wits about you." He drew her away from the crowds of shoppers going about their business. "I'm sorry. If I'd known you were with Fiona, I wouldn't have brought him here."

"You have done nothing wrong. Nor has he." She looked up at the handsome cousin who had been her champion when she'd left Brian. "I hate that I involved him in this. I am ashamed I acted dishonorably. To both him and my husband."

"Ah, Gillian, you were confused. Andres understands."

"Does he?" She shook her head in disbelief. "I really did care for him . . . but my bonds to Brian are stronger. I don't know why, especially since lately, he has not been the easiest person to live with."

"I never thought you rubbed each other well," Holburn said. "I assumed that's why you left him."

"You assumed wrong. Indeed, you will believe I am a perfect ninny when I confess I love him."

"You do?"

"With all my heart."

Holburn's initial shock changed into a broad smile. "Then you have no problems."

"Why is it that men seem to think everything is so simple? He doesn't love me, Nick. But he *needs* me, and perhaps that is enough for him. Perhaps it must be enough for me."

"Perhaps you aren't being fair to Wright," her cousin said.

Fair? Gillian shook her head. "Are you hinting that I am suffering from some sort of wounded female sensibilities?"

Holburn's expression grew guarded as if he sensed he'd overstepped his bounds. He raised a conciliatory hand. "Gillian, I am not accusing you of anything. Or taking sides —"

She shook her head, not wanting him to back away from the question. "Since you have been in London, have you noticed anything in my husband's behavior that would tell you, another man, that he cared deeply for me?"

"He has set up a household with you," Holburn answered.

Gillian had to raise her eyes heavenward for patience at all he was ignoring. "I want *more,* Holburn. I want it *all* — lover, friend, confidant. Someone who cares about me, the *real* me. But the terribly confusing thing is, I want it from *only* him. And for some reason I don't understand, everything has gone horribly wrong between us." Dear Lord, tears were forming in her eyes. She took a swipe at this with her gloved hands. "I'm sorry. Seeing Andres, knowing what I did to him, I —"

She broke off. There were no words to describe the quagmire her life had become.

"Gillian," Holburn said comfortingly. "Don't be so hard on yourself . . . or Wright." He would have placed an arm around her but when he moved, she saw Andres standing there. He'd probably heard everything.

Shame washed through her. She seemed determined to bludgeon Andres with her fickle emotions — and she hated herself for having involved him. "I'm sorry," she whispered to him and turned on her heel to run for the coach.

But Andres wouldn't let her leave. She hadn't gone far when he caught up with her. Taking her arm, he forced her to face him. They were five feet from the coach and Gillian was very aware that Ruby could see them. "I can't talk now," she said.

"When can you talk?" Andres demanded.

"I mustn't —"

"Please, Gillian. I need to know you are happy. That's all."

"And you won't take my word now?"

"Not after what I've overheard."

"Andres —" she started, pleading her case again but he cut her off.

"This evening, at the Covent Garden. You are going? I know Her Grace was to invite you to join our party in their box."

"She did."

"I will see you then."

He didn't give her the opportunity to say no but let go of her arm and walked away to where Holburn waited with his brow burrowed with concern.

Inside the coach, one of the hardest tasks of Gillian's life was to pretend in front of

Ruby's curious eyes that all was as it should be.

When the driver delivered them to her front door, she asked him to wait a moment while she penned a note to the duchess offering her deepest regrets to her friend that she and her husband would *not* be able to attend the performance at Covent Garden with them that evening.

"I'm glad you could join me," Lord Liverpool said to Brian as they sat down to lunch at Boodle's. The club was known for its food and, since it did not have a political bent, its convivial atmosphere. Brian was Liverpool's guest. He assumed this meant the cabinet minister had reached a decision concerning his wish to be appointed to his staff.

"I'm honored that you invited me," Brian said, placing his napkin in his lap.

It was a late lunch and Liverpool had requested a table away from the others in the dining room — another good omen — but still close to the warmth of the fireplace to fight off the chill out of doors.

For the first few minutes they talked about their wives. Liverpool commented again on how much he and his lady had enjoyed their dinner.

"I've known Gillian since she was as high as my knee," Liverpool said. "I had no doubt she wouldn't turn out to be the poised and exacting young woman she is. She has a good head on her shoulders, Wright. You were wise to marry her."

"I consider myself most fortunate," Brian murmured.

"The two of you are a formidable team," Liverpool continued. "I daresay that you are both perfectly able to travel in any social circle you might wish."

"Thank you, my lord."

"Oh, it is much more than a compliment," Liverpool said, waving away his words with his knife before cutting into his beefsteak. "It's an art. You see, I've found that in government service, we must consider both husband and wife. If the wife is not happy, then her husband will grow disenchanted with the long hours and the frustrations that go into leading this great country of ours."

"That is true," Brian agreed, making a pretense of cutting his beef and eating. He was waiting.

Liverpool turned his attention to his meal, dropping his gaze from Brian's. "I know you wished for a position on my staff."

Brian didn't like the past tense of the word "wished."

"It *is* my sincerest desire."

The cabinet minister took a bite and chewed it thoughtfully, and at that moment, Brian knew he did not have good news to deliver. He lowered his head, staring at the weave in the cloth of his napkin. "Was it my father? Has he talked to you?"

"Perhaps you should read this first before we speak," Liverpool said, and placed an opened letter beside Brian's plate. Brian immediately recognized the handwriting as Wellington's.

He picked up the letter and unfolded it.

His general had written a letter of reference on Brian's behalf, noting that he would serve a good purpose in any position England had for him.

I cannot say too much in favor of him. He was one of the best officers under my command. I agree with you (and many others) that Wright should be used to further advance the concerns of our country. Holland would be a very good posting.

Brian refolded the letter. "I have no desire for a diplomat's life," he said carefully. "I do not wish to appear ungrateful, but my heart, my mind is with the men I served

322

and who served under me."

"I understand," Liverpool said.

"I beg to differ, my lord, because if you did, you would not suggest the diplomatic corps to me. My request is not motivated in an interest for a political career. I'm thinking of the men I left behind in Portugal, men who are battling with their lives for this country. They need my voice on your staff. An army runs on money. The government continuously makes promises that it has, so far, failed to deliver. I wish to right that wrong."

"And you believe I have a desire to send men with empty stomachs and no boots into war?" Liverpool demanded, leaning forward, his voice no louder than a whisper.

"I believe you are the *one* man who understands the difficulty," Brian answered. "And for that reason, I wish to side with you."

"There are no sides here, Wright. We all work toward the same purpose. Government is nothing but compromises, one after the other. But there are decisions that need to be made on a higher plane. One of those decisions is how to take talented men with intelligence and loyalty and use them for the good of the empire."

"I have no desire to sit out this fight against Napoleon as a diplomat," Brian said, letting his own temper show. "I do not wine and dine with my enemies."

"Sit out?" Liverpool motioned for the porter to refill his wineglass. He sat back in his chair, tossing his napkin on the table. "Don't ever demean the diplomatic corps with such a statement."

"I mean no disrespect but I am a soldier, a fighter. I do not have the politician's patience."

A ghost of a smile curved the cabinet minister's lips. "That was a skillful recovery. Patience. Is that what we politicians have? I doubt that — or at least I grow as impatient as yourself. And I'm certain you know how Wellington feels about waiting. However, politics is the means we use for accomplishing our goals. A skilled politician is an asset, Wright. That is why we believe you should be sent to Holland."

Brian could have groaned aloud. "I have no desire to —"

"Hear me out." Liverpool leaned forward. "Holland could be pivotal for us. You know Napoleon's brother Louis is on the Dutch throne."

Brian nodded.

"He has actually been a good ruler to the Dutch," Liverpool said. "He has ignored Napoleon's orders to prosecute those caught trading goods with England and continually considers the welfare of the Dutch people. For that reason, we assume his days in Holland are numbered. Napoleon is not a man to be ignored for long, even by a brother. But when that happens, we must take advantage of Dutch discontent. Wright, let me worry about prying money for our army out of Parliament. What I want from you, what England *needs* from you is help loosening Napoleon's hold on the Continent country-by-country. First Holland and then Belgium. Your father's wishes aside, you truly are the best man for this task." He drew a sip of his wine. "I knew your brothers. You are the one most like your father of the three of you."

"I'm not certain that is a compliment, my lord," Brian said.

"Your father is meddlesome, Wright. And he does as he pleases —"

"He takes pride in trampling on people."

"He's also a very effective politician. Nor is he alone in trampling on others. We all do in one way or the other. Some people deserve a good trample. And yes, he does want you to have this ambassadorship. However, don't believe me so simple as to make such a decision on his say so. You possess the tact, tenacity, and intelligence needed for this role."

It was flattering to have a man like Liverpool praise him. Brian still held Wellington's letter. Had he been too hasty in rejecting an ambassadorship? Diplomacy had not interested him before but if it helped the battle against Napoleon, should he not at least consider the idea?

And then he thought of Gillian.

He'd be leaving her.

He thought of last night. There had been a sadness in her touch. They always seemed to hurt each other. Perhaps it would be best for both of them if he *did* leave.

"I see you are thinking of your family," Liverpool observed. "It is up to you if you wish to take them with you. Some diplomats find their wives assets to their duties. Others, for various reasons, leave their families here in England."

Brian nodded, not trusting his voice to speak. The thought of leaving Gillian, even knowing she didn't love him the way he loved her, filled him with sadness.

"So, what shall I tell Castlereagh, Canning, and the others?" Liverpool asked. "Will you take the post?"

"May I have some time to think? At least, perhaps, overnight?"

"Of course. In fact, why don't you and

Lady Wright join my wife and I in our box at Covent Garden this evening? It's *Macbeth* and some musical entertainment called *The Quaker.* I never found Quakers entertaining but my wife wishes to see the performance. This will give us another opportunity to know each other better. You come highly recommended and Wellington thinks the best of you. Of course, for me, a man wise enough to marry Miss Gillian Hutchins is one I can admire."

Brian laughed silently at himself at the trick fate had played on him. "I am indeed blessed," he admitted. "However the wisdom was my father's."

"He may have steered you to the match, but it is obvious your wife dotes on you."

"As I do her," Brian responded perfunctorily.

Fortunately, Liverpool was too preoccupied with other matters to listen closely. Their meal at an end, they left together on cordial terms. Liverpool had a driver waiting for him at the door.

Brian paused on Boodles's front step. So, it appeared his only option would be playing the diplomat in Holland. It was a good offer and Liverpool had placed it in terms that made Brian willing to consider it.

In addition, it would be good for his political career, the same one he'd professed not to have. Still, a man should keep an eye on his future.

He pulled on his leather gloves and set off in the direction of home. It was a good stretch of the legs but he enjoyed the exercise. However, he had not gone far when he noticed Jess's cabriolet coming toward him. It had been sitting at a corner, apparently waiting for him. He slowed his step.

She lowered her window as her vehicle drew alongside him. "Would you please join me?"

"No," Brian said, barely able to look at her.

"My lord, I have information of importance I believe you would want to hear."

"Jess, matters are done between us. You have nothing I want."

She pulled a pretty pout, taking offense to his rejection. "I only wish to help."

"Accosting me on a public street is no help. What if my father were to see you? After all, this carriage he gave you draws more attention than a beacon lamp. I warn you, he can be a jealous man."

"I already know that." She leaned out the window. Her hat was a fashionable thing of feathers and pearls. It was attractive. *She* was attractive . . . but she no longer *attracted* him.

"Please, my lord, hear me out. You owe me that much."

Brian came to a halt. "I owe you?" He shook his head with a bitter laugh. "I owe you nothing, Jess. And I wish for nothing from you in return."

"You don't understand. You have never been alone or afraid," she accused.

"Neither have you. You have always had me, or my father." He didn't hide his disdain.

Jess placed pink leather gloves on the edge of the window. "I would wish that you return to me," she confessed. "Except I know you would reject such an offer."

"And you would be right."

She frowned. "It's because of the baby, isn't it?"

"The baby is one part. Jess, you weren't loyal. You didn't wait for me."

"I couldn't," she said, her expression hurt. "You were gone for years."

"I was fulfilling my duties."

She waved his words as if to erase them from the air. "And how would I know how long that would take? I grew lonely. Besides, a woman who lives by her looks has to earn her keep where she can."

"Not an honorable woman."

"Or one such as your wife?"

Brian's temper soared at the sly peevishness in her tone. He took a step into the road to confront her. "Don't mention my wife. You would never understand a woman of her qualities."

"I know she isn't as beautiful as I am," Jess answered.

"I disagree. Gillian's beauty surpasses yours in the same way the sun outshines the moon."

"And of course, she is more *honorable* than I?" she said, mimicking his earlier words.

"Definitely."

A smile spread across Jess's face. "Then why was she making an assignation with a gentleman not more than an hour ago in front of the Exeter Change?"

"You lie," Brian said, almost laughing at the accusation.

"A tall man, with dark, good looks. One of the most handsome men I've ever seen. He appeared Latin." She brought her brows together. "Do you know him? The beadle told me he had an accent."

"Why are you watching my wife?" Brian charged, shoving aside the rampant jealousy the description of Ramigio set off through his veins.

"Because I want you back," Jess said and for a bleak moment, he could see beneath the paint and powder, the velvet and the silks to the young girl he'd once protected. "We meant a great deal to each other. You loved me."

"I did. But you can't have me, Jess. My father might betray me, but I won't betray him." He took a step back to the curb. "And I'll never betray my wife."

The light in Jess's green eyes hardened. "You did once."

"I was a fool."

"Or perhaps you aren't a good judge of women. You trust too easily. Oh, wait," she said, raising a hand to cover her lips in mock alarm over her words. "I forgot. Your wife is an *honorable* woman." She pulled back into the coach. "Beware, my lord. All that trust means people will laugh harder when you are cuckolded. *Drive,* Jeremy."

Her coachman didn't hesitate but immediately set the vehicle in motion.

Brian was so angry he could have grabbed one of the wheels and turned the fussy cabriolet over. Instead, he marched down the street, disgusted with himself for having taken a moment to have listened to anything Jess said. Her words were like a poison, spreading through every fiber of his being.

He stopped, ignoring the pedestrians brushing past him in their haste to reach their destinations.

If Gillian was going to leave him, well, so be it. He couldn't live with this jealousy or he'd become a crazed man. Instead, he needed to focus on Anthony, *his son,* and that is all he wanted . . . or so he told himself.

He kept that lie alive until he reached his front door, his *home.* Even then he could believe the falsehood, until he discovered Gillian in the nursery feeding Anthony. She was speaking to him with such tenderness, even the sound of her voice was music to Brian's soul.

This was the woman he wanted for the mother of his children. Gillian was all that was good, all that was honest. She would not betray him. He should not believe anything Jess spread in malice —

Gillian looked up at him in greeting and there was such sadness in her eyes — he knew Jess had not been lying.

And he realized he had a decision he must make. He could confront her, or not. It was his choice. He decided to pretend all was right. He did not want to know the truth. "Hello."

"Hello," she echoed and then motioned for him to have a peek at Anthony. The baby had fallen asleep in her arms, his hands clenched into fists.

"Here, let me help you move him to the bed," Brian offered.

"No, not yet. I like holding him." She smiled shyly as if embarrassed to admit such a thing.

"Did you have a good day?" Brian asked, hoping there was no edge in his voice.

"I did. I spent the afternoon with the duchess of Holburn."

"Shopping?" He had to ask.

"Among other things," she replied easily.

No knife could twist in the heart as deeply as jealousy. It took all of Brian's willpower to say, "Well, I hope you had a good afternoon."

"I did."

He started to leave, thinking a strong drink might be in order right now, but stopped. "I had an interesting afternoon. I met Liverpool for lunch. He wants me to be the ambassador to Holland."

"But that isn't what you wanted," she replied.

You are what I wanted, he could have responded but held silent. "It is what I'm being offered. I have the evening to think upon it."

"Brian, I'm so sorry."

He shrugged. "It might not be a bad thing. It will mean leaving England for at least a year, perhaps longer."

A frown line formed between her eyes. "What of us?" she asked.

"What would you like to have happen with us?" he dared to ask.

"May we go with you?" she said, indicating herself and Anthony.

The weight on his chest over Jess's words lifted. If she was with him, she would not be with Ramigio. Jess had it wrong. "Gillian, I would wish nothing more," he said fervently and was rewarded with her smile.

"Then I believe I would like to be an ambassador's wife," she said. "I've longed to travel outside of England. It'll also be good for Anthony. He'll grow up without being —" She paused, searching for a word. "Watched."

The doubts Brian had been harboring fell away. Gillian was right. Anthony would be safe from his father and any difficulties he might consider presenting in the babe's future.

And Gillian would be away from Ramigio. She'd chosen her marriage. It was all Brian could do to not dance around the room.

"Liverpool wants us to join him and his wife this evening. You may have questions and he will be able to give us more information."

"That would be good," Gillian said, rising and picking up the silver pap feeder she must have used feeding the baby and a teacup and saucer she'd used for herself. "I would like a nice quiet evening."

"I don't know how quiet it will be," Brian said. "He has a box at the Covent Garden. He wishes us to join him there —"

His words were interrupted by Gillian dropping the pap feeder and cup in her hand. The china broke while the silver feeder bounced across the floor.

Fortunately, the clatter didn't wake Anthony. Brian immediately set about helping Gillian clean up the mess. "That was clumsy of me," she murmured, but he noticed she didn't meet his eye.

It wasn't clumsiness that had startled her, but what he'd said.

Kneeling beside her, he said, "Gillian, look at me."

She ignored him for a moment, and then slowly raised her gaze to his.

"Is everything all right?" he asked, willing her to tell him anything Jess had said was true.

Gillian laughed, the sound forced. "Other

than I stumble over my own feet, all is fine," she answered.

And he knew she was lying.

CHAPTER EIGHTEEN

Gillian usually adored attending the Theatre Royal at Covent Garden. The theater had burned down in 1808 and the rebuilt building had just opened the past September. She'd wanted to see the new interior but had not had the opportunity since returning to London. She had even thought she'd like to see *Macbeth,* which was on the bill with *The Quaker.*

However, she was not anxious to see the play with Andres somewhere in the crowd.

Nor was she going to tell Brian about Andres. Their existence together as man and wife was too fragile to be disturbed by reopened wounds. That was one of the reasons moving to Holland sounded like a very good idea.

There, she and Brian would start anew.

So, she wouldn't mention Andres's presence in London and if their paths should cross at the theater, then she'd pretend surprise. It was the best plan.

The theater was very crowded to overflowing. Coachmen jockeyed for the best position to deliver their passengers. The entrance to the boxes was under the Portico on Bow Street and it was a very busy place indeed.

Brian appeared devastatingly handsome in black evening dress. Gillian had chosen a green muslin gown trimmed in gold thread for herself with a velvet paisley shawl to match. She could feel eyes turn and stare in admiration as they made their way up the grand staircase to Liverpool's box. Almost furtively, she slipped her kid-leather–gloved hand in his. His reassuring squeeze was all she could have wished.

Lady Liverpool was delightfully welcoming. Their box was on the second tier and had an excellent view of the stage. The men quickly went off to speak with their friends and political acquaintances out in the foyer.

"They must do that," her ladyship confided, patting a place for Gillian to sit in the light blue upholstered chair beside hers.

Gillian took the seat and looked around the newly decorated theater, which was teeming with life. The milling crowd was noisy and a bit raucous in the shilling gallery below them. The boxes were just as full and busy as people leaned around the gilt pillars to call a greeting to each other.

"They've done away with the boxes that protrude out from the others," Gillian observed, taking in the gilt and cream decorated boxes that formed a half circle around the gallery. "I like that. Some seats were difficult to see the stage because of them. And I like cream and gold. Very elegant."

"A bit understated for my tastes," Lady Liverpool answered. "Although I do like the cut glass chandeliers. I hear this exact form has become all the rage in homes across the city since the theater opened. Ah, I see we are about to start," she observed, as Mr. Kemble, the theater company's manager and principal, came out onto the stage in the robes of Macbeth. She glanced back at the door and settled into her chair with a sigh of resignation. "Sometimes my husband doesn't return until well into the play. Such is my life."

"He holds a demanding position," Gillian observed.

"He does, but he handles it so well, most feel he isn't working hard. Ah, something must not be right," she said as Mr. Kemble walked back off the stage.

A beat later, a gentleman came out and

informed the still unsettled crowd there would be a minor delay but to please take their seats since the play would start momentarily. Catcalls from the shilling gallery greeted his announcement and he hurried off the stage lest someone begin throwing orange peels or anything else at hand.

"I can't imagine being on the stage," Gillian said. "There is so little respect for the performers."

"It seems more so lately, such is modern times," Lady Liverpool responded. "So, now that we don't have the men around and a bit of time, tell me about yourself."

Shyness rose inside of Gillian. "I wouldn't know what to say."

"Talk to me about when you first met Wright. I adore those stories. Funny how all couples meet each other in many of the same ways and yet, no two stories are ever alike."

"You are a romantic," Gillian accused her, laughing.

"I am. Now speak. Tell me all."

"Only if you will tell me yours in return," Gillian answered.

"Oh," Lady Liverpool said, lightly tapping her fan on Gillian's arm, "mine is very romantic. His father was set against the marriage and Liverpool and I considered eloping."

That statement caught Gillian's attention. "You would have eloped?"

"For him? Yes. His father objected to the match for reasons I still don't understand. It no longer matters. Family is family. Pitt and the king both spoke on our behalf and evidentially his father gave his approval. Of course, shortly after that, his father was named earl of Liverpool. I wouldn't be surprised if that bit of coercion was what changed his mind. It doesn't matter to me. I'm just pleased that everything worked to our advantage." Lady Liverpool's expression turned dreamy. "I swear I can never tire of the sight of my husband's face."

"That is the way I feel about Wright," Gillian said, and it was true.

"Now your story," Lady Liverpool ordered.

Gillian told her about meeting Brian at the ball and how the moment she set eyes on him, the rest of the world had faded away. "I loved him before I knew him."

There, she'd finally said the words aloud. She'd laid out her heart in front of a stranger. She was thankful he wasn't here to overhear them. He would think her truly foolish then.

It was at that moment that she looked

across the theater and realized the Duke of Holburn's box was in a direct line of sight from the Lord and Lady Liverpool's. Fiona hadn't noticed her yet. She was very busy directing the seating arrangements of her large party of guests.

Richard Lynsted was among their number. His presence surprised Gillian since Richard's father and uncle had had words with Holburn over Christmas and been asked to leave Huntleigh. Richard had left, too. He usually did as his father instructed. He was a giant of a man who always acted as if he felt a bit awkward. Gillian didn't know if that was on account of his size or his father's overbearing manner.

Whatever the reason, she was surprised to see him — and just as intrigued when, instead of hanging back the way he usually did in a social setting, he grabbed a seat at the front of the box closest to the stage. She'd not known him to be interested in theater.

In fact, she'd not thought him interested in much of anything other than the accounts and ledgers his father and uncle foisted off on him. He'd been betrothed for what seemed like forever to Miss Abigail Montross, a wealthy banker's daughter. Gillian had never seen the two of them together.

However, if Richard was developing a taste for theater and happier, lighter pursuits, perhaps there was hope that he would escape his father's strict dictums. He was not unhandsome. More masculine in appearance than given to true male beauty . . . and the evening clothes became him in spite of his appearing ill at ease —

And then all thoughts fled her mind.

She saw Andres. He came to the front of the box and stood there, a dark, dramatic figure searching the crowd in the pit and gallery below him. She was not the only one who noticed him. Women's fans began fluttering. A whisper seemed to go through the theater and heads turned in his direction.

She drew back into the shadows of her box, not wanting him to see her. He would form the wrong opinion and assume she was there for an assignation.

Unfortunately, Lady Liverpool's eye caught sight of the tall, handsome Spaniard. She gave a soft sound of appreciation. "Who is the gentleman in Holburn's box?"

"A friend of his. A Spaniard," Gillian said, surprised at how easy it was to keep her voice neutral.

"A Spaniard?" Lady Liverpool laughed and opened her own fan. "And one of Holburn's friends. He will set hearts afire. I've heard many complaints that there is nothing of true interest amongst the men of this year's Season. I think matters are about to change."

Gillian prayed it was so. Andres finding a new love would assuage her guilty conscience. "Few of us are immune to the looks of a Latin man," she murmured and Lady Liverpool laughed.

"Truer words have rarely been spoken."

Thankfully, there was a clap of stage thunder — the obviously missing ingredient to his earlier entrance — and Mr. Kemble as Macbeth strode out onto a deserted Scottish heath and began the play.

All eyes turned in his direction and Gillian drew her first full breath since seeing Andres. He hadn't noticed her and hopefully, now the play had started, he wouldn't. "Here, let me move to the back so your husband may sit beside you," Gillian said, starting to rise.

"Absolutely not," Lady Liverpool said. "The men may sit in the chairs behind ours. Enjoy yourself up here with me." Gillian had no choice but to stay where she was, hoping Andres would not notice her.

A few minutes later, the door at the back of the box opened and closed and Lord Liverpool and Brian joined them.

Gillian found it hard to concentrate on the play. While the witches on stage brewed their spells, she sensed her own doom. The audience in the shilling gallery knew most of the lines by heart and would shout out comments here and there, some of them witty enough to elicit laughter. The actors played on.

The play was almost over when Gillian felt the hair at the nape of her neck stir.

She did not want to, but could not help herself from glancing in the direction of Holburn's box — and found herself looking straight in the silver gaze of Andres Ramigio.

"He's been watching you all evening," her husband's voice said by her ear.

Gillian thought her heart would stop. *Brian knew.* She turned to her husband, fearing the worst. The features of his face could have been carved from stone. She clasped her hands tightly in her lap to keep them from trembling. "It's not what you think."

Brian rose. "Excuse us," he said to their hosts and left the box. Gillian followed.

All was quiet out in the hall. Brian hadn't waited for her but walked toward the main hall which led to the grand staircase — and the row of boxes on the opposite side of the theater where Andres sat. Gillian charged after him.

"Where are you going?" she demanded, worried.

He stopped at the head of the wide, curved staircase. The play was over. She could hear cheering and some shouts. Any second, the crowd would come streaming out for an intermission.

"Not where you think," Brian answered her.

"Gillian," Andres's voice said. She turned to see that he had come from his box and stood at the opposite end of the hall, not more than twenty feet from her.

"Go to him," Brian said.

"What?" Gillian turned on her husband.

"Go to him," he repeated.

She shook her head. People were starting to come out of the doors from every which way, but must have felt something of the tension in the air. They pulled up short. Heads swiveled back and forth as they took in the sight of Gillian and Brian on one end of the hall and Andres at the other.

If Brian knew they had an audience, he gave no indication. Instead, he took her by the arms. "I can't live my life this way. He's right there, Gillian, waiting for you. *Leave.* Be with him. I won't hold you."

Gillian's throat tightened with the horror

346

of what he was saying. He released his hold. A bit of the hardness left his expression.

"I'm not angry, Gillian. I want you to be happy. I want you to have the man you love. Go to him."

He started down the steps. Andres moved toward her, but Gillian held him back with a shake of her head. She chased after her husband, who had almost reached the ground floor.

"Wright," she shouted.

Brian kept moving, although a good number of people in the foyer looked up at her.

"You stop right there," she ordered.

He didn't obey.

In desperation, Gillian shouted at the top of her lungs, wanting him to hear her over the growing noise of the crowd, *"You* are the man I love, Wright. *You are."*

That caught his attention along with the attention of everyone else in the foyer. Conversation stopped. Gillian had never been so humiliated but then, what else could she do? Her pride meant nothing if he left her.

And her sacrifice had not been in vain. Brian stopped. He looked up at her. "What did you say?"

He was going to make her repeat it. Gillian had never felt more vulnerable. And yet this time, the words were easier to say. She leaned over the railing, enunciating each word with honest emotion. "I love you. I have from the first moment we met."

"That's true," Lady Liverpool's voice chimed in from the staircase above Gillian. She and her husband had come to stand along the railing overlooking the foyer. "She told me exactly that before the play began."

Heads looked to Brian for his response. If he noticed that they had become the center of attention for a good four hundred Londoners, he gave no indication, but climbed three steps toward her.

"I thought I'd killed that love, Gillian," he said, "with years of indifference."

Tears choked her. Did he believe she would make love to him without loving him? The idea made her angry. "You came close, but you earned it back and now, you are throwing it away. No wait. Go on. Leave. I can't live like this, Brian. I can't live with a man who would walk away from me."

The crowd murmured its disapproval of him.

Brian ignored them. He climbed three more steps toward her. "I'm not walking away, Gillian. I want *you* to be happy. I love you too much to force you to stay if you don't want to be with me."

Where earlier the crowd's sentiment had cast him as villain, it now started to change its perception.

Gillian changed hers, too.

"What did you say?" she demanded, taking a step down the stairs toward him.

"I said I won't force you to stay with me —"

"No, *not that part,*" Gillian corrected him. "The part when you said *you loved me.*"

Brian rocked back slightly.

"I want to hear you say that again, Wright," Gillian said. "I won't believe it until I hear it clearly and distinctly from you."

Her challenge was echoed with encouragements from their audience.

Brian looked around as if just now noticing the crowd gathered around them. Gillian braced herself, uncertain how he would react . . . but once again, her husband surprised her.

The tightness left his face. He leaned on the curved handrail so that he could look up at her and said in a voice that echoed throughout the hall, "I love you, Gillian. I love my wife."

Claps and cheers met his announcement.

She closed her eyes, letting the words sink in. It hadn't been her imagination. Everyone else had heard them, too. Still . . . "Say it again," she pleaded.

This time, he charged up the last two steps to speak to her alone. "I love you. I have for so long now, I can't remember a time when I didn't love you. You are my heart. My soul. Without you by my side, my life is empty."

The tension left her, replaced by joy at hearing her husband speak such wondrous things aloud.

"One more time, please," she asked, daring to open her eyes. Yes, there he was, her noble, handsome, *loving* husband.

"*I* love *you*, Gillian."

"Then why haven't you said any such thing sooner?" she demanded.

"I don't know. Pride. Stubbornness —"

Any other suggestions he would have made were cut off as she threw her arms around him, right there in front of the whole theater, and kissed him.

Incredibly, blessedly, he kissed her back.

Cheers around them grew louder and more enthusiastic clapping than had greeted the actors in the play.

Gillian didn't care that they had created a scene. All she knew is that for the first time, she was completely certain of herself and Brian. Wrapped in his arms, she glanced up the stairs and saw Lord and Lady Liverpool clapping with the others.

Holburn and Fiona were there, too, and equally as happy.

The person who wasn't there was Andres. He'd left. It pained Gillian to have hurt him so . . . and yet, her heart belonged to Brian.

Her husband added to the spectacle of the moment by swinging her up in his arms to the roaring approval of their audience, but instead of taking her back up to the box, he walked down the stairs, and through the crowded foyer. Well-wishers followed them.

"We've made a terrible scene," she whispered to her husband as he carried her out the front door and onto the street where coaches and hired vehicles waited.

"Good," he answered. "Let it be in the papers on the morrow that Lord Wright loves his wife. I'll buy a dozen copies for your perusal alone so that you will never, ever doubt my love for you."

"Perhaps we shall start a new fashion," she suggested, "of husbands and wives truly caring for each other."

"I hope that we do," he answered, setting her into a hack.

The ride home was one of the most memorable in Gillian's life. The man who had never spoken those simple three words to her, now couldn't say them enough. Nor could she hold back from telling him how marvelous, wonderful, and precious he was to her.

At home, they hurried up the stairs, throwing off clothes as they went, laughing and giggling like children at a fair.

And then Brian made love to her.

Gone was the restraint, the doubts, the sadness. This time, their love was a celebration, a promise, a bond.

In the aftermath, as they both had returned from the heavens back to the earth of their bed again, they heard Anthony crying.

"Let me fetch him," Brian whispered and slipped on breeches to do so.

Gillian brought the sheets up over her nakedness, waiting for him. She heard him speak a few words to Kate who sounded happy to fall back to sleep. A moment later, her husband returned with the baby. He settled Anthony on the bed between them.

The baby was very bright-eyed at this time of night, almost as if he shared his parents' newly discovered love. He looked from one to the other, his eyes shiny in the candlelight and gave them a coo while he reached for

his toes.

Brian and Gillian laughed. Her husband reached over to place his arm around her. "I've never been happier," he confessed.

Neither had she. In fact, her heart, once so lonely and full of sadness, now seemed to encompass the world with its bounty. She took his hand, lacing his fingers with hers. "I think I could make you happier."

"How could you do that?" he wondered, his smile spreading across his face.

"Not in the way you are thinking," she chided, laughing. "Not with the baby in bed."

"I can take him back to his room."

"Leave him here for a moment. Instead, let me tell you this." She leaned over and whispered in his ear her belief she was pregnant.

Brian's reaction was all she could have wished it. He bounded from the bed with a loud whoop of joy. Taking Anthony in his arms, he said, "You will have a brother or a sister. It doesn't matter which or perhaps *both*. We'll have *herds* of children."

Gillian came up on her knees, pushing her hair back. "Don't be too excited. It's just a suspicion I have. I could be wrong."

"If you aren't, my lady, then let me take this wee one back to his bed and I'll make

353

certain you are on the morrow," he promised her.

And so he did.

And so she was.

ABOUT THE AUTHOR

Cathy Maxwell spends hours in front of her computer pondering the question, "Why do people fall in love?" It remains for her the mystery of life and the secret to happiness.

She lives in beautiful Virginia with her children, horses, dogs, and cats.

Fans can contact Cathy at *www.cathymaxwell.com* or PO Box 1135, Powhattan, VA 23139.